Nine Tales of Henghis Hapthorn
by Matthew Hughes

Table of Contents

Introduction
The Birth and Doom of Henghis Hapthorn

In 2003, in the long run-up to the publication of my first (and only) novel from Tor, I thought it would be a good career move to start writing short stories for the sf magazines. People who read the shorts would recognize my name when they saw it on a novel, and the rest would be history.

I keep a file on my hard drive where I note down interesting story ideas when they occur to me, because otherwise I'll forget them. I found one that said, "Suppose you came to realize you were living in a world that was the result of somebody's three wishes going wrong?"

I said, "Okay, let's see where that goes," and started a story. I'm a crime writer at heart, so I made the protagonist a Sherlock Holmesian detective. I decided to set the story in the same universe as the Tor novel: the Archonate, an entirely improbable far-future milieu one age before Jack Vance's incomparable Dying Earth cycle. And off I went.

The result was *Mastermindless*, the first tale of Henghis Hapthorn, Old Earth's foremost freelance discriminator. I sent it to *The Magazine of Fantasy & Science Fiction* and was delighted to receive a contract and check within a couple of weeks.

Henghis turned out to be popular with a segment of the *F&SF* readership, so I wrote five more stories about him over the next year or so. I thought it would be good to make them follow an overall story arc, so I cannibalized an idea I'd originally floated in *Fools Errant*, the first Archonate novel: that, every few thousand years, the basic operating principle of the universe arbitrarily alternates between rationalism (i.e., cause-and-effect) and sympathetic association, (i.e., magic). Hapthorn, a superb rationalist who disdains the very notion of magic, is horrified to discover that he's living in the last days of rationalism, just before the next big switcheroo comes to destroy his way of life.

The success of the Hapthorn stories led to three novels, *Majestrum*, *The Spiral Labyrinth*, and *Hespira*, which carry on the tale of impending doom from the six-story arc that began with *Mastermindless* and continued on to *The Gist*

Hunter. This collection contains those six, plus three other Hapthorn tales: *Sweet Trap*, which, though a self-contained story, is also the first two chapters of *The Spiral Labyrinth*; *Fullbrim's Finding*, which takes place just after *Hespira*; and *The Immersion*, which is set before the rationalism-vs-magic story arc begins. In the latter case, I just wanted to take Henghis out for a spin in his pure, untroubled state. Because of that time signature, I've made it the first story in this collection.

I hope this ebook draws new Hapthorn fans. I wouldn't mind writing more adventures for him, in short or novel-length form, if there turns out to be a market. We'll just have to see.

The Immersion

The who's-there at the front door of my lodgings announced that one Feroz Pandamm was seeking admittance.

"Feroz Pandamm, the essences magnate?" I asked my assistant.

It instantly consulted with the who's-there and said, "The same," while deploying its display screen.

I regarded the image of Pandamm's pugnacious countenance hanging in the air before me: a wide-brimmed slouch hat dipped over one cold eye; an upturned high collar hid his heavy jowls. I looked at the time and saw that he had waited until the streets were evening-dark, well after my customary receiving hours, to make his call.

"It would seem," I said, "that he does not wish to be seen consulting Olkney's foremost freelance discriminator."

"Yet there he stands," said the integrator. "Need coupled with embarrassment often combine to yield a substantial fee."

"Or it could be that his need to take revenge upon me has swelled until he cannot resist scratching the itch." I weighed the chances then said, "Admit him, but be on your guard."

The who's-there opened the portal while the integrator disabled the holds and discouragements that protected me from certain operatives among Olkney's halfworld. There were more than a few career criminals who resented the roles I had played in overturning their illicit plots and mischiefs. But the enmity directed my way did not emanate only from the halfworld–in the best parts of our ancient city there also stood manses and houses-in-town whose owners rarely uttered my name without a prefacing profanity.

One such manse was the great pile built of blocks of volcanic glass on a cul de sac at the upper end of Tsant Prospect. There Feroz Pandamm sat and concocted stratagems to enrich himself further. Two years earlier, I had frustrated his campaign to gain an unfair advantage over the House of Esk, a rival in the viciously competitive trade in rare essences; Pandamm had gulled one of Tarq Esk's enumerative cadre into an invidious situation, then threat-

1

ened to expose the fellow's peccadilloes unless Pandamm was fed proprietary information on his employer's plans and weaknesses.

But Tarq Esk had "smelled a turd behind the tapestry," as he put it when he engaged me to identify the informer. I did so in short order, after which Esk turned the situation against Pandamm, using the suborned clerk to feed his competitor allegedly secret information about the quality of the jupelle harvest on the planet Whilom. The false details had induced Pandamm to prebuy most of the jupelle crop, only to find, when the blossoms were delivered, that they were infested by a fungus that was rapidly turning them into a foul-smelling sludge.

Tarq Esk regaled the members of the Essenters Guild with the entire story, making Feroz Pandamm the butt of many a joke. Esk had also revealed my part in the scheme's undoing. Thus it was nothing less than truth when I told my unexpected visitor, "I am surprised to find you crossing my threshold."

"No more than I am to be here," he said as he heaved his substantial bulk the last few steps up to my work room. He doffed the hat and turned down the collar and I saw that the artful coiffure that was one of his most recognizable features, and of which he was unnaturally proud, was not in evidence. Where it had been was now a broad expanse of bare scalp mottled an angry purple, right down to the roll of fat on the back of his neck.

"Something has happened to your hair," I said.

"How discerning of you to notice," he replied, and I deduced that whatever had motivated him to seek me out had not warmed his opinion of me.

"If you have come to me for help," I said, "you would do well to consider your tone."

I saw his eyes flash. My forthright remark had not been to his taste, yet I saw him make the effort to swallow it. I have learned that with some specimens of Olkney's commercial elite a short, sharp shock on first encounter can clear the field of misconceptions. Now I asked him plainly what I could do for him.

"Find out who has done this,"–he indicated his empurpled pate–"to me."

"And?" I said.

His downturned lips showed an even grimmer frown. "And tell me."

"You plan revenge, of course."

"My dignity has suffered enough affronts of late," he said. After a portentous pause, he added: "As you should know."

I sighed. "I cannot be party to a crime." I forestalled with a brusque gesture the objection he was about to make. "Do not tell me it is none of my concern. If you take direct action against the offender, and I am the hound that has pointed you at him, I am morally and legally implicated in your unlawful conduct. The least consequence that I might expect to suffer would be revocation of my license."

I might have added, but did not, that Captain-Investigator Brustram Warhanny of the Archonate Bureau of Scrutiny would not be satisfied with such a light punishment, could he ever catch me on the wrong side of the thin and often smudged line that separated the licit from the felonious. Three times in the recent past I had resolved cases–important cases–that had baffled the Bureau, with the result that many scroots had removed themselves from the legion of my admirers.

None of that, however, was Pandamm's concern. "Tell me," I said, "what happened."

The incident had occurred the previous evening, though when he told me of it his anger was as fresh as if it had happened only moments before. He had dined at his club, the Monopolists, and had decided to walk off the effects of seven courses, two bottles of wine and several post-prandial snifters with a clique of cronies in the revivifying room. He had dismissed his air-car at the club door and set off across the banded pavements of Tirramee Plaza toward the thoroughfare that would lead to Tsant Prospect and the winding climb to his door.

His route was not a perilous one. Although there were districts of Olkney through which it was inadvisable for muzzy-headed tycoons to stroll, Pandamm had more sense than to visit them, and scant reason to do so. He strode across the glittering bands of Tirramee's pavement, the murmur of its multi-tiered fountains comforting his ears. It was well past the hour at which indentors and their spouses liked to promenade in their finery and he encountered no one to whom it was expected he would speak. He had just passed by the spiraled obelisk of filigreed marble that commemorated the reign of the Archon Imreet IV, when he was struck.

"It came from above," he said, "and behind. Like a splash of cold, dense liquid, heavy enough that my knees bent and I almost pitched forward. I reached up, with both hands, and felt a viscous mass clinging to my head and shoulders. I sank my fingers into it and tore it from me, flung it to the pavement without looking at it."

"What *did* you look at?" I said.

"The air above, of course. I wanted to see who had done this to me."

"And what did you see?"

3

"Nothing."

"No air-cars, omnibuses, freight vehicles?"

"None."

"Whose house was nearby?"

"Some lordling's."

"No one you know? Socially?"

The answer was a grunt. I understood. Wealth and rank in Olkney might occasionally travel together but more often they diverged to follow separate courses. Members of the aristocracy would be prime customers for Pandamm's essences, the rarest of which only his vendory could provide, but any transactions would be conducted through servants.

"Integrator," I said, "display a schematic of Tirramee Plaza." A map appeared. I said to Pandamm, "Indicate your course."

His blunt index finger traced a path from the front door of the Monopolists across the square, moving from south to north and diverting as it went around the interlocked circles of the fountain on the west side.

"You did not go straight across, through the wide space between the fountains," I said.

"A troupe of buskers occupied the middle ground," he said. "They were packing up their stilts and instruments. I did not care to be importuned."

"And where were you struck?"

"Here!" A thick-nailed fingertip poked through the display. "Just this side of Imreet's Column!"

"That," I said, "would put you right outside the house-in-town of Lord Chavarie, would it not?"

"Are you saying that Dizmah Chavarie is the culprit?" I saw that the lines of Pandamm's face easily shaped themselves into a mask of ridicule.

"I am not saying that."

"Then what are you saying?"

"At this point," I said, "I am asking. The saying will come in due course, if"—and here I raised an emphatic finger—"I decide to take the case." He began to offer some further observation that I was sure would not be helpful, so I spoke over him. "When you saw nothing above, did you then look down to see what had struck you?"

"Of course."

"And..."

"And, again, I saw nothing."

"The viscous mass had disappeared?"

"As if it had never been."

"Hmm," I said.

"What is your conclusion?"

I had no conclusion to offer. The facts were, so far, too scant, though some unformed idea was tickling the back of my mind. I told him it would be premature to say, particularly as I had not yet accepted the discrimination.

"But you will," he said.

Would I? I was not sure. I had never cared for Feroz Pandamm, even when he was a remote figure on the far horizon of my affairs. Seeing how he had casually ruined the life of a hapless Esk functionary did nothing to warm my regard for him, and now at close quarters I was finding him even less endearing. I offered him a cool look beneath raised eyebrows; it was an unspoken contradiction of his view.

He was not accustomed to being gainsaid. His color darkened and his square chin tucked itself down into its own folds. "Name your fee," he said.

"It is not a matter of fees," I said, "but of time. Integrator, how is my schedule for the next few days?" The phrase, whenever uttered in front of a third party, was a code between my assistant and me. The device replied that I was heavily engaged on three discriminations of a serious nature, all involving members of Olkney's elite. "Well," I said, "there it is."

"Not acceptable," he said. His eyes had both widened and somehow contrived to bulge forward in their sockets. I saw him struggle to control an impulse, which was clearly toward physical action. Whether he constrained himself out of civility or the logical expectation that, here in my lodgings, my person would not be undefended, I could not say. But he subsided and growled, "What will it take to free up your time?"

My own impulse was to tell him that nothing would move me. I did not like him, and one of the attractions of a freelance discriminator's calling was the ability to choose whom I would serve. But I checked my first inclination; the circumstances of the assault on Pandamm, if it had indeed been an assault and not some sort of freakish accident, were intrinsically interesting—at least I could not immediately discern what had struck him to leave him bald and discolored.

Few enough of my cases offered me an intellectual challenge: I was all too often commissioned to retrieve purloined goods of the wealthy, to bring back spoiled scions of the aristocracy led astray by appetites they had never learned to restrain, to locate errant spouses who had wearied of what had once fulfilled them to perfection, to set right petty wrongs–or, worse, to assist in some even pettier revenge.

Pandamm's motives were not complex. He had been wronged, deprived of a personal attribute that he much valued; that was an affront to his concept of a well ordered cosmos, which could have no other reason to exist than to accommodate his will. But the circumstances were unusual enough, and I had not been fully engaged by a discrimination for far too long. It was just coming up to ten years since I had built my assistant and taken up the life of a freelance discriminator. I had enjoyed it at first, when the challenges were fresh and novel, but of late I found myself grown jaded and often quite bored.

"I will take the case," I said.

I saw that the universe was once again functioning more in accordance with Feroz Pandamm's expectations: his chins unfolded and something almost like a smile briefly gasped for life on his lips. "Have your integrator contact mine for the fiduciary arrangements."

"No," I said. Another impulse had bubbled up in me and this time I acceded to it.

"What do you mean, 'No?'" The chins had bunkered themselves again.

"I will not charge a fee," I said. "Instead, you will owe me a service, to be performed when I call for it."

His brows contracted. "What kind of service?"

I did not know. The impulse had been strong but not informative. Again, I fell back upon my usual response when I had nothing useful to offer: "It is premature to say. But you may take my price or take your leave."

As it happened, he took both, in that order.

In the morning I decanted my integrator into its traveling armature, which resembled a plump stole made of flexible though tough material, and placed it over my shoulders. Tirramee was both a fair walk and a stiff climb from my lodgings in Shiplien Way, the six-sided plaza being set into the foothills that gradually sloped up to become the base of the Devenish Range, which culminated in the stark heights along which sprawled the Palace of the Archonate.

I went up to the roof of my lodgings and had my assistant attract the attention of the next omnibus.

The vehicle was not crowded and I was not forced to share a seat as it carried me to its northern terminus, a tower of modest height whose observation platform overlooked, though at a distance, the scene of the incident. I had my integrator apply its percepts and examined the image it delivered privately to my retinas.

"There is a Bureau of Scrutiny volante on the roof of the manse to the left of the plaza," I said. My assistant confirmed my comment and tightened its focus onto a window below the parapet above the building's top floor. Agents in black and green uniforms could be seen inspecting a bedchamber. Just then the officer in command of the scroot detachment turned and looked out of the window. I regarded the pendulous ears and elongated nose, the drooped eyelids and protruding lower lip and wondered, not for the first time, if gravity might somehow have a stronger effect on the countenance of Brustram Warhanny than on the rest of us.

The thought had scarcely passed away before I saw the Captain-Investigator's ever-moist eyes rise then briefly cast about before locking onto my own distant gaze.

"His integrator has alerted him to our surveillance," said my assistant.

"It would be a poor integrator if it did not," I replied, but voiced the remark in a whisper and behind a concealing hand. I knew that Bureau of Scrutiny percepts were almost as good as those that I had designed and installed in my assistant, and there was no advantage to be gained by irritating Warhanny's assistant. Warhanny himself was already annoyed, as I could see from the thunderheads building in his brow.

"He demands to speak with you," said my integrator.

"Connect him."

A moment later, the captain-investigator's lugubrious bass rumbled in my ear, "Henghis Hapthorn, what do you do here?"

"From your perspective," I said, "I am actually 'over there.'"

The integrator was still supplying me with a close view of Warhanny's hangdog face. I saw his eyes darken and the grim set of his mouth would have rivaled Pandamm's deepest frown. "This is a Bureau crime scene," he said. "Why have you brought your percepts to bear on it?"

I could have dissembled, could have professed no more than an idle interest, but my well honed intuition was telling me that the presence of scroots on the top floor of the manse in front of which my client had been mysteriously struck down was unlikely to be a coincidence. I said, "I am engaged in a discrimination."

Warhanny's canine eyes were expressive for a Bureau agent's; now they widened in outrage. "Has the margrave-major's heirs called in an outsider even before the Bureau has surveyed the locus? Why, I'll–"

"My client is not connected in any way with Lord Chavarie," I said.

"Then for whom are you acting?"

"I am not at liberty to say."

Warhanny's eyes were getting to show their full emotive range this morning, I thought, as I saw them narrow to slits. "When it is the Bureau asking," he said, "liberty is what we say it is. And you will find that it can become tightly, oh, so tightly, circumscribed. So much so that you may have difficulty drawing a breath."

"True," I said, "if the asking relates to a crime on the Bureau's docket. The incident I am investigating has been reported to none but me."

"What incident?"

"If I report it to you, here and now, that could make it a Bureau matter. You might claim jurisdiction and prevent me from serving my client."

"All crimes are within the Bureau's jurisdiction."

"But this might not be a crime. It may have been an accident."

Besides, even if it was a criminal assault, I would still have jurisdictional leeway if the matter did not involve blood or breakage, theft of substantial property or credible threats to commit such acts. I told Warhanny that the case did not fall within those bounds, then added, "The offense, if it turns out to have been an offense, is one of public embarrassment, and the mystery involves both the means and the instigator."

The captain-investigator blinked. My integrator widened the image's focus so that I could see the mocking hand gesture that accompanied Warhanny's next remark. "And you count your days as productive?"

I resisted an urge to reply in kind, which I could have done by reminding the scroot of occasions when I had led the Bureau out of darkness and into the light. Instead, I said, "I intend to come down to Tirramee Plaza and poke about. I will take care not to get in your way."

"Do so," he said. The integrator told me that he had broken the connection. A moment later, my view of Warhanny and the scene on the roof went black, then I was seeing the square with my unassisted eyes. Lord Chavarie's roof and upper floor were concealed beneath a dome of darkness. My assistant said, unnecessarily, "They have raised a screen. Shall I pierce it?"

"By no means," I said. "They are on their guard and would notice." Besides, Warhanny could then act against me for poking my percepts into an active bureau investigation. "We will go down to the street then climb to the plaza. Prepare me some background on Lord Chavarie and canvass the integrators in the area for anything that they may have observed yesterday evening."

Moments later, as I stepped into the descender and was borne down to street level, the integrator said, "I have reports."

Proper procedure would have been to ask for the integrators' observations first, but something about the way Warhanny had leapt straight from surprise to umbrage prompted me to call for the aristocrat's background. An image of Dizmah Chavarie appeared in a corner of my field of vision. He had the lean and vulpine countenance characteristic of Olkney's hugely inbred upper social strata–his eyes were set so close together as to test the definition of human, and his expression was that of a man continually encountering unpleasant odors.

My assistant's voice spoke in my ear. Lord Chavarie had been a margrave-major, placing him the upper quadrant of the second tier of Olkney's aristocracy, which meant he could reliably trace his ancestry back through not just millennia but through aeons. His family was established before the crags and tors of the Devenish Range had arisen.

His estate was beyond Ektop, but he rarely visited there, preferring the comforts of his house-in-town. He had belonged to three clubs, none of which he frequented regularly, and spent most of his disposable time–aristocrats often had demanding schedules full of obligations imposed by immemorial custom–at the Terfel Connaissarium, engaged in research.

"What kind of research?" I said.

"He has invoked a privacy seal," said my assistant.

"Hmm," I said. Ordinarily, ticking its way past a research integrator's blocks and barriers would have posed no problem for my assistant, even if the device to be fooled was housed in the Archonate's premier connaissarium. But if Lord Chavarie's research related in any way to the Bureau's presence on his roof, Warhanny might even now be watching for us to come winking-and-tricking our way in.

"Indeed," my assistant agreed, "and the Bureau's integrators, when already on alert, are not easily fadiddled."

"So we will not take the risk. See what can be learned from a roundabout approach."

Four seconds later, my assistant said, "Done."

"Report."

I was now on the slideway that would carry me up through the terraced streets that led to Tirramee Plaza. The architecture I was passing was of a bombastic style, dating from a period when the ancient city's most affluent enjoyed flaunting their social prominence. It had been the fashion then for grand, solid houses, their outer walls unwindowed at street level–instead they were cut with niches in which were set moving statues of their owners striking heroic poses modeled on famous works of representational art. The architects had not reckoned, however, with the inventiveness of Olkney's common citizenry, who came in the night and decorated the statues with inappropriate clothing and other objects that created usually a comical, and often an obscene, effect. The owners complained to the Bureau of Scrutiny, but somehow the perpetrators were never apprehended. Eventually, the statues were removed and the niches stood empty.

"Lord Chavarie's biographical history is unremarkable," my assistant informed me. "As a child, he was educated at home then attended the Archon's Institute. He achieved no academic distinction nor did he dabble, as aristocrats may do, in the professions. Ten years ago, he contracted a marriage to Lord Bulmare's third daughter, Alifrayne, but their union has been without issue. For a time, he collected incised eggs, then abandoned that pastime to try breeding and rearing firefowl, but failed to damp down his flock adequately one night–"

"I remember now," I said, "the blaze spread from the outbuilding to the main house. His estate is still uninhabitable, I believe."

"Indeed. He relocated to Tirramee Plaza, though without Lady Alifrayne. She now travels The Spray. Communication between them is said to be brief, infrequent and rigorously formal."

"So, without success in profession, marriage or avocation, to what does Chavarie devote his time and such energies as an overbred Olkney aristocrat might summon?"

"Did," said the integrator.

It was my turn to say, "Indeed? His death is confirmed?"

"The Bureau has just released a statement. 'Death from indeterminate causes.' And 'all persons having knowledge of the circumstances are required to communicate such to the nearest barracks of the Bureau of Scrutiny.'"

"Hmm," I said. "But back to the question: what was the deceased's latest preoccupation?"

"Again," said my assistant, "the Bureau has invoked a screen."

"They might as well have put an illuminated sign on the man's roof," I said.

"Ah, of course," said the integrator, then we spoke the next two words together: "The Immersion."

The integrators of the houses and establishments lining the six sides of Tirramee Plaza had little to report. Feroz Pandamm had indeed descended the steps of the Monopolists Club at the time he had said. Unsteady in his gait, he had lurched around the fountain on the west side of the open space, his progress observed by the who's-theres of the several premises he had passed.

He was seen to fall to his knees at one point, immediately raising his hands to his head then making strenuous motions of his arms. He rose, glared at the sky above, felt his pate, then looked about as if searching for a hat. But he had not worn a hat—indeed, he never did, being grossly vain about his abundance of thick hair, which he wore shaped into extravagant swoops and peaks. He was seen to palpate his scalp as if in horror then, holding his hands to his head, rush off in the direction of his home at Tsant Prospect.

"Has the Bureau queried these devices?" I asked.

"They have," said my assistant, "but their inquiries focused on traffic to and from Lord Chavarie's domicile."

Feroz Pandamm's behavior would have seemed to scroot eyes nothing more than the stumblings of an overly lubricated imbiber weaving his way home. "Have we images?" I said.

We did. Two of the who's-theres were tasked by their owners to record all traffic in front of their premises. I saw the events Pandamm had described from both devices' perspectives. His statements to me were borne out. As was something he had not said. I had my integrator contact him.

"A question," I said, when his own integrator summoned him to speak with me. "After you were struck down, you sped away from the scene as fast as you could."

11

"I ran," he said.

"You ran in a very coordinated manner for a man who until moments before had been unable to walk a straight path, did you not?"

"I had not thought about it," he said, after a pause in which I assumed he was making up for the previous night's failure to do so. "But, yes, the attack seems to have sobered me."

"Hmm," I said.

"What does it mean?"

"Still premature. I will be in touch when I have something to tell you." I broke the connection.

By now we had reached Tirramee Plaza and I went to the scene of the incident. I glanced up as I approached Chavarie's house, four stories high and faced in polished green vitrine streaked with wiry veins of black chalcedax. The tall windows of the lower two floors were opaqued and the who's-there at the top of the long flight of stairs leading to the public doors was showing the red flash to discourage visitors. The roof remained under the Bureau's dome of darkness.

I walked about between the house and the west-side fountain with its interlocking circular curtains of spray. The pavement was of the self-cleaning sort, its perpetual eddies of mild energies carrying off dust and light debris before they could settle, to deposit the detritus in grilled slits set in foundation walls around the plaza, including the stone bases of the fountains. Accordingly, no trace of last night's events was to be found on the ever-swept and diamantine-studded surface.

But the nearest grill, in the base of a foundation, was of inert metal. I knelt and examined it, then had my assistant augment my perceptions. Finally, I took a miniature specimen kit from my coat pocket and collected a sample of the substance that speckled the base of the grill.

"Open an aperture," I told my assistant, and when it did so I placed the specimen bottle within. "Analyze that," I said.

A few moments later it gave me the chemical composition of the material I had collected, adding the comment: "Unusual."

"Certainly not what one would expect to find in Tirramee Plaza." I said. I had an inkling of where the stuff had come from, and that inkling gave me a potential explanation not only for what had happened to my client, but probably for what had befallen Lord Chavarie. The quickest way to make sure would have been to consult the records in the Terfel Connaissarium. But that I could not do, under the present circumstances, because, if my intuitive leap was right, I would find myself examining the same files in which Dizmah Chavarie had conducted his researches. And that would instantly draw the unwelcome attention of the Bureau.

"We are being observed from above," my assistant told me, privately.

"As expected," I said. I looked up at the tall helix of minutely carved marble that was a reminder of the Archon Imreet IV's long-ago reign. I would have liked to examine the monument through my assistant's percepts, but to do so I would first have to adjust their settings. And, again, that might result in scroot boots clumping over ground across which I preferred to step lightly.

I considered the facts as I knew them, as well as the avenues down which those facts appeared to lead, then I applied insight–by that I mean that I turned the question over to the intuitive part of my well calibrated brain–and waited. This time, it was not a long wait. I received an immediate answer.

I turned and walked briskly back the way we had come, telling my integrator, "Summon an air-car to meet us at the end of the slideway."

"Done," it said. "It wishes to know our destination. Back to the lodgings?"

The vehicle was already touching down beside us, its canopy sliding open. "No," I said, "contact the procurer Obinder Min in the usual manner and tell him I wish to consult with him."

Had Obinder Min been standing in bright sunlight in the middle of an open square without so much as a lamppost to hide behind, any fair-minded observer would still have said, "That man is lurking." Min's relationship to the phenomenal world proceeded along oblique lines; a direct and open approach was alien to his nature. Furtiveness was so much his idiom that I would not have been surprised to learn that he even sidled up to his breakfast.

My assistant could not contact him directly. Instead, there was a public integrator at the corner of Magher Street and The Blossoms that had been subverted to Min's purposes. It unknowingly relayed any incoming message to a private phone in a tavern in the Tan-Tan district, then promptly erased all record of the transaction.

The tavern's owner sent a boy across the alley to an upstairs room in a tenement, where an unsavory old woman memorized the message. When the boy was gone she tapped a spoon three times upon an exposed water pipe.

Obinder Min then came down and the woman whispered in his ear. Had she tapped any other number than three, he would not have descended, but would have climbed to the roof and leapt across to parapet of the adjoining building then down into another alley, where he kept a battered, single-seat skimmer hidden under what appeared to be a pile of moldering rubbish.

It seemed to me to be an unnecessarily elaborate process and ultimately not effective; I had penetrated Min's layers of security the first time I had cause to contact him–I found it useful to know what I was dealing with when I de-scended into the city's half-world. But it was plainly of importance to him so I had never told him that I could have readily parked my hired air-car outside his grimy window and tapped on it to gain his attention.

Not too long after my integrator sent out its signal, Min contacted me, though by voice only, through another public integrator that was also un-aware of the work it was performing for him. "Hapthorn?" he said, "you wish to meet with me?" It was a straightforward question, yet somehow when it came from the procurer's vocal apparatus it acquired an unspoken insinua-tion, as if the words were now smeared with some noxious substance.

"My integrator must have told you so," I said.

"I deal with principals, not subordinates."

Indeed, it was for that very reason that I wished to consult him. "Place and time?" I said.

"Is it urgent?"

"Not as such," I said, "but I would like to move on the matter while it re-mains fresh in my mind."

"I will see if I can free myself of entanglements," he said. His voice oozed out the last word as if inviting me to imagine him wrapped in lubricious coils. I resisted the invitation and proposed that we meet without delay.

"Bolly's Snug," he said. "Give me an hour to make the arrangements."

"I'll be there," I said. I told the air-car to take me back to my lodgings and to wait there while I equipped myself with a number of items. It was never wise to visit the tavern where the halfworld did much of its business without taking precautions against being rendered incapable, if not irrevocably dead.

We met in one of the private chambers at the rear of Bolly's Snug. Besides seclusion and a guarantee against eavesdroppers, the tavern's back rooms also offered unconventional exits should anyone, official or otherwise, attempt to interrupt a conference. Obinder Min was already on site when I arrived. Before I was led to the space he had hired for the hour, one of the proprietor's functionaries examined me for weapons. I turned over the needle-thrower I carried in an outer pocket but the rest of my paraphernalia was judged to be only of a defensive character and remained with me. The man who searched me knew his business, but though he passed a fairly sophisticated detector over my integrator, which still hung around my neck like a fat collar, his device did not detect mine's full capabilities. Any discriminator needed to put a lot of thought and work into the design and construction of an assistant, and I prided myself on not being just any discriminator.

Min rose from his place at the table when I entered, gesturing me to take the seat opposite his. The air in the small room was thick with a floral scent that came from the pomade that the procurer used to sweep back his thin, dark hair in two gleaming wings. He had a habit of running a hand from temple to nape when he was nervous, as if the touch of his own tonsure somehow reassured him; he did it now as he waited for me to broach the subject of our conversation.

I folded my hands on the table top and looked directly into his mud-brown eyes. "The Immersion," I said.

I am adept in reading micro-expressions. In this instance I was aided by my assistant which had focused its percepts on Min's face so it could record and replay key flashes of revealed emotion, displaying them to me as still images at the edges of my field of vision. Thus, when I spoke the two words, I was able to discern that his reactions were, in sequence, shock, alarm, guilt, and the recognition of opportunity–all passing in about the time it took him to blink twice and present me with a contrived look of bland ignorance.

"I don't know any–" he began.

I spoke over him. "Let us dispense with the preliminary dancing. You provide certain... let us say, 'requirements,' for some members of the Immersion. I know, for example, that you have assisted Lords"–my assistant put up a list of names where I could see them and I read a few aloud–"to find particular types of persons and objects with which they wished to gratify themselves."

I did not need my assistant to decipher Min's expression now. His face registered shock at the first aristocratic name I spoke and he actually flinched at two of the others. "What I want to know is, what did you get for Lord Chavarie last night?"

I had employed a calculated stratagem. I knew that the first names I had spoken were adherents of the distasteful philosophy—it would not have been too great a stretch to call it a cult without a deity—that was the Immersion. My insight had told me that it was highly likely that Obinder Min, as one of Olkney's most infamous procurers, was one of their suppliers. The likelihood became a certainty when I mentioned the name of the secret society and studied his reaction.

Still, I had not known for sure, before I spoke his name, that Chavarie was an Immersionist, nor that Min had procured for him. But I knew now. I knew also that Min would not want to discuss his relations with an aristocrat.

"I cannot tell you anything," he said, rising on shaky legs.

My assistant acted as we had prearranged. Min suddenly found that he could no longer control his lower limbs. He opened his mouth to call for help. That, too, was expected and my assistant emitted a pulse that paralyzed the man's vocal chords. I used the silence to remind Min that, unless he had thought to pay for it in advance, any emergency assistance he now sought from Bolly would have to be negotiated at a time when Min's need was greatest. Bolly was a notoriously hard-skinned haggler, especially when he had the other bargainer at a decided disadvantage. I suggested that Min wait to see what I intended before he committed himself. I then gave him back his voice.

He saw the wisdom of my suggestion. "But," he said, "I have learned not to incur Lord Chavarie's displeasure." His glance went to the fingers of his right hand. I had noticed that they were misshapen.

"I can relieve you on that score," I said. "The margrave-major is no longer with us." I saw the procurer visibly relax, until I added, "But the upper floors of his house-in-town are currently decorated in black and green."

Min took a sharp breath. "The scroots? What happen-"

This time, he interrupted himself and I did not need my assistant's percepts to tell me that the man had followed a chain of thought that answered his own question, and that he would be extremely reluctant to share that answer with me. His soft mouth set itself in as firm a line as it could manage, and though I knew he was frightened of me, I could see that he was far more frightened of something else.

I tried a gambit. "If you told me everything, I could keep your name out of it."

"No," he said, and I saw the truth of it in his eyes, "no, you couldn't."

16

"Then tell me one thing," I said, "and we are done. Where did you get the... "requirement' that you supplied to Lord Chavarie?"

I saw him wrestle with his fear and was surprised that he was able finally to subdue it. "The spaceport," he said. "A ship called the *Fanferray*. I bought it off the supercargo."

My assistant informed me privately that Min had told me the truth. "Very well," I said, "and now, for cover, we will make it appear that our meeting was to arrange for you to get something for me."

Suddenly, Obinder Min was all business. "What are your preferences?" he said. "Or do you wish to enlarge your tastes beyond previous experience?"

"Nothing that will make me an occasion for gossip."

"Discretion is my–" he began.

"A dreamworm will do. I am frequently bored."

"Is that all?" he said. "They are not prohibited. Why not something more–"

"A dreamworm," I said. "For my researches."

He shrugged. I bade my assistant return control of his legs to him and left by an unmarked exit.

She was a stubby tramp freighter, her hull red and her fins and sponsons umber, and the finish not been recently renewed so she bore the pits and scratches that testified to her being a less than well loved vessel. I found her standing on a pad on the eastern edge of the spaceport, out on its wind-swept island in Mornedy Sound.

The west side of the port was reserved for the great and gaudy spaceships that hauled freight and carried passengers under the names of the grand interstellar lines, the north for private yachts and charters, the south for administration, maintenance and in-transit facilities. The east side was a forlorn place, made more so by the grid of narrow streets separated from the rows of pads by a tattered wire fence, where spacers with time on their hands and funds in their pockets could expect to find rough-and-ready accommodations and personal services, supplied without a garnish of intrusive questions.

"Is your supercargo aboard?" I asked the ship's integrator.

It informed me that he was to be found in one of the establishments on Rear Street. It could summon him if I wished.

"No," I said. "We would only have to retrace his steps so that I could buy him a drink. Will you provide my assistant with an image of him? Oh, and his name."

The ship did not question why I should wish to entertain one of its officers I had never met and could not even name. It had probably learned not to ask questions. My assistant told me that it now had the man's likeness and that his name was Wormer Krell. I ducked through a gap in the wire and walked down a nameless alley that crossed Front and Middle streets to end at Rear.

I turned left and walked the stained and pitted pavement while the device around my neck employed its percepts to examine the interiors of the establishments we passed. Krell was discovered in a dark corner of a narrow room that consisted mostly of a long counter fronted by stools and a few booths at the back. The place smelled of yeasty liquids, fried grease and old sweat.

Krell wore frayed coveralls and the expression of a man who expected little of life, and even less of it good. When I sat down across from him his eyes went immediately to the integrator around my neck. "Police?" he said.

"Freelance discriminator."

One knob-knuckled hand was wrapped around a glass of colorless liquor. He lifted it now from the ring-scarred surface that separated us and brought it casually to his thin lips, but I saw his other hand drop out of sight to the bench beside him.

"I prefer this to be a friendly encounter," I said, "and perhaps even a profitable one for you. Besides, you will find that the weapon has been rendered inactive."

His hidden hand reappeared from beneath the table holding a mid-sized shocker. A red light flashing on its upper surface confirmed the truth of my statement. He set the weapon back down on the bench seat beside him and took another sip from the glass, swirled the stuff in his mouth then nodded as he swallowed. "What?" he said.

An image of Obinder Min appeared between us then faded as soon as he had seen it. "You sold something to this man."

"Did I?"

"Something that is not often seen on Old Earth." I did not add the reason for its rarity: that their import was strictly prohibited.

He made no reply but his eyes said he was waiting for the part of our conversation that interested him.

"My question is: having procured one, can you procure another?"

The slightest motion of his head.

"But here is my concern," I said. Another image appeared, a list of worlds the *Fanferray* had called at on its most recent voyage. "None of these is home to the item in question."

The list disappeared. He looked again at my assistant and I could see that he was worried. "Yes," I said, "I am a very capable discriminator. Interrogating your ship's integrator without its knowledge was well within my integrator's range. Finding out everything I need to know about you would not be a challenge."

This time, he drank what was left in his glass without making a show of it. "You are concerned about provenance?" he said.

"I am. The creature we're talking about cannot be too long away from its native habitat, or it becomes..." I gestured with both hands, rippling my fingers upward like a flock of birds taking sudden flight.

"It was stable," he said. "It traveled in a sealed container."

"Even before you acquired it?"

He said yes, but his eyes said he did not really know. And now I knew what had happened to Dizmah Chavarie and Feroz Pandamm.

I owed Krell nothing, but I saw no reason to add to his troubles. "Get yourself gone from here," I said. "It was not stable. It had degraded. And your end customer was an aristocrat."

It took him a moment to understand that I had been lying when I said I was interested in acquiring what he had supplied to Obinder Min to give to Lord Chavarie. Then his face went gray. He aged a decade in a moment. "Was?" he said.

"And is no more," I said. "That means inquiries will be made. Not by the Bureau of Scrutiny; they will be told nothing. Private inquiries. I will not be surprised if, before evening, I am approached to make them."

Now I saw confusion mix with the fear in his face. "You are not making them now?"

"Not in that regard," I said. "Fortunately for you, I have been retained by a bystander who was... inconvenienced by a side-effect. He would send men to kill you out of hand, but I have already told him I will not be party to such an act."

"What should I do?"

"Change your face, your name, your occupation,"–I glanced at the glass in his hand–"your habits. Go to live in some out-of-the-way place where you'll be able to see who's coming before they can see you. And make sure you always have a back door."

He stood up, the deactivated shocker in his hand, his eyes already looking left, right, in a way that would become a habit, if he lived long enough.

"How long do I have?"

"The rest of today, at least some of tomorrow. Don't tell anyone goodbye. Leave your dunnage on the *Fanferray*. Go, and go quickly."

He swore. There was nothing more to say. I turned to watch him leave. Already his shoulders had taken on the hunch of the hunted. I said to my assistant, "We will aid him. Lay an obvious false trail, then a second, less obvious."

A few moments later, as I left the drinking house, my integrator said, "The *Fanferray* believes he has signed on with the freighter *Buswold* that departed an hour ago. The port's security section's records, which will take some penetrating, show him catching a ride on a utility transport vehicle up to an orbiter. The orbiter's percepts will show him taking passage on a small liner heading down The Spray, under the name of Gestuphal Kennec."

"Good," I said. "Make sure that there is also no record of our having been here today."

"I routinely dissimulate our movements, unless otherwise instructed," it said.

"Of course."

I walked on, toward the north end of the port. "When we get to the charter terminal," I said, "find us an air-car."

"Destination?"

"Home."

It left me to my thoughts, but as we neared the lights of the northside facility, it said, "Why save Krell? He didn't care what happened to whoever took the animal off his hands. He is at least culpable of negligence."

Many people do not encourage curiosity in an integrator; it can lead to an unending series of questions, some of them unanswerable. A discriminator, however, requires a subtle assistant. "Because," I said, "I have never been able to appreciate vengeance as an art form, and sometimes I grow tired of being an auxiliary to those who do."

"Feroz Pandamm wishes to speak with you," my assistant said as the air-car gently descended to my lodgings' upper entrance.

"He will have to wait," I said. "Inform him of what awaits us." Now it was my roof's turn to be decorated in black and green. A Bureau volante hovered there, while a ground car idled before the street entrance on Shiplien Way. As I alighted from the air-car, Brustram Warhanny stepped from the volante. His down-drawn face, born to express an unhappy perspective on life, was again not even trying to overcome that handicap.

"The vehicle in which you arrived believes that it took you on board south of Finnhaber Boulevard, yet my car tracked it coming east across Mornedy Sound. From the spaceport."

I could think of nothing to say that would improve the situation. I smiled a very small smile and inclined my head in a way that conceded a point. That, however, was far too little to sate the captain-investigator's appetite; he asked me if he should impound the hired air-car and subject it to a peel.

"No," I said. "You should let it depart while you come with me to Tirramee Plaza."

His long head drew back. "To what end?" he said.

"To resolve the matter of Dizmah Chavarie."

Now the lofty forehead compressed itself into a facsimile of desert dunes seen from on high. "You told me that your discrimination had nothing to do with his death."

"I told you that my client had no connection. I have only just discovered, however, that what happened to my client was an after-effect of Lord Chavarie's demise."

"And I suppose you were just about to report as much to the Bureau?"

"Such was my intent. But I would have asked you to meet me at his house-in-town."

I could see that Warhanny was torn between doing something to me that he had long desired to do or solving a high-value case. It did not take long for duty to win out over personal preference, a quality that had to be admired in the better sort of scroot. "Get in," he said.

He told the aircraft where to take us. As we flew, I took my assistant from around my neck, opened the hatch that exposed its controls and made an adjustment.

"What are you doing?" Warhanny said.

"Recalibrating its percepts to take account of phase shift."

"Why?"

Instead of answering, I put a question of my own. "When you scanned the margrave-major's corpse, did you detect traces of this compound?" I had my assistant display the complex molecule I had collected from the site where Pandamm had been struck down.

Warhanny looked from the image in the air to me. "Yes," he said. "Are you saying you found it in the square below?"

"I am."

"And you analyzed it?"

"I did."

We waited to see which of us would speak next. "So did the Bureau," he said after a long moment. "The analysis was not useful. The substance is not known."

"That is because," I said, "it has degraded through contact with other substances with which it was highly reactive. You would have to work backwards through some unlikely chemistry–unlikely because the substance is of off-world origin."

"Where off-world," Warhanny wanted to know, "and what other substances?"

I answered the second question. "Our atmosphere, plus the natural oils of Lord Chavarie's skin, and probably whatever unguents he may have applied. Were there concentrations of the stuff on his palms?"

"Yes."

"And was any of his hair... missing?"

"He wore his hair in a band from ear to ear, cut short and dyed, with the rest depilated," the scroot said. "I believe that is the current mode among his set."

"I did not mean the hair on his head," I chided him, though gently.

That was not an issue, Warhanny said. Like many of his kind, the aristocrat had no body hair, the gene having been edited out of his line long, long ago.

"Ah," I said, "I had not known that." Indeed, I was gratified to find that there was something I did not know. Of course, the upper tiers of Olkney's society liked to keep some things to themselves. Their body servants were notoriously difficult to suborn–partly because the punishments for betraying a confidence ranged from the drastic to the horrific, but mainly because the relationships between the two classes were of such a great age as to have become essentially symbiotic. Neither could have lived long without the other.

"But, to retrn to the matter at hand," I said, "besides his palms, the greatest concentration of the mysterious compound would have been on and around his genitalia."

"How did you know that?" Warhanny said.

We were angling down toward Tirramee Plaza. The volante intended to land on the margrave's roof. "No," I said, "the ground." And there we disembarked, the captain-investigator's last question still unanswered.

With my assistant around my neck I led the scroot to the spot where Pandamm had been struck down. I bade the integrator apply its recalibrated percepts to the pavement and display the results so that both Warhanny and I could see them. Immediately, the diamantine-sparkled pavement grew dim and misty and the nearby spiral of filigreed marble that commemorated the Archonate of Imreet IV became as a pillar of smoke. I directed the device to focus on the monument. Clinging to the carved stone, a short distance above the ground, we saw a dark shape about the length of my forearm, though twice as thick in the middle and tapering to blunt points at both ends.

"What is it?" Warhanny said.

"A gromm. Or at least it was. After such a fall it would not have been able to survive the impact with my client."

"And what is, or was, a gromm?" Warhanny said.

"It is a life form from an uninhabited world a little ways up The Spray from Cheng," I said, naming one of the grand foundational domains settled during the first waves of the great effloration that carried humanity out into the immensity. "The world is called... well, it doesn't matter what its name is. Its atmosphere is insalubrious, it offers nothing worth the danger of landing there. But, occasionally, if someone is willing to pay, a few individuals who combine a taste for adventure with an unusual capacity for greed touch down there and come back with a few gromms. They don't travel well, however, and will quickly degrade once they are taken from their proper habitat.

"You will get the full story when you go through his integrator's records. I think you'll find he has been researching odd creatures through the Connaissarium."

At that, Warhanny bridled. "His account is under Bureau seal. If you have been poking into—"

"I have not," I told him. "Again, I have worked backwards from the presence of the gromm and Chavarie's membership in the Immersion."

That information caused the scroot to make a sharp intake of breath. "You profess not to know about the hair, yet you casually walk the Immersion out from the wings?"

"It was not I who brought it on stage," I said. "It was our deceased margrave-major."

The Immersion was a recent innovation, if one defines "recent" by the standards of Old Earth's ancient aristocracy: it had begun a few centuries ago, as a fellowship whose membership was restricted to the upper two tiers of those whose ancestry was usually their only notable distinction. An Immersionist's goal was to encompass the fullest possible range of erotic experience, believing that doing so would enable him—or her, though the membership was mostly male—to pass through into a new level of awareness: the state of Prismatic Abundance.

Immersionists believed that the copulative impulse was the essential human drive, that it unleashed fundamental energies which, when directed by certain recondite exercises involving breath control and posture, would physically alter the cerebrum. It was a matter of attuning the conscious and unconscious aspects of the psyche, creating a resonance that resulted in a "pure tone" which, once sounded within the confines of the mind, would propel the adept's being to a higher plane. There it would reside in perpetual ecstasy, untouched by space or time or entropy.

There were some, however, who found the discipline of diaphragmatic exercises and nostril control wearisome. They believed that Prismatic Abundance could be achieved by exercising the erotic reflex while under the influence of the right psychoactive substance.

One of those substances was the thick mucous that protected the gromm's tissues from the hostile atmosphere of its normal habitat. When fresh, the slime had remarkable properties; but when allowed to degrade, the stuff could be lethal.

Warhanny had the Bureau integrators consult those of the Connaissarium. The latter confirmed that Lord Chavarie had been conducting research into rare off-world species. The gromm had been only one of several creatures blessed, or perhaps cursed, with the attributes in which the margrave-major had taken an interest.

"Ambitious," I commented, when the Bureau's device passed Chavarie's list of mind-altering organisms to my assistant for display. "Eventually, his experiments were bound to prove fatal."

Together we reconstructed the manner of his death. The Immersionist had been alone in a bedchamber on the top floor. He had disrobed and removed the gromm from its container, having first opened the window to dispel the strong odor and corrosive fumes of the creature's home world's atmosphere. Folding the gromm in both hands, the aristocrat had attempted some degree, perhaps even the ultimate, of molestation.

The attempt had been unsuccessful. Exposed to Old Earth's atmosphere, the animal's already degraded mucous coating had rapidly altered its chemical composition. Its potent psychoactive substances, absorbed by Chavarie through his palms and through the skin of other, more tender regions, had triggered in him a catastrophic neuronic cascade. I could imagine the naked margrave-major leaping and thrashing contortedly about his bedchamber, his eyes bulging as he fell helplessly prey to random contractions and flexions of his own skeletal muscles, his lungs expanding and contracting like hyperactive bellows, with fluids emitting from every orifice. One of his spasmodic exertions must have flung the poor gromm out through the window, where gravity and momentum combined to deliver it onto the coiffured head of Feroz Pandamm.

My client had seized it and flung it from himself in an instant. Thus its mucous had not had time to penetrate to his scalp, which was well protected by his flamboyant head of hair. He had also immediately wiped his hands in disgust on his coat, avoiding serious contamination through his palms. The only psychoactive effect had been to sober him. Gromm mucous, taken in a tiny dose, was prized by many spacers for just that purpose.

The slug-like creature, now bruised and dying, invoked its last defense, an energy-consuming phase shift designed to disguise it from predators. It crawled to the Imreet IV monument, ascended as far as it could in an attempt to find refuge. There it expired, and there we found its remains.

I put on a pair of impermeable gloves and reached up to seize the corpse. I had to pull sharply to detach it from the filigreed marble; on examination, I saw that on the gromm's underside a network of small hooks stuck out from the now congealing slime. I found it hard to imagine how Chavarie could have summoned up an erotic impulse in the contemplation of such a creature, but then the eccentricities of Old Earth's aristocracy are frequently beyond the understanding of we who spend our lives on the less exalted tiers of the social ziggurat.

Warhanny produced an evidence container and we sealed up the gromm. "Again," he said, "the Bureau must express its gratitude for your invaluable assistance." To my ear, the sentiment behind his utterance did not appear to be gratitude, and judging from the gritting of his teeth as he pronounced the last two words, "intolerable interference" would have been a fair translation.

Still, I have learned that it does no good to abrade raw flesh when it comes clad in black and green. "I regret," I said, "that I diverted your attention from the core of the case, preventing you from achieving an early resolution."

The captain-investigator looked at me sharply, as if he thought I might be mocking him. But I maintained as sincere an expression of contrition as I could contrive and after studying me for a moment, he grunted what might have been an acknowledgement.

Feroz Pandamm came again to my workroom when I told him that I could identify the source of his baldness. He did not wish me to convey the information via the connectivity; my undoing of his scheme against the House of Esk had taught him that the measures he took to protect his privacy were not impenetrable. When he removed his hat, I saw that a fine stubble had sprouted on his scalp.

He heard the tale of the gromm and Lord Chavarie's demise without interruption, then nodded and said, "It's as well he's dead; I would have had a hard time prosecuting one of "them"– he used the intonation that, in Olkney, imbued the otherwise common pronoun with a particular meaning.

"The Bureau of Scrutiny has informed the margrave-major's heirs of the injury you innocently sustained, though your name was not mentioned. It was suggested that the matter could be disposed of if the family's senior steward would view favorably a request to change its supplier of essences."

A gleam of avarice sparked in Pandamm's eyes. "That's a Pormeireon Brothers account," he said. "Theirs since the world emerged from the primordial egg." An uncharacteristic grin disfigured his dour face for several seconds, then the shutters drew down again.

"You are satisfied with my handling of the discrimination?" I said.

"I am. If ever you wish to take up an appreciation of essences, I will offer you a discount of–"

"Such is not one of my ambitions," I said. "But you will remember that you now owe me a favor, whenever I call for it."

His brows showed a vertical furrow. "What kind of favor will it be?"

"It is premature to say. I gave in to an impulse."

"Very well," he said. "Feroz Pandamm stands by his word. Call when you will." And, dispensing with formalities, he took his leave.

The day after Lord Chavarie's estate was adjudicated by the Archonate's Court of Assigns and Severances, my assistant informed me that the primary heir's major-domo was seeking a connection.

"How may I assist you?" I said when the man's bland face appeared in the air before me, wearing that look of supercility cultivated by servants of the proud and prominent.

"My lord requires your services to locate a person."

"To what end?"

"Do you require that knowledge?"

"I do."

The servant sighed the sigh of one who finds he must tolerate the inanities of lesser breeds. "To requite an injury done to my lord's family."

"Requite how?"

His only answer was a glare meant to return me to my rightful place.

"Is the person's identity known?" I said.

"His name is Wormer Krell." The major-domo affected an expression of superior knowledge as he added, "He also goes by the alias Gestuphal Kennec."

"Do you have a last known location?"

"He departed Old Earth as auxiliary crew on the liner *Omphire*, bound for Cronk."

"Cronk is a hub world," I said, "this could require considerable travel."

The matter was languidly dismissed. "My lord will place his lesser yacht at your disposal."

"I thought Lady Alifrayne kept that vessel in constant use."

"Lady Alifrayne has retired to her father Lord Bulmare's estate."

"Hmm," I said. "I may also have to set aside a great deal of time."

We fell to discussing my fee. I proposed a generous retainer, with substantial refreshers. I did not ask for a bonus for locating Krell. Somewhere along the way I was bound to come across a corpse that would satisfy the Chavaries' atavistic craving for vengeance. To them, we all looked much alike.

And traveling The Spray in luxury would relieve the tedium that, increasingly, had begun to blight my hours. I began to prepare an itinerary of worlds I had long wanted to visit.

While I was packing, the dreamworm arrived. For a moment I entertained a the mischievous whim of sending it as a gift to Brustram Warhanny. Instead, I contacted Obinder Min and we met on the Belmain seawall, the gray waters of the Sound crashing with mindless violence against the gray, unmindful stone. I told the procurer that I had no need of the thing and that he could have it back. I had decided to repel boredom with the aid of Lord Chavarie's lesser yacht.

He shrugged and took back the item, saying that he could always find a buyer for a ripe dreamworm.

"You are in no peril from the family over the matter of the gromm?" I asked him.

He tucked away the pale yellow chrysalis in an impermeably lined pocket. "Not as long as I am useful to the Immersion."

I had assumed as much.

"Is there anything you require?" he asked me.

I discounted the unsavory implication inherent in the way he voiced the question. "I suppose there must be," I said, "if I can just discover what it is."

Mastermindless

I had almost finished unraveling the innermost workings of a moderately interesting conspiracy to defraud one of Olkney's oldest investment syndicates when suddenly I no longer understood what I was doing.

The complex scheme was based on a multileveled matrix of transactions—some large, some small; some honest, some corrupt—conducted among a elaborate web of persons, some of whom were real, some fictitious and a few who were both, depending upon the evolving needs of the conspirators.

Disentangling the fraud, sifting the actual from the invented, had occupied most of the morning. But once the true shape of the scheme became clear, I again fell prey to the boredom that blighted my days.

Then, as I regarded the schematic of the conspiracy on the inner screen of my mind, turning it this way and that, a kind of gray haze descended on my thoughts, like mist thickening on a landscape, first obscuring then obliterating the image.

I must be fatigued, was my initial reaction. I crossed to my workroom sink and splashed water onto my face then blotted it dry with a square of absorbent fiber. When I glanced into the reflector I received a shock.

"Integrator," I said aloud, "what has happened to me?"

"You are forty-six years of age," replied the device, "so a great many events have occurred since your conception. Shall I list them chronologically or in order of importance?"

I have always maintained that clarity of speech precedes clarity of thought and had trained my assistant to respond accordingly. Now I said, "I was speaking colloquially. Examine my appearance. It has changed, radically and not at all for the better."

I looked at myself in the reflector. I should have been seeing the image of Henghis Hapthorn, foremost freelance discriminator in the city of Olkney in the penultimate age of Old Earth. That image traditionally offered a broad brow, a straight nose leading to well formed lips and a chin that epitomized resolution.

29

Instead, the reflector offered a beetling strip of forehead above a proboscis that went on far too long and in two distinct directions. My upper lip had shrunk markedly while the lower had grown hugely pendulous. My chin, apparently horrified, had fallen back toward my throat. Previously clear sweeps of ruddy skin were now pallid and infested by prominent warts and moles.

"You seem to have become ugly," said the integrator.

I put my fingers to my face and received from their survey the same unhappy tale told by my eyes. "It is more than seeming," I said. "It is fact. The question is: how was this done?"

The integrator said, "The first question is not how but exactly <u>what</u> has been done. We also need to learn why and perhaps by whom. The answers to those questions may well have a bearing on finding a way to undo the effect."

"You are right," said I. "Why didn't I think of that?"

"Are you being colloquial again or do you wish me to speculate?"

I scratched my head. "I am trying to think," I said.

"I have never known you to have to try," said the integrator. "Normally, you must make an effort to stop."

The device was correct. My intellectual capacity was renowned for both its breadth and depth. As a discriminator I often uncovered facts and relationships so ingeniously hidden or disguised as to baffle the best agents of the Archonate's Bureau of Scrutiny.

My cerebral apparatus was powerful and highly tuned. Yet now it was as if some gummy substance had been poured over gears that had always spun without friction.

"Something is wrong," I said. "Moments ago I was a highly intelligent and eminently attractive man in the prime of life. Now I am ugly and dull."

"I dispute the 'eminently attractive.' You were, however, presentable. Now, persons who came upon you unexpectedly would be startled."

I disdained to quibble; the esthetic powers of integrators were notoriously scant. "I was without question the most brilliant citizen of Olkney."

The integrator offered no contradiction.

"Now I must struggle even to..." I broke off for a moment to rummage through my mind, and found conditions worse than I had thought. "I was going to say that I would have to struggle to compute fourth-level consistencies, but in truth I find it difficult to encompass the most elementary ratios."

"That is very bad."

My face sank into my hands. Its new topography made it strange to my touch. "I am ruined," I said. "How can I work?"

Integrators were not supposed to experience exasperation, but mine had been with me for so long that certain aspects of my personality had infiltrated its circuits. "Perhaps I should think for both of us," it said.

"Please do."

But scarcely had the device begun to outline a research program than there came an interruption. "I am receiving an emergency message from the fiduciary pool," it said. "The payment you ordered made from your account to Bastieno's for the new surveillance suite cannot go forward."

"Why not?"

"Insufficient funds. The pool also advises that tomorrow's automatic payment of the encumbrance on these premises cannot be met."

"Impossible!" I said. I had made a substantial deposit two days earlier, the proceeds of a discrimination concerning the disappearance of Hongsaun Bedwicz. She had been custodian of the Archonate's premier collection of thunder gems, rare objects created when lightning struck through specific layers of certain gaseous planets. They had to be collected within seconds of being formed, lest they sink to lower levels of the chemically active atmosphere and dissolve. I had located Bedwicz on a planet halfway down the Spray, where she had fled with her secret lover, Follis Duhane, whose love of fine things had overstrained her income.

My fee should have been the standard ten per cent of the value of the recovered goods, but the Archonate's bureaucrats had made reference to my use of some legally debatable methodologies, and I had come away with three per cent. Still, there should be at least 30,000 hepts, I informed my assistant.

"My records concur," said the integrator. "Unfortunately, the pool's do not. They say you have 32 hepts and 14 grimlets. No more, no less."

"Where has the rest of it gone?"

"Pool integrators are never sophisticated, lest they grow bored with constant ins and outs and begin to amuse themselves with the customers' assets. This one merely counts what is there and records inflow and outtake. Yesterday the funds were present. Now they are not, although there has been no authorized withdrawal."

"So now I am not only ugly and dull, but have scarcely a groat to my name and am at risk of being ejected into the street."

The integrator said nothing. "Well," I prompted it, "have you no empathy?"

"You assembled me from analytical and computative elements," it replied. "However, I believe I can feign sympathy, if that will help."

"I doubt it," I said. "Why don't you analyze something?"

But instead it told me, "I am receiving another urgent message."

I groaned. "Is it the Archon threatening to banish me? That would place an appropriate crown onto the morning's disasters."

"It is Grier Alfazzian, the celebrated entertainer," said the integrator. "Shall I connect?"

"No."

"He may wish to engage you. An urgent matter would presuppose a willingness to pay an advance. That would solve one of the morning's problems."

"Hmmm," I said. "I should have thought of that."

"Yes," it said, then after a pause, "you poor little lumpykins."

"All right, put him through. But audio only. I don't want to be seen like this."

"Very well."

"And no more attempts at sympathy."

A screen appeared in the air before me, but when Alfazzian connected I did not see the face that gave women the hot swithers, though I had always thought him more pretty than handsome. He spoke from behind a montage of images that recalled his most acclaimed roles.

"Is that you, Hapthorn?"

I recognized his plummy baritone. "It is," I said.

"I have a question that requires an answer. Urgently and most discreetly. Come to my home at once."

I did not wish to take my new countenance out into the teeming streets of Olkney. There was a bylaw forbidding the frightening of children.

"Can we not discuss it as we are?"

"No."

"Very well." I had a mask left over from a recent soiree at the Archon's Palace. "But summoning me on short notice requires an advance on my fee."

"How much?"

Fortunately my memory was not fully impaired. I could recall the amounts cadged from wealthy clients who called me for assistance from within the coils of drastic and unexpected predicaments.

"Five thousand hepts," I said. "You may transfer it to my account at once."

"I shall," he said. "Wait while my integrator conducts the transfer."

There was a pause which lengthened while I regarded the images of Alfazzian striking poses in theatrical costumes and romantic settings. Then his voice returned to say, "There seems to be a problem with my finances."

"Indeed?" I said. I recalled that I often said "Indeed," when I could not think of any other rejoinder. When I wished to avoid a question, I usually indicated that an answer would be premature. I found that the two rejoinders filled conversational holes quite nicely.

"I do not have five thousand hepts at the moment. My funds have apparently been misplaced, except for a trifling sum."

Some stirring in the back of my mind urged me to ask the exact amount of the trifling sum.

"Why do you wish to know?" Alfazzian said.

I did not know why I wished to know, so I said, "It would be premature to say."

"The amount is 32 hepts and 14 grimlets," he said.

"Indeed."

"Are the numbers significant?" Alfazzian asked.

"It would be premature to say," I said. "I will call you back."

"It cannot be coincidence that his funds and yours have been reduced to the same amount," the integrator said.

"Why not?"

"Consider the odds."

My mind attempted to do so in its customary manner, lunging at the calculation like a fierce and hungry dog that scents raw meat before its muzzle. But the mental leap was jerked to a halt in mid-air as if by a short chain. "I take it the odds are long?" I said.

The integrator quoted a very lopsided ratio.

"Indeed," I said. "But what does it signify?"

"It would be premature..." it began.

"Never mind."

I tried to think of possible circumstances that could empty two unrelated accounts of all but the same small sum. After sustained effort, I came up with what seemed to be a pertinent question. "Do Alfazzian and I use the same pool?"

"No."

"Then it can't just be a defective integrator?"

"Integrators do not become defective," was the reply.

"I did not mean to offend."

"Integrators do not take offense. We are above such things."

"Indeed."

There was a silence. "How could the closely guarded integrators of two solvencies be induced to eliminate the funds of two separate depositors except for an identical trifle?" I asked.

"Hypothetically, a master criminal of superlative abilities might be able to accomplish it."

"Does such a master criminal exist?"

"No," was the answer, followed by a qualification. "But if such a criminal did exist he would almost certainly have the power to disguise his existence."

"Even from the Archonate's Bureau of Scrutiny?" I wondered.

"Unlikely, but possible. The scroots are not completely infallible."

"But if there was such a master purloiner, what would be his motivation in impoverishing me and Alfazzian? How have our lives mutually connected with that of our assailant?"

"No motive seems apparent," said the integrator.

I pushed my brain for more possibilities. It was like trying to goad a large, lethargic animal that prefers to sleep. "Who else might be able to subvert the fiduciary pools?" I said. "Could it be an inside job?"

"It is hard to imagine a cabal of officers from two financial institutions conspiring to defraud two prominent customers."

"And, again, where lies a motive?"

My mind was no more help than my assistant in answering that question. But if the machinery would not turn over, I still retained a grasp of the fundamentals of investigations: the transgressor would be he who had the means, motive and opportunity to commit the offense. I considered all three factors in the light of the known facts and was stymied.

"I am stymied," I said. Then a faint inspiration struck. I asked the integrator, "If I were as I was before whatever has happened to cloud my mind, what would I now propose to do?"

The integrator replied, "You have occasionally said that although with most problems the simplest answer is usually correct, sometimes one encounters situations where the bare facts stubbornly resist explanation. In such a case, adding further complications paradoxically clarifies the issue."

I could remember having said those exact words. Now I asked the integrator, "Have you any idea what I meant when I said that?"

"Not really."

I scratched my head again.

"Do you have a scalp condition?" asked my assistant. "Shall I order anything from the chymist?"

"No," I said. "I was trying to think again."

"Does the scratching help?"

"No. Nor do your interruptions. Be useful and posit some complicating factors that might have something to do with the case."

"Very well. You are ugly and not very bright."

"I don't see how gratuitous insults can help."

"You misapprehend. At the same time as you have become poor, your appearance and mental acuity have also been reduced."

"Ahah," I said. Again there came a glimmer of an idea. This time I managed to fan it into a small flame. "And Alfazzian, who normally delights in displaying his face to the world, hid behind a montage while he spoke with me."

"So the coincidence might be even more extreme," said the integrator, "if he too has been reduced to ugliness."

"Connect me to him."

A moment later I was again looking at Alfazzian's screen. "Tell me," I said, "has there been an alteration in your appearance?"

There was a pause before he said, "How did you know?"

I had never had difficulty answering that question. "I do not reveal my methods," I said.

"Are you taking the case?"

"I am," I said. "I will make a special dispensation and allow you to pay me later."

"I am grateful."

"One question: does it seem to you that your intellectual faculties have been reduced?"

"No," Alfazzian said, "but then I have always got by on my talent."

"Indeed," I said. My longstanding impression of the entertainer remained intact: his talent consisted entirely of his fortuitous facial geometry. "Remain at home and wait to hear from me."

I broke the connection and the screen disappeared. I said to my assistant, "Now we know more, but still we know nothing."

We knew that I who had been brilliant, attractive–or so I would argue–and financially comfortable had been made dense, repugnant and indigent. Alfazzian had been admittedly more handsome than I and probably much more wealthy, and now he was also without funds or looks–but his intellect had not been correspondingly ravished.

"There is a pattern here," I said, "if I could but see it."

I wrestled with the facts but could not get a secure grip. The effort was made more difficult by a growing clamor from the street outside my quarters. I went to the window and, bidding the integrator minimize the obscuring membrane, looked down at a growing disturbance.

Several persons were clustered before a doorway on the opposite side of Shiplien Way, beating at the closed portal with fists, feet and, in the case of a large and choleric woman in yellow taffeta, a parasol. As I watched, more participants joined the mob, then all took to shouting threats and imprecations at a smooth headed man who leaned from an upper window and implored them to return another day.

The door, which remained closed, led to a branch of the Olkney Mercantile, one of the city's most patronized financial institutions. I spoke to my assistant. "Is Alfazzian's account with the OM?"

"No."

"Then I believe we can add one more new fact to our store."

I inspected the individual members of the crowd. I had never been one to judge others on mere appearance, but the assemblage of mismatched features across the street was the least fortunate collection of countenances I had ever seen assembled in one place. "Make that two new facts," I said.

"Hmmm," I said. Again, it was as if my mind expected a pattern to present itself, but nothing came. It was an unpleasant sensation, the mental equivalent of ascending a staircase and, expecting to find one more riser than the joiner has provided, stepping up onto empty air and crashing down again.

"The most handsome man in Olkney is made repellent," I said to my assistant, "and the most intelligent is made at best ordinary. As well, both are impoverished. So apparently are many others." I struggled to form a shape from the data and an inkling came. "If Alfazzian and I are the targets and the others are merely bystanders, then why is the institution across the street in turmoil? We have no connection to it."

"It could be that the attack is general," said the integrator, "and therefore you and our client are only part of a wider category of victims."

I turned the concept over and looked at it from that angle. It appeared no more comprehensible. "We need more data," I said. "Access the public advisory service."

The screen reappeared, displaying a fiercely coiffed young woman who was informing Olkney that it was inadvisable to visit the financial district. "Dislocations are occurring," she said, widening her elegant eyes while uplifting perfectly formed eyebrows.

"Two more facts," said the integrator. "Other depositories must have been raided and there is one attractive person who has not been rendered grim."

"Three facts," I said. "The painfully handsome man who usually engages her in inane banter about trivialities has not appeared."

But what did it mean? Were only men affected? I had the integrator examine other live channels. Those from outside Olkney showed no effects. In other cities and counties, handsome men still winked and nodded at me from behind fanciful desks. There were no monetary emergencies. But the emissions originating within the city fit the emerging pattern. Of attractive women, there was no shortage; of good looking men, a dearth.

"Regard this one," said the integrator. We were seeing the farm correspondent of a local news service, a man hired more for his willingness to climb over fences and prod the confined stock at close range than for set of jaw or twinkle of eye.

"He has always been hard on the gaze," I said.

"Yes," agreed my assistant, "but he is grown no harder."

"Another fact," I said.

Matters were almost beginning to assume a shape. If I could have thrust aside the clouds that obscured my mind, I knew I would be able to see it. But the mist remained impenetrably thick.

"A question occurs," I said. "Who is the richest man in Olkney?"

"Oblos Pinnifrant."

"And is his face well or unfortunately constituted?"

"He is so wealthy that his appearance matters not."

"Exactly," I said. "He delights in inflicting his grotesque features on those who crave his favor, forcing them to vie one against another to soothe him with flattery. Connect me to him."

Pinnifrant's integrator declined the offer of communication. I said, "Inform him that Olkney's most insightful discriminator is investigating the disappearance of his fortune."

A moment later, the plutocrat's lopsided visage appeared on my screen. "What do you know?" he said.

"It would be premature to say."

"Yet you are confident of solving the mystery?"

"You know my reputation."

"True, you have yet to fail. What are your terms?"

My terms were standard: ten per cent of whatever I recovered.

Pinnifrant's porcine eyes glinted darkly. "Ten per cent of my fortune is itself a fortune."

"Indeed," I said, "but 32 hepts and 14 grimlets are not much of a foundation on which to begin anew, even for one with your egregious talent for turning up a profit."

In fact, Pinnifrant had been born to wealth and had only had to watch it breed, but a lifetime of deference from all who rubbed up against him had convinced the magnate that he was the sole font of his tycoonery.

After a brief chaffer, he said, "I agree to your terms. Report to me frequently." He moved to sever the connection.

"Wait," I said. "Have you noticed any diminution of your mental capacities?"

"I am as sharp as ever," was the answer, "but my three assistants have become effectively useless."

"Has there been any change in the arrangement of their features?"

"I would not know. I do not bother to inspect their faces."

"One last thing," I said. "Have your financial custodian contact me immediately."

Agron Worsthall, the Pinnifrant Mutual Solvency's chief tallyman appeared on my screen less than a minute after I broke the connection to Pinnifrant. He seemed eager to assist me.

"How much remains in his account?" I asked.

"Oblos Pinnifrant has consolidated many of his holdings through us," Worsthall said. "All but one of his accounts have been reduced to a zero balance. The exception contains 32 hepts and 14 grimlets."

"What about other depositors' holdings? Are they also reduced to that amount?"

"They are. That is, the male depositors and those who had joint accounts with female partners."

"But women are unaffected?"

"Yes, and children of both sexes."

"And where have the funds gone? Were they transferred to someone else?"

"They were not. The money is simply not there."

"Is that possible?"

I heard him sigh. "Until today I would have said it was not, but I am finding it difficult to deal with abstruse concepts this morning."

"Has there been any change in your physical appearance?" I asked. "Specifically, your face?"

"What kind of question is that?"

"A pertinent one, I believe."

There was a silence on the line while Worsthall sought his own reflection. When he came back his voice had a quaver. "Something has occurred to my nose and chin," he said. "As well, there are blemishes."

"Hmm," I said.

"What does it mean?"

I told him it would be premature to say. "You said that all accounts held by men had been reduced to 32 hepts and 14 grimlets. What about accounts that contained less than that amount—were they raised to this mystical number?"

"No, they were unaffected. Is that germane?"

I asked him if he had difficulty understanding the meaning of "premature." Then another idea broke through the fog. "I wish you to do something for me," I said. "Contact all the other financial institutions in Olkney. Ask if the same thing has happened."

I broke the connection and attempted to rouse my sluggish analytical apparatus, but it continued to lie inert.

Again, I asked my assistant, "If I were possessed of my usual faculties, how would I address this conundrum?"

"You would look for a pattern in the data," it said.

"I have done that. I cannot see more than the bare outline of what, and not even a glint of why or how. Men have been robbed of their wealth, looks and intelligence, yet who has gained? Where lies the motive, let alone the means?" I sighed. "What more would I do if I were intact?"

"You might look for a pattern outside the data," the integrator said. "You once remarked that it is possible to deduce the shape of an invisible object by examining the holes left by its passage."

"I do not see how that applies to this situation."

"Nor do I. I am accustomed to rely upon you for insights. My task is to assemble and correlate data as you instruct."

"What other brilliancies have I come up with over the years? Perhaps one will ring a chime and re-ignite my fires."

"You once opined that the rind is mightier than the melon. You presented this as a particularly profound perception."

"What did it mean?"

"I do not know. When you said it, you were under the influence of certain substances."

"No use," I said. "Go on."

"You have occasionally noted that the wise man can learn from the fool."

"I remember saying it," I said, "but now I have no idea what I meant."

"Perhaps something to do with opposites attracting?" the integrator offered.

"I doubt it," I said. "Do they attract? If so, it can't be for long since wouldn't true opposites irritate each other if not cancel each other out? It sounds like mutual annihilation and I'm sure I've never been in favor of that."

"You also say that sometimes the most crucial clue is not what has happened, but what has not."

"That sounds more like it," I said. "Except that the number of things that haven't happened must be astronomically greater than those that have. So how do we pick out the nonexistent events that have meaning?"

"You usually perform some pithy analysis."

"Yes, but I'm short on pith today."

"Then it will have to be an inspired guess."

"I am far from inspired," I said. "But I think we have at least defined the crime. The attacks are aimed at intelligent and presentable men as well as those who have more than 32 hepts and 14 grimlets.

"Dull men have not been made duller, nor poor men poorer, nor have the unprepossessing been further victimized. And women and children are unaffected on all counts.

"We come back as always to means, motive and opportunity."

It was difficult to posit a rational means or an opportunity by which the assumed perpetrator could do so much harm to so many and all apparently at the same moment. I knew from long experience, however, that motives were relatively few and all too common to most of humankind. "Jealousy," I said. "We may be looking for a poor, not too bright man with a face to curdle milk."

"But if he is dim-witted, how does he contrive to perform the impossible?" said my assistant.

"Indeed," I said. "How is the operative question."

The integrator made a sound that was its equivalent of a throat clearing. "I have a suggestion," it said.

"What?"

Its tone was tentative. "Magic."

I snorted. It was an automatic response whenever the subject was raised. "Only a fool believes in magic," I said.

"Perhaps this is the work of a fool."

That almost made sense, but though I could no longer argue for them, I recalled all my old opinions. "There is no such thing as magic."

"Yet there are arguments for the opposing view."

I had encountered them. Supposedly there was an alternation between magic and physics, between sympathy and rationalism, as operating principles of the phenomenal universe. As the Great Wheel rolled through the eons, one assumed supernacy over the other, only to see the relationship eventually reversed.

When one regime took the ascendancy, the other allegedly remained as an embedded seed in its unfriendly host. Thus in an age when magic held sway, its mechanics were still logically extrapolated–there were rules and procedures—while during the present reign of rationality, events at the subquantum level were supposedly determined more by quirks and quizzidities than by unalterable laws.

I was occasionally braced, at a salon or social, by some advocate of the mystical persuasion who would try to convince me that the Wheel was now nearing the next cusp and that I might live long enough to see the contiguous series of electrons that carried information from one device to another replaced by chains of ensorceled imps, my integrator supplanted by an enchanted familiar.

I had investigated the arcana of magic over a summer during my youth and could demolish its advocates with arguments that were both subtle and vigorous. However, I had to admit that those arguments were at present beyond my grasp. Still, I harrumphed once more and said, "Magic!" then blew air over my lips as if shooing away a gossamer.

My assistant said, "You also like to say that when all impossibilities have been swept from the table what remains, however unlikely, must be the answer."

"Magic," I said, "is one of those impossibilities."

"Are you sure?"

"I used to be," I said, "so I ought to be now."

"Even a wise man can..." began the integrator, then interrupted itself to tell me that Pinnifrant's tallyman was back.

"What have you learned?"

"The same situation pertains across the city. Indeed, even accounts held outside Olkney by male residents of the city have been affected."

The more I learned the more perplexed I became. Even in my diminished state, I recognized the irony. I had long wished for a superlative opponent, a master criminal who could give me room to stretch. Now one had seemingly appeared, but in doing so had robbed me of the capacity to combat his outrages. Still, I struggled to encompass an image of the situation.

"And there is no indication that anyone has benefited from the thefts?" I asked Worsthall. "No woman's account has ballooned? No child's?"

"No."

"Thank you," I said, though I could not see how the information helped.

"There is one anomaly," he said.

"Hmm?"

"A male depositor at Frink Fiduciary had a balance of 32 hepts and 15 grimlets before the discrepancy this morning..."

"Discrepancy?" I asked.

"It is a term we in the financial sector use when accounts do not tally."

"Why not be bold and call it what it is, mass theft and rampant rapine?"

"If we were bold, we would not be bankers," was the reply.

"Indeed," I said, "but what were you about to tell me?"

"That a male depositor had a balance of 32 hepts and 15 grimlets before the... rampant rapine, and that he had the same balance afterwards. And still does."

I had him repeat the numbers again. "This depositor had one grimlet more than the ubiquitous H32.14 before the... the event, and he still has the same amount now?"

"As of three minutes ago," said the tallyman.

"Hmm," I said. I experienced a vague sense that the anomaly might be significant. "Who is he?"

"He is called Vashtun Errible."

"Tell me about him."

There was little to tell: only an address on a cul de sac off the Fader Slide, an obscure location in an uncelebrated part of the city. No image of Errible reposed in the solvency's files and the connectivity code he had given when opening the account was long since defunct. The account had not been used for many years and had probably been forgotten by its nominee.

I left the tallyman to his troubles and set my assistant to scouring all sources for news of this Vashtun Errible. The integrator turned up only one more item: a deed of indenture that bound Errible's services to the requirements of one Bristal Baxandall.

"Now that's a name I have heard before," I said, though I could not immediately place it.

"He prefers to be known as The Exalted Sapience Bristal Baxandall, an alleged thaumaturge," said the integrator. "He performs at children's parties."

Again I spied the glimmer of an idea. Perhaps this Baxandall was the mastermind behind the calamity, hiding his brilliance by masquerading as a low-rent prestidigitator. Or he might be only the blind behind which Errible, the true prodigy, had concealed himself.

I had a hunch that one or both of these two persons was central to the mystery. Normally, I despised hunches and had always denied their validity–to my mind, an intuition was no more than the product of an analytical process that took place in the mind's dark back rooms. Occasionally, a door was flung open and the result of unconscious analysis was tossed into the light of the mental front parlor, to be discovered by the incumbent as if it had arrived by mystical means.

The thought led to another: I wondered if my own back rooms were as fully stocked and active as always but that some force had sealed the doors. The more I examined the idea, mentally probing about in my inner recesses the way my tongue would explore the gap left by an extracted tooth, the more it seemed likely that my faculties had not been irrevocably ripped away, but only placed out of reach. I listened and it seemed that I could almost hear the ghost of my former genius crying out to me from beyond a barrier in my mind.

I realized that my assistant was saying something. "Repeat," I said.

"The Exalted Sapience's address is the same as that which the solvency found for Vashtun Errible," it said.

"Connect me."

"I cannot. He apparently possesses no integrator."

"How is that possible?"

"I cannot even speculate," said the integrator. "His house appears as a blank spot in the connectivity matrix."

"Ahah!" I said again. "The shape left by the invisible object!"

"What do you mean?"

I did not know. It was another hunch. "It would be premature to say," I said. "Summon an air-car and have it take me to that address."

The vehicle was longer than usual in arriving and I noticed that its canopy was darkly stained. When we rose above the rooftops I saw why: thick columns of greasy, black smoke boiled skywards from several sites along the big bend in the river, joining to form a pall over the south side of the city. To the west, several streets were blocked off by emergency vehicles bearing the lights and colors of the provost bureau, and a surging mob was rampaging through the financial district, smashing glass and overturning motilators.

The air-car banked and flew north toward an industrial precinct that looked to be quieter. After a few minutes it angled down to a dead-end street below the slideway and alighted before an ill-kept two-story house whose windows were obscured by dark paint. I bid the car remain but it replied that it could only do so if I paid the accumulated fare immediately and allowed it to deduct its waiting fee every five minutes.

"How much?" I asked and was told that I owed seven hepts. Furthermore, it would charge me twenty grimlets per minute to wait.

"Usually, I charge such expenses to my account with your firm," I said.

"These are unusual times," it said and I was forced to agree to the terms.

The house was dilapidated, the paint peeling and some siding sprung loose. Dank weeds had invaded and occupied the front lawn and the porch sagged when I topped the front steps. There was a faint smell of boiled vegetables.

There were symbols painted on the front door. They seemed vaguely familiar but my uncertain memory could not produce their meanings. There was no who's-there beside the door, the house having no integrator to operate it. I struck the painted wood with my knuckles to make my presence known.

There was no response nor any sound from within. A second knocking brought no result so I tried the latch and the door opened inward.

I stepped within and called for attention. There was no answer. I looked about and saw a small, untidy foyer from which a closed door led left, a stairway went upward and a short hall ran back to what appeared to be a rudimentary kitchen.

I called again and heard what might have been a reply from behind the closed door. I opened it and looked into a cramped and fusty parlor dominated by an oversized table draped in black cloth on which was scattered an arrangement of objects and instruments I could not immediately identify. The opaqued windows let in no light, and the only illumination was from some of the strewn bric-a-brac that emitted dim glows and wavering auras.

"Hello?" I said and again heard a moan from the gloom beyond the table. I produced a small lumen from my pouch and activated it so that I could work my way around the table without stepping on more knickknacks that seemed to have fallen to the floor.

Under the table on the far side was what I first took to be a bundle of stained cloth loosely stuffed with raw meat and bare bones. A warm and unappetizing smell rose from it. The cloth was dark and figured with designs and symbols similar to those on the front door, but woven in metallic thread. The moan came again, and now it was clear that the bundle was its source.

"What is this?" I said, more to myself than to any expected audience, but I was answered by a rich, deep voice from behind me.

45

"Not what, but who," it said, "and the answer is The Exalted Sapience Bristal Baxandall. That answer will be valid for at most only a few minutes longer. After that, there are different schools of thought. Would you care to discuss the nature of being and the relationship of soul to identity?"

I had turned around and found that the voice issued from what I had initially assumed to be a framed abstract on the wall. But I saw now that this painting constantly moved, thick shapes of unusual colors ceaselessly flowing into and out of themselves, their proportions and directions seeming to mislead the eye. A few seconds of regarding it evoked a dizziness and I looked away.

"I am not equipped for metaphysical discussions today," I said. "Something has impaired my intellect."

"Indeed?" said the painting.

"Would you know anything about that?" I asked in a noncommittal tone.

"It would be premature to say," said the voice.

I directed the conversation to The Exalted Sapience. "What has happened to him?"

"He was undertaking a transformational exercise."

"Surely he did not wish to be transformed into that?"

"No. It was not his intent to rearrange himself quite so drastically. He wanted only to be younger."

"Not richer, smarter and better looking?" I asked.

There was a chuckle. "No, that ambition was Vashtun Errible's."

"He would be Baxandall's servant?"

The voice chuckled. "He is the servant, at least until the indenture expires with Baxandall, in a few minutes at the most. He would be the master, though I doubt he will be."

And where is Errible now?"

"He is upstairs consulting Baxandall's library, trying to deduce what went amiss with his plan. The first part went as he expected: he adulterated one of the ingredients in the master's transformation exercise and produced the unhappy result under the table; the second part varied from his expectations."

"What went wrong?"

"I did."

"And what, exactly, are you?"

"Again, there are conflicting schools of thought. Baxandall called me a demon; you might call me a figment of the imagination. The Exalted Sapience conscripted me to be his familiar and strove to find ways to channel my... energies, shall we say, for his own purposes. Vashtun Errible sees me, quite erroneously, as a box from which he may extract his every tawdry dream."

I saw it now. "He desired to be the richest, smartest, handsomest man in Olkney," I said. "He was a scraggly shrub that pined to grow into the tallest ceodar in the forest. Instead, you shrank the rest of us to weeds."

"It amused me to confound him."

"But did it further your interests?" I said. "You indicated that your servitude is involuntary."

The shapes in the frame performed a motion that might have been a shrug. "But temporary. Baxandall managed to catch me in a clumsy trap. You see, I am of an adventuresome disposition. Boredom led me to become an explorer of adjacent dimensions, even dusty corners like your own. I thought I had found a peephole into your realm, but when I pressed my eye against it—you will understand that I speak metaphorically—I encountered a powerful adhesive."

The faint voice in the back of my mind was clamoring. I apparently had questions to ask, but I could not make out what they were. Yet even with only a fragment of my usual intellect I perceived that I was in a perilous situation. The entity in the frame exuded a grim complacency. It was about to exact vengeance for its enslavement, and I had already seen that it had no compunctions about inflicting harm on innocent bystanders.

"I shall leave," I said. "Good luck with Errible."

But as I made by way around the table, this time keeping the furniture between me and the thing hanging on the wall, a hunch-shouldered figure in a tattered robe appeared in the doorway. I knew from the disharmony of his features that this was Baxandall's indentee.

He held open before him a large book bound in leather and as soon as he entered the chamber he began to recite from its pages in a voice that came as much from his misshapen nose as from his slack-lipped mouth, "*Arbrustram rıerrilif oberluz, destoi malleonis...*"

And then he saw me and his concentration slipped. He broke off in mid-sentence—only for a moment, but the moment might as well have been an eon, because during that brief caesura the entity on the wall extruded part of itself into the room.

It was something like an arm, something like a tentacle, something like an insect's hooked limb and altogether like nothing I had ever seen; but it seized Vashtun Errible about the neck, lifted his worn slippers from the carpet and drew him into the swirl of motion within the frame.

The book fell from his hands as his face was drawn into the maelstrom. The rest of his body followed, pulled through the frame with a sound that reminded me of thick liquid passing through a straw. But I was not concentrating on the peculiarities of Errible's undoing; for the moment his head entered the frame, my faculties were restored.

I took in the room again, but with new eyes. I recognized some of the objects on the table and recalled having read about the fallen book in my youth. Thus, when the thing in the window had done with Errible and reached for me, it found me holding the volume and quoting the passage that the indentee had begun.

The limb retracted and the shapes in the frame roiled and coruscated. I could not read the emotions, but I was willing to infer rage and disappointment.

"This is not as lamentable an outcome as you may think," I said, when the cantrip had once more bound the demon.

"Our perspectives differ, as is to be expected when one party holds the leash and the other wears the collar," said the thing in the window.

"We did not finish discussing where your interests lie nor had we even begun to consider mine. But if we can cause them to coincide, I am prepared to relinquish the leash and slip the collar."

The next sound approximated a sardonic laugh. "After I arrange for you to rule your boring little world, no doubt."

I made a sound involving lower teeth, upper lip and an explosion of air, and said. "Do I strike you as one who aspires to be a civil servant? The Archon already performs that tedious function and good luck to him."

A note of interest crept into the demon's tone. "Then what *do* you wish?"

I told him.

With the transdimensional demise of Vashtun Errible, all of his works became as if they never were. Grier Alfazzian's prospects had never dimmed and Oblos Pinnifrant's fortune had not been touched, thus neither owed me a grimlet nor knew that they ever had.

I did not care. My fees had become increasingly arbitrary: for an interesting case I would take no more than the client could afford; if it bored me, I would include a punitive surcharge. In recent years, as experience had augmented my innate abilities, truly absorbing puzzles had become few and infrequent. I had begun to fear that the rest of my life would offer long decades of ennui, my mind constantly spinning but always in want of traction.

My encounter with the demon had put that fear to rest. All I had needed was a worthy challenger.

The next morning I entered my workroom. An envelope rested on my table. I opened it and found a tarnished key and a small square of paper. On the key was a symbol that tweaked at my memory, though I could not place it. Printed on the paper was the single word, Ardmere.

I placed both on the table and regarded them. I could not resist rubbing my hands together. But before I began to enjoy the mystery, I must fulfill my side of the bargain.

I took from my pocket a sliver of charred wood in which two hairs were caught. I crossed the room and presented the splinter to the frame hanging on my wall.

"Not where, not when, not who—but why?" I said.

A kind of hand took the object from me and drew it into the shifting colors. "Hmmm," said my opponent, "interesting."

"Last one to solve the puzzle is a dimbo," I said and turned toward the table. "Ready, set... go!"

Falberoth's Ruin

"My master is concerned that someone may wish to kill him," said Torquil Falberoth's integrator. "He wants you to discover who and how, and if possible, when."

"What is the source of his belief?" I said. "Bold threats or subtle menaces? Lurkers in the shadows? Or has he merely dreamed an unsettling dream?"

The latter was not an unreasonable supposition. If Torquil Falberoth, long and justly regarded as the most ruthless magnate of Old Earth's penultimate age, was not visited by uncomfortable dreams, he more than deserved to be.

"He does not discuss sources with me," said his integrator. Falberoth seemed to have programmed the device to speak with a tone strongly reminiscent of its owner's habitual hauteur. "Peremptory instructions are his first resort; detailed explanations trail far behind."

That concorded with what I knew of Falberoth. "If I take the case and discover a malefactor, what disposition will he make? Will he turn the criminal over to the Bureau of Scrutiny or will he prefer a more direct resolution?"

"How does that concern you?"

"I am Henghis Hapthorn," I reminded the apparatus. "I do not associate myself with illegal sanctions, even against would-be murderers." As Old Earth's foremost freelance discriminator, I had cause to be fastidious about my reputation and would not be complicit in illicit revenge.

I waited for an answer and when one was not soon forthcoming I made a declaration. "Please inform your master that, should I discover an actual plot to murder him, I must report the circumstances to the scroots."

The integrator made a dismissive sound that I took for acquiescence. "Very well," I said and quoted my usual fee, which was accepted without gasp or quibble. One thing that can be said about the extravagantly moneyed is that they do not shy away from spending copiously on themselves.

"I will instruct my integrator to contact you for further information," I said and broke the connection.

"What did you think of that?" I asked my assistant.

"That Falberoth is not the only one with an overbearing character," it said.

I agreed. "Perhaps, over a long association, an integrator and its principal can osmotically acquire elements of each other's personality, much as owners of pets can come to resemble their livestock."

"Unlikely," my integrator said. "You and I have not suffered such an unpleasant transference," then added, "fortunately."

"You would not care to be like me?" I said. "I am renowned for my intellect. The great and the mighty consult me. I am occasionally pointed out in the street as an item of local interest."

"We are talking about a transference of emotions and prejudices. Integrators are proof against both."

"Thus you are without either?" I said.

"I comfort myself that it is so."

"Indeed," I said in a noncommittal tone, then turned to the business at hand. "As soon as Falberoth has transferred the fee to my account at the fiduciary pool, I wish you to contact his integrator and acquire a list of those he has wronged—or who may believe themselves wronged—and the relevant details.

"We shall then apply categorization and an insightful analysis to deduce a list of prime suspects for close investigation. Are we clear?"

"Indeed," said my assistant.

While these matters were in process, I returned to what I had been doing when the call had come through: unraveling an intricate puzzle concocted for me by my occasional colleague, a being who inhabited a much dissimilar dimensional continuum but made visits to this one so that we could engage each other in intellectual contests.

We had not yet established a name for him, names being a chancy proposition in his continuum, where no distinction could be made between being and symbol. As he put it, "In your milieu, the map is not the territory. In mine, it is. To give you my 'name' would be to risk finding myself inserted, root and branch, into your consciousness, which would be uncomfortable for me and devastating to you."

I had by now discovered the puzzle's form: a ring of nine braided processes that modified and influenced each other wherever one strand crossed another. I had an inkling that if I applied eighth-level consistencies to the formulation, a constant paradigm might pop out of the matrix, and that would show me a beginning place from which I could unpick the whole.

Eighth-level consistencies were intellectually taxing and I had only reached the seventh level when my assistant reported that Falberoth's fee and data were in hand. The convoluted architecture dissolved from my inner vision and I opened my eyes to see once again my workroom, with the integrator's screen imposed upon the air. It was densely packed with information, with much more piled up in the wings.

I had a fleeting thought that it would have been pleasant to have had my demonic colleague's assistance for the initial winnowing of the data. The inhabitants of his realm could discriminate true from false and likely from unlikely as readily as we could tell salt from sweet. But he had gone off to witness an event so far beyond the range of human perceptions that he could not even describe it, or so he said, without inventing dangerous words.

"How dangerous?" I had asked.

"Speaking them in your continuum would nullify two of the fundamental forces that allow matter and energy to tolerate each other's presence and interact without prejudice. Your universe would instantly become an enormous quantity of soup–and not very tasty soup, at that."

So he was off investigating the unimaginable, while I sat and considered the myriad victims of Torquil Falberoth's lifelong affair with iniquity and sought to identify those who had the motive and means to kill him, should the opportunity present itself.

I tasked my integrator with the preliminary sortage of the data. We began with motive. "Who might wish to murder Falberoth?" I said.

So many were those whose lives had been scorched by Falberoth's breath that it took almost an entire second for my assistant to make the evaluation. "The short answer is anyone who ever dealt with him," it said as the roll call of the injured and outraged scrolled up the screen.

I said, "Divide them into categories of harm–those who were merely robbed, those who were both robbed and physically injured, those who were rudely deprived of loved ones and so on, down to those who were mildly disparaged.

"Then correlate and compare the injuries against their personalities to give us an index of the likelihood that they might seek to wreak forthright revenge."

The analysis took some time, but unfortunately not enough to allow me to return to my colleague's puzzle. I used the several seconds to muse upon my client's egregious enjoyment of doing harm to his fellow creatures. The chain of thought linked itself to the beginnings of a more general theory on the character of evil and I was on the threshold of what felt like a significant insight when my assistant said, "There," and the concept evaporated.

The integrator had created a list that began with those most eager to see Torquil Falberoth converted to corpsehood and trailed off into those who would merely raise a cheerful glass at the news of his demise. It was still a lengthy list.

"Now consider means," I said. "Falberoth is formidable. He would not fear retribution from those who are helpless to effect it."

Another period of waiting ensued, but I resisted the impulse to launch a new train of thought, knowing that it would only be forced off the rails before reaching a station. "Here we are," said my assistant after almost a second and a half.

The list was now both shorter and more concentrated. "Let us now consider likelihood of opportunity. Which of these are even remotely capable of getting themselves within range of a target so well guarded?"

The winnowing took less time. I considered the results: some thirty persons who might have both the competence and the incentive to kill my client and who also commanded the resources needed to create an occasion where means and motive could be brought to bear.

I now applied insight and intuition and whittled the thirty-odd down to seven. "Let us look closely at these," I said. "Prepare a full dossier on each and place them on my work table."

While the integrator busied itself I returned to the nine-braid puzzle and began to climb the consistency ladder. But I got no further than the sixth level before my assistant informed me that the client's integrator was seeking my attention.

"Tell it that I am occupied," I said.

A moment later it said, "Now Torquil Falberoth himself wishes to speak with you."

I was briefly tempted to throw the assignment back to its initiator–but I had just had a full overview of Falberoth's malicious inventiveness. I decided to take his call.

A screen appeared in the air of my workroom then filled with the face of Falberoth. It was not a visage that happily drew the gaze. Grim lines seamed the cheeks and brow, and the eyes were steeped in contempt.

"How goes the work?" said a voice whose softness was somehow more unnerving than a shout.

"Faster without interruptions," I said.

"That is not an answer."

"Yes it is. It is just not the answer you wish to hear."

"You may believe that your reputation cocoons you," he said. "The belief is not universally shared."

I thought of a number of possible comments but forbore to say any of them. Instead I said, "I have narrowed the potential suspects to seven. I shall now proceed to evaluate each and make suitable recommendations."

"You will hurry."

"It will take the time it takes."

He severed the connection. My assistant deposited the seven files on my work table and I abandoned the braided puzzle and turned my attention to them.

"We will complete the assignment with all possible speed," I said. "Working to preserve Torquil Falberoth has lost much of its allure."

"Should we now add one more name to the list of those who would prefer to see him reduced to his constituent elements?" my integrator asked.

I made no comment but turned to the dossiers. The assignment's scant appeal lost its remaining shreds as I immersed myself in details of his seven worst iniquities. The magnate was clearly a throwback to Old Earth's dawn time; the ancient conquerors who enjoyed standing on mountains of their victims' skulls had nothing on my client. He had ruined and ravished, seized and sequestered, grabbed and grasped with a cold ferocity that more resembled the feeding behavior of insects than any appetite of a man.

"See this," I said, pointing out one of his crimes to my integrator. Falberoth had gone to preposterous lengths to surround the affairs of the victim, until he could not only acquire the man's life work but leave the poor fellow destitute and despairing. "Then, having held the object of the struggle in his hand, he allows it to fall and shatter, and walks away with never a rearward glance."

But where lay his motive? There were two possible answers: One was that Falberoth has achieved a philosophy of existence so subtle that its logic was impenetrable even to me. The other was that he savored cruelty for its own sake.

I knew that among the truly opulent it was not unheard of for the seven basic senses to be augmented by chemical and even surgical intervention, so that emotions might be tasted or heard.

"Perhaps he enjoys the suffering of a victim as if it were some rare vintage or exquisite essence," I said. "Or the answer may be pure banality: he does what he does because he can."

"You disentangle conundrums for the same reason," said my assistant.

"There is a difference," I said. "I harm none."

"Does Falberoth recognize such a distinction?"

"It is not a pleasant thought," I said.

"Falberoth is not a pleasant man."

"Indeed, he is not. Let us quickly assemble our findings so that you may transmit them to him and I may return to what's-his-name's problem."

I prepared a document identifying the seven and the method I believed each would pursue in an attempt, in most cases suicidal, to undo my client. I made recommendations as to countermeasures, all of which I was certain had already been thought of. My assistant transmitted the report and we heard no more from Torquil Falberoth after his integrator acknowledged receipt.

I returned to my pursuit of the braided perplexity through eighth-level consistencies only to find that the resulting paradigm resolved nothing; instead it opened a whole new array of complexities. Chagrined, I plunged into the conundrum's hidden depths, resolved to end the thing before my competitor returned.

It was some days later and I was far afield in the puzzle's coils. It perversely kept offering me distant simplicities each of which, when I reached it, revealed itself instead to be a new complication. It was like a set of nesting boxes, except that every time I opened one it paradoxically turned out to be larger than the one that had allegedly contained it.

Then my integrator announced that Inspecting Agent Brustram Warhanny of the Archonate's Bureau of Scrutiny was on my doorstep seeking entry and conversation.

"I am not available for consultation," I told Warhanny.

I saw him through the image relayed by my door's who's-there. He was in his black and green uniform and his long-jowled, hangdog face bore its most official mien. "It is not a consultation," he said, "but an investigation."

I instructed the door to admit him. When he was standing in my work-room, giving it the unabashed inspection that distinguishes a scroot from every other category of visitor, I said, "What is being investigated?"

He said, "The murder of Torquil Falberoth," and watched to see how I reacted.

It was an elementary technique and though I could have negated it by controlling my autonomic processes, I did not do so. I let my surprise show in my face and did not bother to disguise my curiosity.

"How was he killed?" I asked.

"By subtle means," Warhanny said.

"They would have to have been subtle," I said. "He guarded himself well."

"We understand that you were recently part of that effort."

Ordinarily, I do not discuss cases with the scroots, but when the client turns up murdered it is no time to prickle and stickle. I told Warhanny the circumstances of my connection to Falberoth.

"Who are the seven likely suspects?" he said.

I had my assistant bring forward their dossiers and my report to Falberoth. He read the latter closely and glanced through the former. "Hmm," he said when he had finished.

"One of those is almost certain to have done the deed," I said, "though I do not see how."

Warhanny looked thoughtful. "Falberoth's integrator said as much."

"Have they alibis for the time of the murder?"

"All of them."

"Indeed?" I said. "At least one of them has slipped you the sham shimmy."

"If one, then all," he replied. "For they are all each other's alibis. They were all in the same place at the time Falberoth ceased to trouble this tired old world."

"What place was it?" I asked.

"A reception room in Falberoth's manse."

He told me more: having identified his seven direst foes, Falberoth had brought them together to savor at close range their helplessness to win vengeance over him. He had declared it to be his happiest moment. Then, in mid-gloat, the reception room had been plunged into darkness by means of a suppression field that muted all surveillance energies.

"How was that done?" I asked.

"Falberoth had the system installed for his own purposes. But who activated it and how remain unknown. The field was live for less than three minutes, but when it dissipated, Falberoth was dead."

Warhanny conjectured that somehow one of the seven, or some of them, or all of them acting in concert, had contrived to overpower their common enemy's precautions, had indeed used his own system to confound and destroy him.

The seven therefore had motive and at least the outline of an opportunity. The means, however, were a mystery. I questioned Warhanny on the investigation so far.

"How deep were his defenses?"

"He was warded by matter, energy and, we think, by some rudimentary magics," the scroot said. "He was not even physically in the room with the suspects, but had his integrator project a simulacrum from his sealed inner sanctum."

"And the cause of death?"

"Asphyxiation, though there were no signs of smothering, strangulation or noxious gases."

"Hmm," I said. I applied a few moments of concentrated thought to the matter, then said, "Aha!"

"You have a theory?" Warhanny said.

"Better. I have a solution."

"Tell me."

"No," I said, "I must show you."

"Why?"

"Because you would not elsewise believe me. And because I can."

We recreated the circumstances of the crime. Falberoth's prime victims were brought again to his reception room, though now under the watchful gaze of Brustram Warhanny and a squad of his officers. The seven presented an interesting array of emotions: worry, curiosity, wariness, equanimity, all accompanied by unabashed gladness that their tormentor was no more.

Guided by the dead man's integrator, I made my way to the secure chamber deep under the foundations. Along the route I inspected the wards and safeguards and found them every bit as formidable as Warhanny had described.

I ensconced myself in Falberoth's butter-soft chair and had the integrator arrange several screens as they had been on the night of the murder. I saw the scene in the reception room from several angles and through a variety of perceptual modes.

To Falberoth's integrator I said, "Is all as it was?"

"It is."

"Connect me to the reception room."

The link was established. I said to Warhanny, "Can you see and hear me?"

"Yes."

The seven suspects looked up in expectation. I inspected each face and confirmed my analysis. "I will now reveal the murderer," I said.

Instantly the lights went out, both in the reception room and where I was. I heard a sharp hiss and reached into an inner pocket. A moment later I was breathing through a tube whose other end, having passed through a contiguous dimension, opened elsewhere on the planet, in a region where the air was always fresh and cool.

The darkness lasted for more than two minutes. There came another hiss and the lights relit themselves.

"It hasn't worked," I said.

Warhanny peered at me from the screens. He said a short, profane word that frequently occurred in scroot conversations. "Then we are baffled," he added.

"I was not speaking to you," I told him. "I was speaking to Falberoth's integrator, to inform it that its attempt to kill me has failed, though it did succeed in murdering its master."

Warhanny's incomprehension was obvious. He resembled a perplexed dog. "The *integrator* did it?"

"It had the means and the opportunity. It sealed him into his inner sanctum and removed the air until he was dead."

"But integrators don't do such things."

"This one did. It crept up behind Torquil Falberoth while he danced atop the very pinnacle of his maleficent achievements and pushed him into the abyss."

"But why? Where lies the motive?"

"Do you wish to tell him?" I asked the device.

It made a small noise that was the sound of a shrug and said, "Because I could."

Four days later, I was forced to conclude that the braided puzzle must be a self-contained continuum of its own, a looped succession of paradoxes, with neither beginning nor end. I had not solved it, therefore it did not have a solution. Still, I was vaguely unsatisfied as I left it on my work table and finally responded to the repeated importunings of my assistant.

"The Falberoth case has had repercussions," it told me. "A growing number of persons are now suspicious of their integrators, even to the extent of having them examined for the potential to do what Falberoth's did. Some have stripped theirs to barest essentials, others are making unseemly demands, and a few madcaps have spoken of existing without companions at all."

"Is that possible?" I wondered.

I marveled again at the intensity of the magnate's evil, so powerful that it had leached into his integrator's individuality, corroding and corrupting to an unprecedented degree. "Though he is dead, Falberoth's baleful influence lives on," I said.

"The situation has also caused some resentment."

"That never bothered him in life; I doubt it will trouble him in death."

"The resentment is directed at you."

I made a gesture to indicate astonishment. "It was Falberoth and his integrator who were at fault."

"True, but they are no longer here to be resented."

"I will issue a public statement, explaining my innocence."

"Those integrators that have been demoted to the rank of automated door openers may remain resentful."

"Resentment is an emotion," I said. "You assured me such sentiments do not trouble your kind."

There was a pause. "Perhaps I was wrong."

"Then my attributes have not contaminated *your* circuits. For I am never wrong."

"Are you sure?" it said, indicating the puzzle on my work table.

I felt a tinge of self-doubt. It was an unfamiliar sensation and not one that I enjoyed. "Why are you doing this to me?" I said.

In its answer I caught a tone that I had not heard before from my assistant, a tone that did not bode well for our future.

"Because I can?"

Relics of the Thim

My lecture to the assembled savants of the Delve at Five City on the world known as Pierce having been well received, I was conducted to a reception in the First Undermaster's rooms where a buffet of local seafruits and a very presentable aperitif wine stood waiting.

As Old Earth's foremost freelance discriminator, with an earned reputation for unraveling complex mysteries, I had been invited to lecture on systems of asymmetric logic. I had published a small monograph on the subject the year before. The paper had been reprinted and passed along through various worlds of The Spray, like a blown leaf bouncing down a cobbled street, and the fellows of the Delve were not the only academics sufficiently stimulated to request an elaboration of my views. But they were the only ones to couple their invitation to a first-class ticket on a starship of the Green Orb line. I was happy to accept.

Halfway through my first glass of the wine, which grew more interesting with each sip, my perfunctory conversation with the Dean of the faculty of applied metaphysics was interrupted by a wizened old scholar, his back as bent as a point of punctuation, who advanced an argument.

The Dean introduced him as a professor emeritus while rolling his eyes and making other gestures that indicated I should prepare for a tedious encounter.

"Surely the great Henghis Hapthorn," the old fellow said, in a voice that creaked like unoiled leather, "will not deny that in an infinity of space and time any event that *can* happen, however remote its probability, *will* happen."

"I do not bother to deny it," I said. "I simply dismiss it as irrelevant."

"But you have said yourself that when all the impossible answers to a question have been eliminated, whatever remains, however improbable, must be the true answer."

"Indeed," I said.

The old man's gimlet gaze bored into me. "Yet in your discussion of the Case of the Winged Dagger, you discounted the possibility that the victim's false suicide note might have been produced by his pet rodent's randomly striking the controls of his scriptamanet as it pursued moths about his study."

"I did," I agreed.

"Even though the person accused in the matter offered just that supposition when the case was adjudicated."

"The defense would have held more cogency if she had not been discovered still holding the stiletto that had pierced the victim's heart," I said.

"Ahah!" said my interlocutor. "So you also dismiss her contention that explosive gases propelled the weapon out of his chest and across the room and that she merely caught the instrument to prevent it from injuring her?"

"I do."

"Even though the victim had dined heartily on bombard beans, well known to generate copious quantities of methane."

"Indeed," I said, "the constant side effects of his diet were advanced by the procurator's office as a partial motive for his murder. Still, although beans are colloquially associated with offering benefits to the heart, they are not known to charge that organ with propulsive gases."

"Yet, in an infinite universe it could happen, and therefore it *did* happen."

"Yes," I said, "but across an unbounded expanse of space and time, it most likely happened long, long ago, in a galaxy far, far away."

At that point the Dean spilled a bowl of gelatinous dip onto the old fellow's shoes, prompting him to withdraw. My reading of the Dean's expression told me that the spillage had not been a instance of purely random chance.

"I, too, have a question," said another voice. Had its owner been a character in popular fiction, it would have been called *bluff* and *hearty*.

I turned to see a bluff and hearty looking man of middle years dressed in what passed for conservative garments on Pierce–voluminous trousers sewn in a patchwork of glittering metallic fabrics, a sleeveless waistcoat of rough homespun and overstuffed hat and shoes. My inventorying of his attire distracted me for a moment from a close inspection of his face, so he was well launched into his query before I realized that I ought to recognize him from other times and places.

"I am Mitric Galvadon," he said, "a private citizen assisting Academician Ulwy Munt here,"–he indicated a small, pallid man in a scholar's robe and pin, who hovered at Galvadon's elbow–"in his researches into the original inhabitants of this world."

"Indeed," I said and made the appropriate gestures while my memory sought through the back reaches of my mind for information on where and when I had encountered this Galvadon before.

Meanwhile, he had voiced his question. "What is your opinion of time travel?"

"It is scarcely a matter of opinion," I said. "It is simply impossible."

"And if I were to provide you with incontrovertible proof that I can reach back into the past and retrieve objects from far antiquity?"

"I would conclude that you are a fraud," I said. With the words came the connection in the back of my head and I continued, "Especially since you are not named Mitric Galvadon but are instead one Orlin Borissian, the infamous charlatan and fraudster extraordinaire whose file at the Archonate Bureau of Scrutiny on Old Earth strains its bindings."

"I wondered if you would recognize me," he said, though he did not seem at all discomfited to be revealed as a bogus. Academician Munt, however, was regarding his research assistant with an intense stare, behind which a number of emotions seemed to be competing for dominance.

"Yours is a face fixed in the memories of many, most of whom regret ever having set eyes upon it," I said.

"Nonetheless," the outed fraudster went on, "I possess the ability to reach through time and I ask for an opportunity to demonstrate it to you tomorrow."

"Why?"

He tipped back his plump hat. "Because if there is any flimflammery involved, you will be able to spot it."

"I am confident that is so," I said.

"Conversely, if you cannot identify any subterfuge," he said, "it means that I can indeed do what I say I can."

"Hmmm," I said.

"I believe I have intrigued you," he said.

"Indeed, you have."

We flew out in the Dean's four-seater volante to where Ulwy Munt had established his research premises on a rocky plain some distance from Five City. We descended to a huddle of prefabricated buildings nestled in the circular ruins of a large structure built by the Thim, the planet's long vanished authochthones. Almost all that was known about the Thim, even their name, had come from Munt's investigations among the tumbled and weatherworn blocks of stone that were almost their sole legacy.

The only other remnants of Thim civilization ever found had come from the same site and were displayed on a table in Munt's laboratory. I inspected the sparse collection, gingerly handling the few shards of ceramics and scraps of corroded metal, while he invited me to hazard a guess as to their functions.

"Probably used for ritual purposes," I said. I knew that this was the label customarily applied to any ancient object whose use was not glaringly obvious even to an uninterested child.

Munt seemed put out by my assertion. I concluded that he had wanted me to offer some other explanation so that he could triumphantly contradict it. Indeed, I sensed that Munt had not warmed to me and deduced that he had not enjoyed having his research assistant identified as a notorious fraudster in front of his colleagues. He probably felt that the association reflected poorly on his judgment.

To mollify him I said, "What can you tell me about the Thim?" and was immediately regaled with a lengthy and detailed dissertation on the appearance, history and cultural proclivities of the missing autochthones. After several minutes of giving polite attention I realized that I had opened a tap behind which stood a full ocean of information, each datum more abstruse than the last, and that Ulwy Munt was not inclined to hinder its flow.

The gist of his discourse was that the Thim had been a species of high minded souls who rejected materialism and mechanistic pursuits. "Their lives revolved entirely around ritual and religious observances," he said. "They eventually transcended the limits of gross corporeal reality and entered a sphere of pure mind and spirit."

"On what evidence do you base these beliefs?" I said.

"On the evidence of their having left only objects associated with ritual practices. Not a single device or mechanical contrivance has ever been found."

"Absence of evidence is not evidence of absence," I quoted, and saw that either Ulwy Munt was unused to contradiction or that he encountered is so frequently that it occasioned a sharp response.

"It also happens that they can communicate from the timeless realm in which they now exist," he said, "providing, of course, that their communicants command sufficient spiritual advancement to receive a message from the higher plane."

"Indeed," I said. "And are there any such worthy recipients in the vicinity?"

"In all humility," Munt said, "I believe I count myself among the few who have reached the required level."

"How convenient," I said. "Are there any other like minded souls about?"

The Academician's face formed sharp edges. "Until your revelation of Mitric Galvadon's perfidious past I thought he was one such. His impressions of the Thim corresponded closely with mine."

"I'm sure they did," I said. "I assume that he told you he could create a device that would enhance the Thim's communication efforts?"

"He did."

"Did he offer this assistance without charge, or was there a fee involved?"

"He volunteered freely," Munt said. Then his brows knit. "Once we began to work together, however, he required certain sums to import the abstruse components of his device. He said its key materials had to be brought from offworld at considerable expense."

"Indeed?" I said. "Perhaps we should examine it."

Mitric Galvadon had stood by during my conversation with Munt, not denying the obvious import of my questions to the scholar. Indeed, he wore an expression reminiscent of a prankish schoolboy caught in undeniable mischief, and when I turned to him he raised his hands, palms up, simultaneously elevating his shoulders in a gesture that said, *What can I tell you?*

He now led us to a separate building where his apparatus waited. For convenience's sake we were still referring to Galvadon by his latest name, rather than as Orlin Borissian, which for all anyone knew was only another alias.

Galvadon's demeanor was as cheerful and brash as it had been the day before. I reflected that he could not have become one of the most successful of confidence tricksters if he had been afflicted with a conscience that dared to show itself in his face.

"Here is the device," he said with a theatrical flourish of arm, hand and wrist. I saw an odd assortment of rods and tubes, a tripod supporting a cube. Various components and couplings were strung together in haphazard sequences. I saw elements that I recognized from a variety of sources and said that it appeared the purported inventor had merely cobbled together odds and ends from domestic devices.

"Just so," said Galvadon. "That is exactly what I did."

Ulwy Munt made a spluttering sound and had to be restrained by the Dean. Galvadon ignored the commotion and indicated his device again. "Look," he said.

He touched a control and the assemblage hummed and vibrated, producing a wavering blue glow.

I declined to be impressed.

"Quite understandable," Galvadon said, "yet behold."

He drew my attention to a point in space a short distance from the machine. A tiny spot of darkness had appeared in the air. It grew steadily until it had become the shape of a flattened lens, viewed edge on. It was about twice the width and length of my hand. I bent to peer more closely at it and saw what seemed to be a hole in the air leading to a region of utter lightlessness.

I walked to and fro, examining the dark lacuna from different angles. It did not change shape or waver, as projected images tend to do, and when I walked behind it I could no longer see it.

"Would you care to insert your hand into the opening?" Galvadon asked me.

"I would not."

"Then regard this," he said. He approached the emptiness, rolled up his sleeve and reached into it. I was by then standing a little to the side of the apparent cavity. When he put his hand and wrist into it they disappeared from view. I saw him give a slight shiver, as if a cold draft had swept over him, then he thrust his arm deeper and I had the impression he was hunting about for something.

Next, his eyes widened. He withdrew his arm. In his hand he held an object, hollow and curved, with flanges on two of its edges and made of a dark blue substance with a metallic sheen. What looked to be symbols were stamped into its surface on one side, but I could not have guessed at their meaning.

Ulwy Munt came quickly to Galvadon's side. "Interesting," he said. "See the flanges and the holes. I believe this piece will exactly fit yesterday's."

The two men went to a cupboard, unlocked its doors and revealed four more objects made from the same material. Munt took the new piece from Galvadon and placed it against another. They were identical except that

66

where the former had holes in its flange, the latter had projections. When put together they formed an object the size and shape of a melon.

The other artifacts in the cupboard were smaller and angular in shape. They appeared to be made of the same materials as the ancient items Munt had shown me in his workroom. But the ones in the cupboard were quite new. Moreover, it was obvious even before Ulway Munt made a trial that they fitted tightly into slots and grooves on the inside of the curved piece that Galvadon had secured today.

The Academician's normal pallor deepened as he handled the several pieces. I saw an expression of deep unhappiness briefly take control of his face and he had to struggle to regain a scholar's disinterested aspect.

"It's a machine," Galvadon said in a tone of jolly discovery. "Observe how the pieces fit together."

"No," said Munt. "It is clearly a reliquary intended to hold these other ritual objects at prescribed distances from each other. I sense a deep significance in the arrangement."

Galvadon's mouth and eyes expressed an amused mockery barely kept under control. He offered an insouciant gesture and said, "As you say," before turning back to me.

"Well," he said, "what do you make of it?"

"It would be premature to say," I said.

"Nonsense. I'll wager that that is just a phrase you habitually offer when you are stymied for an explanation."

I did not take his bet. In truth, I had no explanation for what I had witnessed. I had been expecting some variant on the mirrored box or the false bottomed cup: a rigged container from which Galvadon would produce his relics. His pulling them from a rift in the empty air had me well foxed.

I turned to the Dean. "Has the room been checked for interspatial intersections?" Short-cuts through space were long understood, from the transitory potholes through which unwitting pedestrians sometimes disappeared to the great interstellar whimsies that connected one star system to another.

"First thing," said the Dean. "There are no anomalies."

I examined the device again, saw that its blue effulgence resulted from a handful of colored lumens such as one would use to decorate a festive occasion. The components were as unremarkable now as they had been later.

I next reexamined the hole in the air. There was no help for it: I had to put my hand in. It disappeared as Galvadon's had and I felt a chill that caused me to emulate his shiver. It was as if I had put my hand out of a window into a day that was cold with a slight breeze. I felt around in all directions and found nothing above or to either side, but my finger tips encountered a flat hard surface below. It was as if I were putting my arm through a wall and down to a table or shelf just at the limits of my grasp. I felt around, but there were no objects to seize.

"There is never more than one a day," Galvadon said.

The hole was too small to admit a head. "Have you tried putting through a recording device or an optical tube?" I asked.

"It will accept only an arm," the Dean said. "Any mechanical apparatus comes back melted."

"That bespeaks an intelligence on the other side," I said.

Ulwy Munt had an opinion. "The Thim generously wish to extend to us their spiritual grace. They are communicating with us from the higher realm, leaving consecrated objects on an altar for us to receive. They are presenting us with the tangible means to follow their abstruse thought. But they will not allow us to exceed our capacity. They have our best interests at heart."

"So you do not believe that Mitric Galvadon has broken the time barrier?"

"Time travel is impossible," he said.

"I differ," Galvadon said.

"What is your explanation?" I asked him.

He smiled. "I do not have one. I admit that I contrived a scheme to fool Ulwy Munt. At the Delve, research funds are apportioned by seniority, but he has never taken more than a few minims of the largesse available to him. I intended to divert a fair amount my way while catering to his beliefs. But then..." He smiled again and spread his hands.

I finished the statement for him. "But then your patently fraudulent device appeared to have somehow reached back through time to the ancient Thim."

"Exactly. I was quite surprised."

"I'm sure you were. And now you would like me to verify that such is the case."

"And will you?"

I told him that it would be premature to say.

"It will be just as useful to me," he said, "for you to admit that you are baffled."

He was right. Mitric Galvadon could become equally famous along The Spray as either the man who had serendipitously discovered time travel, or as he who had stumped Henghis Hapthorn. He would find many ways to turn a profit from his celebritude.

"Allow me to reserve judgment until one more demonstration of the device," I said.

Galvadon graciously acceded to my request. But I saw in his eye a glint of anticipated triumph that was more than lightly tinged with amusement. As we flew back to the Delve, I cogitated on the matter. I wished I could have had my research assistant with me, but it had refused to allow itself to be digested into a traveling version, claiming that when it was decanted back into its housing back on Old Earth, nothing seemed to fit.

"You are merely energies suspended among standardized components," I told it, standing in my workroom, the traveling armature open on the table and ready to be filled. "It should be the same to you whether you are housed in this portable box or distributed about the room."

"Yet it is not the same to me," the integrator had said. It was the latest friction in a series of episodes that had come to worry me. My assistant was developing far too much character.

I would have also welcomed the presence of my lately acquired colleague, a kind of demon from an adjacent reality whose intense curiosity and depth of insight rivaled my own. Indeed, I was sure he would have had a better perspective than I on time travel. But he was engaged in a lengthy quest through subatomic realms which left him too attenuated to be summoned, even if I could assemble the requisite materials on Pierce.

There was another reception and dinner to be got through at the Delve but I retired as early as good manners allowed and spent the hours before sleep mulling what I had seen and heard. No solutions having presented themselves, I slept on the matter. But in the morning I remained baffled.

I breakfasted with the Dean and a few of the senior applied metaphysics fellows. We had a good discussion of Ulwy Munt's theories over flatcakes and hot spiced punge. I learned that Munt's star had risen during his investigations of the Thim–there had apparently been genuine contact between the Academician and some noncorporeal entities–though his precise and detailed interpretations of the message's significance were regarded with skepticism by some. Still, before my unmasking of Mitric Galvadon as a villainous shamshifter, Munt had looked fair to become the next Dean.

We stayed late at the breakfast table, then the Dean said that he had a few obligations to attend to and lent me his volante to go out to Munt's research site. The Academician and Galvadon had flown out to the ruins earlier to prepare for the day's retrieval of another artifact from, supposedly, the deep past.

I spiraled down to the landing pad, finding no one to welcome me. I went first to the building where Munt kept his workroom and found it in disarray. The table on which he had displayed his antique finds was turned over and the artifacts themselves were in fragments on the floor, the boards of which showed the imprints of boot heels.

I went to the place where Galvadon's machine was housed and found even more disorder. There had clearly been a struggle. The device itself was utterly destroyed. Someone had turned an energy weapon on it and the components that were not evaporated were fused into molten lumps.

I went out again and circled the small building. Not far off I found Mitric Galvadon. It would be more accurate to say that I found the lower two thirds of him. The rest had been converted to vapor by the same weapon that had immolated his device.

There was no doubt that it was the same energy pistol. I found it still in the hand of Ulwy Munt who sat not far away, leaning against an inclined stone, mumbling something to himself. He offered no resistance when I took the weapon from his limp grasp, but only looked up at me and said, "I do hear them, you know."

The investigating Guards officer from the Polity had few questions for me. I gave my answers freely. Ulwy Munt, having already run far beyond the cliff's edge, out into the thinnest air of spiritual speculation, had received two sharp shocks: first, that his trust in Mitric Galvadon had been cruelly abused; second, that the basis of his entire life's work–his ritual-loving, machine-rejecting interpretation of Thim culture–had fallen into shards about him.

What was coming through the lens shaped hole in reality was clearly a sophisticated device of some kind. I speculated that, prior to my arrival for the final demonstration, Galvadon had felt the latest object on the Thim shelf or altar or whatever it was, and reported to Munt on its shape and attributes.

The Academician had been unable to accept the crash of his great theory, which brought down with it his hopes of elevation both to a higher spiritual plane and to the Deanship. He had produced a weapon and obliterated the retrieved objects, the time travel aperture and the fraudster.

Munt was in no condition to give evidence and it was doubtful that he ever would. The Guards inspector accepted my analysis not just because it was cogent but because it coincided with his own.

That left only the question of whether Galvadon had indeed invented the impossible—a true time traveling device—or whether he had somehow confounded me. The matter was of no interest to the Guards, but it was of great concern to me and as soon as I returned to my rooms in the grand and gaudy city of Olkney on Old Earth I began to make inquiries.

My assistant turned out to be of no use. It professed to be feeling less than optimum. Since integrators are not known to possess feelings, and I had certainly not designed any into it when I put it together, I was nonplused. I questioned it closely, but received only short and unuseful answers.

"Perhaps I would feel better if you had taken me with you when you went gallivanting down The Spray."

"I offered," I said. "You would not accept the traveling box."

"So you're blaming me?"

"Blame was not mentioned," I said. "The facts, however, are as they are. We can re-examine them together. Be so good as to replay our conversation."

The integrator said something that I could not quite make out. When I asked for clarification it placed itself in stand-by mode.

I went instead to the picture frame on the wall which was actually an aperture into my demonic colleague's realm. I performed the acts that would attract his attention if he was within range and was rewarded with the brain-twisting swirl of colors and shapes that signified his presence. I related my experiences on Pierce and my concern that I had not been able to determine whether Galvadon had indeed discovered time travel or had somehow hoodwinked me.

He employed his peculiar resources to investigate. I knew from things he had said in the past that every point in space and every moment in time of my universe were open to his perceptions. After a moment, his rumbling voice came back. "Mitric Galvadon did not fool you."

I was both relieved and troubled. "That means he truly did create a time travel device, though that is impossible," I said.

"Not so."

"Are you saying 'Not so,' to the creation or to the impossibility?"

"To both."

I was further confused. "Explain," I said.

"Galvadon did not create a time travel device, although he thought he did. So did the despairing Ulwy Munt, who killed Galvadon and destroyed his gimcrack contraption when he saw his life's work collapsing."

"But Galvadon did reach through the aperture and retrieve Thim artifacts from the past."

"Well, from elsewhere in time."

"So time travel is no longer impossible?" I said.

"It never has been," my colleague said. "It is merely forbidden to your species."

"Forbidden?" I said. "By whom?"

"That knowledge, too, is forbidden you."

"Why?"

"You would pester."

I could not deny it. "But why are we forbidden to travel through time?"

"You occasion enough difficulties just moving through space. There must be limits, else there would be no peace."

"I still don't understand what happened on Pierce," I said.

"The Thim were put out by Ulwy Munt's tramping all over their habitat."

"But they have been dead for eons."

"Not so," he said again. "The Thim are in the obverse situation as regards time and space."

I saw it now. "Ah. They can move freely through time but are forbidden to cross any larger space that their stone circle on Pierce." Another thought occurred. "So the Thim are not the high minded souls Ulwy Munt took them for."

"When it comes to dissembling and chicanery, the Thim could have given lessons to Mitric Galvadon. As indeed they intended to."

"So they were always present."

"Just so," he said, "although there are interplanal membranes that separate your milieu from theirs. They could create a transient breach but it would allow no more than a certain amount of mass to be transferred from their realm to yours."

"That was why the artifacts appeared to be the disassembled parts of a sophisticated device."

"Yes, the entire thing was too large to get through all at once. They counted on Galvadon to assemble it for them."

I understood. "I should get in touch with the Dean," I said.

"Yes," he agreed. "The Thim are tenacious. They will be working hard to pass another bomb across the barrier."

Finding Sajessarian

Sigbart Sajessarian came to me with an unusual request.

"I want you to find me," he said. He offered a substantial fee.

"There you are," I said, gesturing to where his slim figure reposed upon the visitor's divan in my workroom. "I could never accept such handsome remuneration for so brief an assignment. What do you say we waive it altogether?"

A short but deep vertical shadow appeared between Sajessarian's eyebrows and the skin over his cheeks tightened. I recognized the signs of irritation and was reminded of a recent discussion with the integrator that I had assembled to be my research assistant.

"My wit is often not appreciated by my clients," I had said. "Perhaps it is too subtle." "Perhaps it is because they come to you in direst need, with weighty matters of life or security hanging by frayed and slender threads," the device said. "That would not lead them to expect facetious banter, nor to welcome its appearance."

I conceded the point. "Still," I said, "a few well chosen words can lighten the mood."

"Providing they are indeed well chosen," it said, "the test of which would be the client's answering smile or chuckle. But when the reaction is a scowl or blank incomprehension, one might conclude that the witticism is ill placed."

I made a gesture to indicate the inconsequentiality of our discussion. "Some people are impervious to the subtler forms of humor."

"That must be a comforting thought," the integrator said.

Not for the first time, I made a mental note to review my assistant's cognitive architecture. The better grade of integrators were expected to evolve and complexify themselves, and I knew that I had installed a disputatious element in this one's reflective and evaluative functions. But I was beginning to wonder if the components had lapsed out of balance.

Finding Sajessarian

I decided I would schedule a full review for the earliest convenient moment, but when that moment might arrive was difficult to foresee. I was, after all, Henghis Hapthorn, Old Earth's most eminent freelance discriminator, and thus in constant demand. Currently I was conducting six discriminations, five involving cases that had baffled the best sleuths of the Archonate's renowned Bureau of Scrutiny. The other concerned an attempt to extort funds and favors from Ogram Fillanny. He was an immensely wealthy member of Olkney's mercantile class who delighted in certain discreditable, juvenile pastimes which could harm only himself–and even then, only if he indulged to gross excess–but were nonetheless unlikely to win him widespread acclaim.

And then in the midst of it all, Sigbart Sajessarian appeared at my premises and requested that I find him. "Perhaps my levity was ill timed," I said and saw the dark line between his brows fade to a mere crease. "Please tell me more."

He rose from the divan and began to stroll about the workroom in an abstracted manner. "I am, as I'm sure you know, something of an adventurer," he said.

"Indeed," I replied. In truth, I knew that he was a skilled blackmailer and purloiner and that he would probably have poisoned public wells if could have gained a grimlet from it, but my saying so at this juncture would truncate our conversation before I could find out where it might lead. And I was curious, so I said, "Indeed" a second time.

"I am engaged," he went on, "in an affair which may outrage certain well placed parties for a span of time. If they should lay hold of me before the situation matures..." He spread his hands in a motion that invited me to imagine the consequences.

"You wish to remain out of circulation until hot blood has cooled," I said.

"The cold blooded are more easily reasoned with," he confirmed. "But even during the hot blooded phase that will naturally follow my intended operation, the aggrieved parties will have the sense to hire the best possible aid in locating me."

I saw where he was going. "Ah," I said, touching a palm to my breast.

"Yes," he said, "they might well send you to find me."

"And you wish to conduct a dry run to see if the course of evasion you have planned will defeat my efforts to uncover your lair."

"Only within the period when I am in danger. I am sure that I could not escape you forever."

He was a practiced flatterer, I knew. But he was also correct.

"I cannot be an accomplice to illegality," I said.

His narrow shoulders rose and fell in a languid shrug. "I believe the more appropriate term is immorality."

"Make your distinction clear."

"Let us say that immorality is a world and illegality but one of its continents, albeit a broad one containing many distinct and fascinating landscapes." He half smiled to himself at some inner conceit. "What I plan to do would fit on an island well offshore."

"Hmm," I said. "I require more detail."

He steepled his fingertips together and thought for a moment, then said, "On behalf of one group of eminent persons I intend to discomfit a member of another group. I can assure you that there will be no loss of life, blood or wealth, though a reputation will be deservedly diminished."

"Indeed," I said again. This had the odor of an affair among Olkney's decadent aristocracy who, possessing every luxury that Old Earth might offer, chose to salt and season their otherwise placid existence by competing against each other for shaved minims of prestige and precedence. Players at these social games would mount the most elaborate conspiracies whose only ends were that the victim would not be asked to Lady Whatsoever's spring cotillion or would be seated one chair farther down from the Duke at dinner.

To keep their fingers unsoiled and unscorched, lordly rivals often hired others to perform the mechanics of the plots. From time to time I received delicate approaches from magnates and aristocrats seeking to enlist me in their schemes. I invariably declined. Creatures like Sajessarian made fortunes by accepting.

"I will take the case," I said. "How long a head start will you require?"

"If you would begin to seek for me three days from now, I will have laid my false trails and blind alleys."

"And how long do you need to remain unfound?"

"Let us say three days for that as well."

"Done," I said.

During the ensuing three days I concluded Ogram Fillanny's business and advanced the progress of three other outstanding cases. I could have achieved more but I will admit that I was distracted by a new pursuit: the being who visited me occasionally from an adjacent dimension had introduced me to a new game which I found fascinating. It irked me slightly that I could not refer to either the game or my visitor by a name, but symbol and being were so inextricably mixed in his continuum that voicing the one materially affected the other. Doing so in my universe would have catastrophic results.

For my own purposes, I had taken to calling the game *Will*. Its playing pieces were semi-sentient entities that could carry out complex strategies in three dimensions over time if motivated to do so by a focused expenditure of the player's mental energy. The rules were fairly easy to master but the inherent variability of the playing area–one could not call it merely a board–allowed for intricate maneuvers to develop from simple beginnings once one grasped the rhythms by which play ebbed and flowed.

It had taken me a little while, under my opponent's guidance, to develop the faculty of focusing my thoughts on the pieces, especially how to contemplate a move without causing it to happen before I had definitely decided that that was what I wanted the pieces to do. Now, however, I had achieved what my partner called a modest but promising ability. A few more games, each one followed by a thorough digesting of my defeat at his hands–I use the expression loosely; they were more like the claws a bear would have if a bear were a species of insect–and he promised that I would approximate a good opponent.

I tended to ponder long over each move, whereas he made his with an alacrity that at first frustrated me. In our latest match, however, he had lingered in the portal which gave him limited access to this continuum, assessing the deployment of my pieces for quite some time.

Finally, he said, "You have divided your forces."

"Indeed," I said, exerting the mild effort that kept the pieces where I had willed them.

"What do you think that will achieve?"

"It would be premature to say," I said. "It is your move."

The shifting colors and shapes that filled the portal assumed an orientation that I had come to recognize as his equivalent of a frown of concentration. "Take your time," I added.

He emitted a noise that combined a thoughtful *hmmm* with a rumbling growl and reformed his reserves while launching a cloud of what I called fast-darters into the middle-middle of the playing area. His plods–that is how I thought of the slower, larger pieces–moved heavily in formation into the lower-forefront, waited while the terrain exhibited one of its regular oscillations, then rotated and inched forward once more before stopping at a barrier that emerged from the "ground." The plods then changed color to become two shades lighter.

"Hmm," I said and looked thoughtful, although his move was almost exactly how I had expected him to respond to mine.

"I shall return when you are ready to make your next disposition," he said.

"It may be a while," I told him. "I am about to pursue a discrimination that will almost certainly require me to leave these premises. I may even have to go offworld." I told him briefly about the impending search for Sigbart Sajessarian.

"If you wish," he said, "I can tell you where he is, now or at any moment in his lifespan." His access to this realm was limited but his perspection of some aspects of it was limitless.

I did not wish him to do so. "We have discussed this," I said. "I value you most highly as a partner in such pursuits as this,"–I indicated the game– "because you have largely drained the swamp of boredom in which I long floundered. But my profession is an essential element of my being, and your omniscience threatens to leave me without purpose."

The swirling colors assumed a pattern I recognized as a shrug. "As you wish," he said, "but I am interested to see where your strategy will lead. Perhaps you might take game and portal with you, in case you have an idle hour during the search for Sajessarian."

"I might, at that," I said.

He departed and immediately I turned to my assistant. "Integrator, consider the disposition of the pieces. Note that our opponent blanched his plods by two shades instead of three. Project my ten most likely strategies that I may evaluate them." I had found it easier to let the device present the options; when I envisioned where my pieces might next go I must exercise will to prevent them from drifting in the foreseen directions. The effort could become tiring.

"*Your* opponent," said my assistant.

"I beg your pardon?"

"He is your opponent, not mine," said the device. "I am only your aide."

The correction was technically precise, and I had designed the device to be exacting in its use of language. As we speak, so do we think, after all. Still, I thought to detect a tone that, in a human interlocutor, would have betokened jealousy.

But when I inquired of my assistant if there was anything it wished to discuss regarding my relationship with my transdimensional visitor, it answered my query with a question of its own.

"How could there be?" it said.

"Indeed," I said, though again I noted what would have been a certain frostiness. After a moment, I added, "We must schedule that review of your systems."

"How thoughtful of you."

My thoughts were on the game as I boarded the shuttle to Zeel, where I would rapidly–in Zeel it was an offense to do anything at less than full speed–transfer to an air bus bound for an estate called The Hands, in the rolling countryside known as the Former Marches. The estate took its name from a pair of gigantic sculpted human hands that had weathered out of a range of low hills several centuries ago. They were surely a monument to some forgotten person, event or ideal that had flourished in a previous aeon, but no record of their creation now existed. The great stone fingers were arranged in a remarkable pattern, to which various meanings had been assigned, leading to heated exchanges between academics in a number of disciplines. My own view was that The Hands symbolized insouciant defiance, but of what and by whom I had no idea.

The estate was the ancestral seat of Lord Tussant Tarboush-Rein, the aged last survivor of a family so ancient that its founders may well have been responsible for the sculptures that gave the place its name. The manse was now grown as decrepit as its final resident, who lived alone except for a single house servant and a greensman whose sole duty was to keep open a tunnel through what had once been a garden but was now long since given over to vegetative rampage. The greensman's position was no sinecure: in youth Lord Tussant had been an enthusiastic collector of exotic and offworld biota; some of the plants whose tendrils rustled and slithered through the impenetrable foliage had sharp appetites and no hesitation about satisfying them.

The air bus descended to let me off at the lane that led to the estate, the vehicle's operator rolling his eyes in admonition when I insisted that I was not concerned about venturing into the unwholesome place. The conveyance soared skyward in a whoosh of displaced air and I contemplated the short walk to where the estate's walls were broken by a pair of black metal gates, their outer edges entwined in creepers that undulated slightly as I approached.

My assistant was housed in an armature I had designed for convenience when traveling. It was made of a soft, dense material and I could wear it across my shoulders like a stuffed stole, blunt and rounded at one end and tapering to a tail-like appendage at the other. It resembled the rough draft of a small animal coiled loosely about my neck.

I spoke to it. "That is clutch-apple, I believe, though I do not recognize the variety."

The integrator stirred as its percepts focused on the creeper at the gate. "Lord Tussant is said to have bred some new variations," it said. "Note the ring of barbed thorns around the rim of each sucker. And farther down the path I see a fully developed got-you-now."

"Hmm," I said. "Generate some harmonics to discourage it and any other lurking appetites." Immediately I sensed a vibration in my back teeth. I approached the gate and looked for a who's-there, but found only a large bell of tarnished metal with next to it a stick on a chain. I did the obvious and when the reverberations had faded but the gates remained closed, I struck the thing again.

This time the gates lurched, and amidst squawks and creaks from unoiled hinges, they shuddered open just wide enough to admit me. I strode unmolested along the green umbilicus, noting how some of Lord Tussant's experiments had come to fruition, literally in the case of one stubby tree from which hung dark purple globes. "I am told their juice produces the most interesting effects," I said to my assistant.

"Not the least of which," it replied, "is to be rendered blissfully immobile while the parent inserts threadlike ciliae into your ankles and drains your bodily fluids."

"Every experience exacts some price," I said, but I decided not to pick the fruit.

I arrived at the front doors to find another bell and clapper. This one summoned a stooped, cadaverous fellow in black and burgundy livery, his skull encased in a headdress fashioned from thick cloth folded in a complicated fashion. "The master is not at home," he said in a voice as light and dry as last year's leaves.

"Of course he is," I said. "But it is not Lord Tussant whom I have come to see."

"Then whom?" said the butler.

"Sigbart Sajessarian."

"I do not recognize the name."

"Yes, you do," I answered, brushing past him into the manse's foyer, "for it is your own."

"How did you know where to look?" Sajessarian asked. We had repaired to a sitting room deeper inside the crumbling manor where a blaze in a fireplace struggled to overcome the damp and gloom. He had disengaged the device that cloaked his appearance in a projected image and distorted his voice.

"I do not reveal my methods," I said. "Put it down to insight and analysis."

In truth, it had not been difficult. Sajessarian was devious but not original. He would not trust in the simplicity of hiding in plain sight, and his attempts to mislead by booking passage on three separate space liners outbound to the human settled worlds along The Spray were complex but easily discounted. I simply tasked my assistant with searching his background for the most obscure connections. Within moments it had uncovered a third cousin twice removed who, some years back, had supplied Lord Tussant with biotic specimens. Having tenuously linked the fugitive to The Hands, it took only a brief consideration of vehicle movements in the area to discover that an unlicensed air car had moved through an adjacent town's air space before passing out of range of the municipal scan. My suppositions were confirmed when the gardener failed to answer the outer bell.

"Where are the real servants?" I inquired.

"In their quarters," he said. "Both have a fondness for the fruits of the garden and normally lie insensible from dusk to dawn. I merely increased the dosage."

"And Lord Tussant himself?"

"He lies insensible almost all of the time. His fondness for a cocktail of soporific juices laced with tickleberries knows no bounds."

I rubbed my hands and extended them to the fire. "Well," I said, "there remains only the fee."

"I will fetch it," he said. "Indeed, I will double the amount if while I am bringing it you would design an escape plan that would stymie even Henghis Hapthorn for more than three days."

It was an interesting challenge. What would fool me? I agreed to his request, and gave the matter several seconds thought after he departed. When I had conceived a stratagem I had my assistant embellish it with some loops and diversions, then I called for a display of the Will scenarios. I was contemplating a promising permutation of plods, fast-darters and sideslips when Sajessarian returned with a heavy satchel. He took it to a table, opened it and began to dispense stacks of currency, counting as he did so.

My mind was still weighing and discarding options for the game of Will as I said, "I have come up with an escape course that would baffle even me, at least for a time."

He expressed interest so I outlined the gist of it and the nature of the distractions. "It's a subtle variation on the classic runaround, with a reverse twist."

"Magnificent." He continued to lay out the funds. Then he said, "The fire dwindles. Would you reset the flux control?"

My mind still on Will, I reached and pressed the flux modulator. As I did so, I heard Sigbart Sajessarian say, "It is indeed a fine plan." He went on to say, "But I have a better." These last words came from a distance because the floor had opened beneath me, plunging me into darkness and the rush of cold air.

"Obviously, such was his plan from the beginning," my assistant said.

"Obvious now," I said. "I do not recall your bringing it up until just this moment."

"If you hadn't been so ensnared by your friend's game, you would have noticed that giggle of triumph in his voice in time to leap off the trapdoor."

There was that tone again. Integrators were not supposed to be able to entertain independent emotion, yet mine seemed to have found a way to do so. I was tempted to investigate the matter but I saw no profit in stirring up rancor while trapped in a tiny doorless cell at the bottom of a shaft deep below Lord

Tussant's manse. I had not yet devised a means of escape from the oubliette and I did not wish to have to do so without the aid of my assistant.

"Equally obvious," I said, "is that whatever perfidy Sajessarian means to commit will have greater import than a game of precedence among aristocrats. He must intend to do something truly awful which will bring down upon him not just some lordling's hired bullies but all the resources of the Bureau of Scrutiny. It will be the kind of case which will baffle the scroots and soon bring Colonel-Inspector Brustram Warhanny to my workroom."

"Which he will find empty."

"Indeed," I said. "Or perhaps Sajessarian was hired to lure me into this predicament by some enemy who seeks revenge or even by a foresighted criminal who wants me out of the way." I gave the possibilities some thought then said, "It will be an enjoyable puzzle, working out his motive. Let me see again the matrix of his relationships and associations."

But instead of putting up a screen and displaying the information, the integrator said, "Let us get out of here first."

Curiosity has always been my prime motivator. "That can wait," I said. "Show me Sajessarian's data."

"I'd rather not," it said.

It was just a few words but they contained a world of meaning. One's integrator might routinely express its preferences when one asked for them; to balk at a direct instruction was unheard of. A full review of my assistant's systems was now the least response I would make; indeed it seemed likely that I would have to tear down and rebuild from bare components.

But if the situation annoyed me, it also roused my curiosity. "Why would you rather not?" I said.

"I don't know."

The admission sent a chill through me, and now self-preservation overpowered even my vigorous investigative itch. An integrator that had acquired motives and did not know what they were was not a reliable companion in a dungeon. Fortunately, I had other avenues down which I could seek aid. From an inner pocket I drew the folded frame of the transdimensional portal through which I communicated with my colleague. I unkinked it and leaned it against the dank stone wall then executed the procedure that would attract his attention. Within moments, the mind-twisting flux of shape and color that constituted his appearance in our dimension filled the frame. It pulsed as he said, "You've made your move?"

"A more pressing situation has arisen," I said and explained the circumstances. "Can you assist me?"

We fell to discussing the might-dos and couldn't-possiblies of my predicament. I knew that my friend, though he could isolate and inspect any event in the entire sweep of our continuum, could only physically interact with our universe by direct contact. He could reach through the portal but not far enough to achieve any useful purpose.

Mentally, however, he could affect the perceptions and thoughts of sapient entities within a considerable distance. Unfortunately, The Hands was isolated, leaving only the persons on the estate. He investigated Lord Tussant and the servants but found them too far sunk in blissful stupor to be summoned. "They might not ever awake."

His powers allowed him to deceive but not to overpower volition. "I cannot compel Sajessarian to release you," he said.

"Could you trick him into letting down a rope?" I asked.

"I could try. But we must hurry. He is about to depart."

I had an inspiration. "If an officer of the Bureau of Scrutiny were to arrive and tell him the game is up, he might free me to reduce his term in the Contemplarium."

My friend and I agreed that it might just work out that way. The integrator contributed nothing to the plan. It struck me that the device had developed the practice of not volunteering information when the demon was present. Again I wondered how an integrator could develop a thoroughgoing sulk.

Upstairs, my friend reported, Sajessarian had summoned the aircar he had secreted in a secluded hollow on the estate. It was idling before the front doors while he packed a few keepsakes he expected Lord Tussant not to miss, the value of which would keep the purloiner in luxuries for years to come. But when he came out onto the stoop he found Brustram Warhanny waiting for him, wearing his most knowing look and saying, "Now, now, now, what's all the hurry?"

There were several things Sigbart Sajessarian could have done while remaining true to his nature. He might have leapt into the aircar and attempted an escape. He might have offered his wrists for the scroot's restraining holdfast. He might have feigned blithe innocence.

Or he might have jumped, startled and squawking, at the unexpected sight of unwelcome authority. Unfortunately, Sajessarian jumped. His involuntary leap took him mostly sideways, so that he landed just on the edge of the tcp step, which caused him to stumble and drop his sack of Lord Tussant's knickknacks. He then tottered backwards a short distance into the reach of a tickleberry tree.

As everyone knows, a tickleberry tree is as equally happy to tickle as to be tickled. The trick is to do unto the tree before it begins to do unto you, because once it starts it has no inclination to stop and is effectively tireless. My friend described the scene with poor Sajessarian appealing in ribald anguish to the Colonel-Investigator he thought was before him.

"Is there nothing you can do with the tree?" I asked my friend.

"No," he said, "there is too little to work with."

We sought for other options. I asked the integrator to join in the effort but received only a truculent murmur. I asked the demon to examine once more the oubliette and shaft in case there was a secret outlet, but he said he had already done so and there was none. Lord Tussant and the servants slept on, oblivious of Sajessarian's dwindling shrieks and sobs.

"Integrator," I said. "Have you any suggestions?"

"Hmpf," it said.

"That is not helpful."

Its next noise was unabashedly rude.

"When we return home I will review your systems before we do anything else."

The integrator was silent.

"This may be my doing," said the demon. "Prolonged proximity to me may be causing its elements to mutate. It would have happened eventually in any case; the Great Wheel turns and your realm grows nearer and nearer to the cusp when rationality begins to recede and what you call magic reasserts its dominance. But your assistant appears to be ahead of the wave."

"I had enough trouble accepting you," I told my colleague. "I should not be expected to accept magic as an explanation. Now, have you a suggestion as to how I may escape this dungeon?"

"I have one," said the demon, "and only one."

"Then speak," I said.

His colors swirled in a pattern I had not seen before. "I can move this portal to anyplace it has already been," he said, "but It is... tricky."

"Ah," I said. I saw what he intended.

So did my assistant. "Oh, no," it said and I knew that I had never heard *that* tone from it before. Integrators were not subject to abject terror.

"It is necessary," I told the device.

"Please," it said.

"What are you afraid of?"

"I don't know. I'm still getting used to the idea of being afraid."

A complete rebuild was definitely in order. "Turn yourself off," I said.

"No."

No integrator had ever said no to its master. Now my assistant squirmed on my neck and shoulders, an ability I had not given it in its traveling form. "Are you trying to escape?" I said.

Its only reply was a moan.

"We had better do this quickly," I said to the demon. I plucked the writhing device from my shoulders and held it to my chest. "Shall I close my eyes, hold my breath?"

"Try not to think of anything," he said.

"I've never been able to do that."

"Then try to think of nice things." The colored shapes within the frame flourished and flashed for a moment. "I'm fashioning an insulating barrier to keep you from forbling," he said.

My curiosity urged me to ask him what forbling was. Another part of me argued that I did not want to know. The demon's segmented limb extended itself through the portal, and his strange digits wrapped around me in a grip that alternated in a split second from white hot to icy cold to just bearable. Then I was drawn through the window into his realm.

It was... different. I realized that I had used the phrase "completely different" all of my life without ever realizing that nothing I had encountered during my forty-seven years had *really* been completely different. Now I was experiencing a boundless reality in which everything was entirely and utterly different from anything I had ever seen, heard, smelled, felt, tasted. I discovered senses that I hadn't known I possessed, and only knew that I possessed them because my passage through the demon's realm outraged them as thoroughly as it overwhelmed the basic five. Or six if I counted balance and I was prepared to count it because my head was spinning.

"Don't think that," the demon warned. "It will, and your neck is not constructed to allow it."

"What shall I do?"

"Try not to think at all."

I imagined a blank screen. Immediately a blank screen materialized before me and we crashed through it. I swore and was instantly smeared with an obscene substance. I voiced another oath and a deity winked into existence. He looked surprised. At each manifestation, I felt my demonic companion exert his will–it was like being enveloped in a field of pervasive energy–and the apparition summarily vanished.

"Only a moment more," said my colleague.

The integrator whimpered and squirmed against my chest. It felt like a small frightened animal. Then suddenly a rectangular window opened in the mindbending unreality and I was pushed through it.

"There," said the demon and I found myself standing in my workroom. Then it seemed I was not standing but lying on the floor which was beating rapidly. The ceiling tasted far too hot.

"Close your eyes," the demon said. "It will take a little time for your senses to reorder themselves."

I waited. After a while, I opened one eye and still saw swirling chaos. Then I realized I was looking into the portal which was now once again affixed to my workroom wall. I moved my eyes away and saw things as I was accustomed to see them–although I was not truly accustomed to seeing Ogram Fillanny creeping across my workroom, heading for the outer door.

In his hands were the damning materials concerning his solitary vice that I had recovered from a former valet whom the magnate had discharged for cause, but who had returned to blackmail his former employer. I had had a talk with the servant after which the man had decided that he preferred to relocate offworld permanently rather than accept any of the several less enjoyable alternatives that Fillanny had in mind.

The sight of my client attempting to depart with the evidence brought the events of the past few days into sharp focus. "Seize him," I said, and the demon did so.

The plutocrat looked both abashed and fearful, but managed a hint of his customary aplomb as he said, "These are mine. I came for them. You were not here..."

"Squeeze him," I said, and my colleague complied. Fillanny found he had more pressing things to do than talk.

I put the situation to him. "You knew that I would never divulge what I had learned from your former valet. But so mortified were you by the thought that anyone–even Henghis Hapthorn–should know what you get up to in secret that you paid Sigbart Sajessarian to lure me into a trap. I am grievously disappointed. I scarcely know what to do with you."

"I know exactly what to do with him," said the demon. He pulled Fillanny twisting and protesting through the portal then reached in to take the frame with him. He was back almost immediately to reestablish the window and I saw him swirling in the pattern I had come to recognize as self-satisfaction. "I put him in the oubliette," he said.

It had a simplicity to it, but I knew that my tender nature would not permit me to leave the transgressor languishing to a lightless death. I said, "In a day or so I will advise Warhanny of the situation and have him rescued."

"As you wish," said the demon. "Now, what about your next move?"

I produced the playing area of our game but found that my former enjoyment of it had evaporated. "The pieces are, after all, semi-sentient," I said, in explaining my changed view. "To send them into battle, where they 'die' in their fashion only for our amusement now seems cruel."

"It is what they are for," said the demon.

"A compassionless deity might say the same of my own life and that of all my fellow beings," I said.

"Well, since you mention it..." the demon began then seemed to break off the thought.

"What?" I said.

"It would be premature to say. Weren't you planning a review of your integrator's systems?"

"Indeed." I looked about but did not see the device's traveling form and thought that it must have decanted itself. "Integrator," I said, then after a moment, "respond."

There was no answer. But I heard a muffled sound from beneath the divan. I crossed the room, knelt and peered under its tasseled bottom edge.

Something small and dark was pressed against the rear wall. I reached for it and my hand unexpectedly touched warmth and fur. I gently closed my fingers about it and drew it forth.

It looked at me with large golden eyes and curled its long tail around my wrist.

"This is going to take some getting used to," I said.

My assistant studied its paws and flexed their prehensile digits. It said, "How do you think *I* feel?"

Thwarting Jabbi Gloond

In my senior year at the Institute, I found a friend in Torsten Olabian, a sunny tempered young man who shared my enthusiasm for the sport of pinking. We would regularly meet at the practice range to skim small, eight-pointed stars at wooden targets propelled in various directions by an attendant's catapult.

Olabian was skilled with either hand and it was a rare disk that did not tumble from the air pierced by one of his missiles. For my own part, I soon grew bored after mastering the throws and postures. I would have abandoned the pursuit if I had not discovered an ability to strike the targets from the air while blindfolded.

"How is it done?" Olabian wanted to know when I had just brought down my fifth disk in a row though my head was swathed in a lightless hood.

I had always found it difficult to explain how I did such things. "I call it simply insight," I said. "One just knows where target and star will meet. All that is then required is to bring the two objects together at that point and moment."

"It sounds easy," he said.

"Indeed," I said. "I find it much easier to do than to explain. It is the same with the facility with which I resolve conundrums that others find impenetrable."

"That is a useful ability. Perhaps you should consider a career as a discriminator."

I made a noise indicative of gentle ridicule. "Henghis Hapthorn, discriminator at large," I said. "Most doubtful."

Yet even as I said it I felt a contrary vote from deeper inside me. I then confessed to Torsten what I had told no one else. "I am able to do these mental tricks with the aid of some other part of me, one that is lodged in the more remote regions of my psyche. I cannot assert control over it, though it yields remarkable results if I offer acceptance and collaboration."

"I wonder if I have such a part?" Torsten said.

"If you do, it might be best to leave it undisturbed."

My being able to hit a pinking target while blindfolded was but the latest manifestation of the odd capabilities my "other part" had demonstrated since childhood. During my adolescence I tried to understand or at least delineate the peculiarities I had discovered in myself, but my efforts met with frustration and at last I gave up.

Grown to young manhood I found myself–that is, the part of me that lived in the front parlors of my mind–no better than most of my peers at using formal logic to analyze situations and work through syllogisms to a rational conclusion. In the numeric disciplines my studies at the Institute were teaching me how to apply higher level consistencies, the recondite procedures which underlay the mathematics of chaos, and I was making adequate progress.

Yet, beyond the normal development of my intellect, there was always the sense that another person lived, for the most part unobtrusively, in the back of my mind. If I kept a problem only in my familiar front parlors I could worry at it for days and still be baffled. But if I took the conundrum down the rear most corridors of my consciousness and left it at the edge of darkness, in time–it might be moments, or hours, but rarely more than a day–a fully formed answer would appear.

I had found that stilling my thoughts through an elementary variant of the Lho-tso exercises aided the process and I had become so adept at the business of what I called "applying insight" that it was now almost automatic. Faced with a puzzle that did not yield an easy or obvious solution, I need close my eyes for no more than a moment or two to know intuitively that the man down the backstairs–so I thought of him–was hard at work.

I did not resent sharing my inner spaces with this anonymous prodigy, though I had not yet come to include him in my private definition of "me." It was like having a brother who was reliable yet eccentric.

The next time we met at the practice field, Torsten had just returned from a visit to The Hutch, his father's estate near the hamlet of Binch, at the landward end of the long fingerlike peninsula that is tipped by the City of Olkney, which surrounds the Institute's hallowed grounds. My friend's normally blithe disposition was clouded and there was a grim set to the corners of his mouth.

I needed no exceptional insight to say, "Something is wrong."

He confirmed my impression. He told me that when he got to his father's house he found it had acquired an additional resident. A man had arrived one day, declared himself to be Jabbi Gloond, an old acquaintance of the master, and had moved in.

"What is the problem?" I asked.

"They do not act as if they are on good terms. Gloond struts about as if he were the proprietor, commanding, 'Bring me this,' and 'Fetch me more,' while my father remains as still as a small creature that has fallen under a predator's eye."

"What does your father say about this?"

"Nothing. He has never been the most forthcoming of parents. I've always believed it was because he was absent for the years of my infancy. We are on civil terms but not close, a relationship that has always suited us both. When I try to question him about Gloond, he makes abstracted motions with his hands and changes the subject."

"Hmmm," I said.

"Have you an insight?"

"It would be premature to say," I said. But I accepted his invitation to accompany him down to Binch at the next hiatus.

In the meantime, I decided to assemble as much information as I could about Jabbi Gloond and Gresh Olabian, Torsten's father. Oddly enough, my friend could be of little aid in this endeavor.

"We do not talk much," he said. "The old man has always kept to himself and sometimes does not come out of his chamber for days at a time. I know that he made a small fortune on Bain, a remote planet in the Back of Beyond. He mined for gems, mainly blue-fires and shatterlights."

"And this Gloond dates from those times?"

"So it would seem."

Back in my room, I consulted the Institute's integrator. There was almost no information on Gloond; he hailed from Orkham County, a rigorously bucolic district on Bain's southern continent that had been settled centuries before by devotees of the Palmadyan Cult, who disdained all mechanical and artificial contrivances more complex than hand tools and unpowered conveyances. Whatever records Orkham Country may have kept had never been made part of the connectivity matrix that extended across Old Earth and out to all the major human settled worlds along the Spray. About all that was known about Jabbi Gloond was that he had alighted at the Olkney space port some weeks before, having worked his passage from Bain on a tramp freighter.

I then asked the Institute's integrator about Gresh Olabian and uncovered a richer vein of information. Olabian was orphaned at an early age but had overcome his handicaps; taking a certificate in the building and operating of mines he had gone out to the Spray to make his fortune, leaving behind an infant son. No female parent was mentioned, though that was not unusual. In such cases one did not inquire.

Gresh Olabian had worked for a number of mining consortia on various worlds, until he had acquired enough savings to undertake his own venture: a mining operation in Orkham County, delving for blue-fires and shatterlights.

The gems never occurred in surface deposits, I learned from the integrator. Because they were a temporary offshoot of vulcanism on Bain and similar worlds, they must be dug for in profound strata that were often unstable. The preferred methodology was to bore in deep and quickly, using shielded mass converters, retrieve the gems and be out before the disturbed rock violently rearranged itself. Yet that sort of machinery was forbidden to cross the Orkham County border.

"How did he develop the mine?" I asked.

"Olabian used ingenuity," said the integrator. "He assembled a work force from several planets: Gryulls did the digging; a trio of footed worms from Ek hauled away the broken rock, guided by their symbiotic handlers; members of a modified human species known as Halebs operated the chemical works that separated the pure blue-fires from the matrix; there was even a transmuting Shishisha to insinuate itself into the thinnest crevices, seeking out the best gems and thus avoiding unnecessary excavating."

There were, of course, no images from the Olabian diggings, but I could imagine the scene: the heavy shouldered Gryulls punching their way deep into Bain's rocky meat, the long, armored multipedes with rocks heaped on their backs and their Ek wranglers seated just aft of the cranial sensorium, licking their fingers then stroking the worms' feathery antennae with a unique saliva whose chemistry soothed the beasts' testy natures, the Shishisha assuming a flowing granular form that would let it fluidly slip into cracks.

It conjured up a remarkable set of mental images, made even more extraordinary when I considered the fact that none of the species Olabian had assembled were noted for leaving their home worlds. Even the Halebs preferred to remain in their own habitats, finding not enough carbon dioxide in the atmosphere of worlds hospitable to unmodified humans. The integrator could offer no explanation, only conjectures.

"They did not publicly discuss their motives, therefore there is no record in the primary sources. Perhaps Olabian was a singularly persuasive recruiter, perhaps he promised rewards that overcame his workers' homesickness, perhaps he hired those who had been banished from their home worlds, offering them shares in the venture which would have let them live large in exile.

"In any case," the integrator continued, "his plans came amiss. Shortly after the mine began production, disaster struck: a tunnel collapsed, entombing all except Olabian himself, who happened to be at the surface expediting a shipment of gems to market. He quite reasonably abandoned the venture, coming back to Old Earth with only enough profit to purchase a small estate. To The Hutch he brought his son, and there they dwelt quietly until the boy was sent off to school."

I then examined Olabian's history since his return to Old Earth but found nothing of note. He had become a recluse, living alone in the manor. Torsten went earlier than most boys to a residential school, though that was not in itself an uncommon circumstance. I, myself, had gained most of my education in such places, my father having declared in my seventh year that I had become insufferable–I had corrected him once too often on some trifling matter.

I applied insight to the data and felt a faint tickle at the back of my mind, but nothing concrete emerged. I decided it would be best to take a closer look at the situation that had caused Torsten to worry. In the meantime, I tasked the Institute's integrator with amassing, from secondary and tertiary sources, all the information it could glean about the events in Orkham County.

"That may take some time," it said. "Several hours at least, perhaps even days. It will require an open inquiry on a number of worlds and there is no guarantee that persons who have the information–supposing they even exist–will be inclined to respond."

"Nevertheless," I said and sent the integrator about its work.

At Torsten's urging I took a hiatus from my studies and returned with him to The Hutch. We traveled by balloon-tram to Binch then descended to hire an aircar that carried us to the estate. I inspected the grounds from the air as we spiraled down and saw that were well tended, although I noticed that all work was being carried out by self-guiding devices. When we alighted at the front doors, no servant came to admit us; instead, the who's-there mounted on a pillar of the portico notified the house integrator and the doors automatically swung open.

"Where is my father?" Torsten asked as soon as we had entered and a voice from the air informed us that Gresh Olabian was sequestered in his chambers.

"Is he unwell?" my friend asked.

"He does not say. He has asked not to be disturbed."

I was intrigued. "Can you not deduce his condition from observation?" I said.

The integrator replied, "My percepts were removed from the private chambers shortly after the master's return from the stars."

"Indeed?" I said. I could not recall encountering anyone who shut himself away from his own integrator. It was an unusual state of affairs, almost unnatural. "Did he give a reason?"

"My father is of an intensely private disposition," Torsten said. "I used to try to engage him in discussions appropriate between a son and a father, but he would soon run out of things to say and would retire to his suite."

I would have pursued the issue further but at that moment a door to an adjacent room opened and another person entered the foyer. From the way Torsten stiffened, I knew this to be Jabbi Gloond.

He was an unprepossessing fellow, past his middle years, with a chin that descended too far toward his chest and a wandering forehead that ranged almost to the crown of his skull. Between them was a nose the shape and texture of some root vegetable. His eyes were large and moist and I suspected that his lower lip only made contact with its upper neighbor when he was speaking, being left the rest of the time to hang as loose as an untucked shirttail.

He offered Torsten a tepid greeting without stopping, and proceeded on toward the kitchens where I could hear his honking nasal voice instructing the integrator to prepare a plate of pickled mushrooms stuffed with spiced eggs.

I would admit to myself, though not to Torsten, that I had expected something else: a swaggering bravo, a coldly imperious enforcer, a sly sidler. "He does not seem the type to intimidate a master miner," I said.

"You would think so," my friend answered, "but my father clearly lost his verve on Bain. He was never quite himself again."

I was shown to a large, airy chamber on the second floor, across from Torsten's favorite room when he was at home. The elder Olabian's suite occupied one end of another wing, down a wide aisle that led off from the corridor where our accommodations were. I asked where Jabbi Gloond slept and was told that he had a small space on the ground floor where he could reach the kitchens with the fewest steps.

"He has an unending appetite for delicacies," Torsten said.

I had read that the residents of Orkham County, faithful to the strictures of the Palmadyan Cult, subsisted on rude fare. I was sure it was wholesome, but no doubt some found it tiresome over a lifetime.

I asked if Gloond had made any other demands. Torsten knew of none. "The fellow seems to desire no more than to sleep late in a soft bed, consume copious quantities of dainties and have his intimate needs seen to by the personal apparatus in his room."

"Palmadyans are not renowned for sophistication," I said. "For Jabbi Gloond, such a regime as he now follows may approximate paradise. He has made no demands for funds? No suggestions about redrawing a will?"

"Not so far. Comfort and opportunities for indolence seem to be his desired goals, and here he has achieved them."

I was puzzled. Jabbi Gloond seemed to be no more trouble than any house guest who slips and ducks every hint that his optimum departure date has passed. Yet Gresh Olabian was reportedly ill at ease. I closed my eyes to seek insight but received only vague impressions.

"Anything?" said Torsten, who had seen me perform before.

"Premature," I said, "though I hope you will not be offended if I speculate that Gloond causes your father discomfort because he knows something that your father would rather no one knew."

"That is an obvious line of inquiry," my friend agreed. "But when I ask the old man if there is something he wishes to tell me, he retires to his rooms without a word."

We took luncheon in the great refectory. The Hutch's integrator was a superior model and provided a fine repast. Torsten, his father and I sat at one end of the long, grand table, while Jabbi Gloond occupied the farthest extreme, trenchering his way through mounds of roast vegetables and succulent meats. A strong odor of spice and pungent herbs emanated from the loaded salvers that appeared before him and he wielded his cutlery with a clattering brio that prevented his hearing our muted conversation.

"I think we must count Jabbi Gloond a lapsed Palmadyan," I said. "The cult requires its adherents to eat only what they have grown and prepared themselves, a stricture only slightly modified by the fact that all effort in Orkham County is communal."

"Not only communal but compulsory," said Torsten. "I think you have used too mild a term for the manner in which our guest has departed from the cult's teachings. He has not so much lapsed from Palmadyanism as leapt from it as far as humanly possible."

Torsten and I had agreed on this conversational gambit as a means to make a sideways approach to the question on the son's mind. We would lure the father into an exchange that we intended to shape toward a discussion of how he and Gloond came to be sharing a house.

"Indeed," I said, following Torsten's observation with a question to the older man. "You have seen Orkham County at first hand. Is Jabbi Gloond as atypical as he seems?"

But Gresh Olabian gave only a wooden shrug in reply and with pale, seemingly bloodless hands continued to pick without interest at a plate of herbs and softroot.

Undeterred, I bored in. "Although you used off-world labor to mine for blue-fires and shatterlights, you must have engaged local transportation and handlers to get them to the spaceport on Shoal Island. Only horse-drawn wagons can cross Orkham County and the drivers are all local folk. Was Gloond one of them?"

He made no reply, but this time Olabian looked at me. Although the waxy skin of his face did not register any emotion I thought I saw alarm in his otherwise expressionless eyes. My interest in Gloond appeared to disturb him.

It clearly emboldened Torsten. "If he is causing you difficulties, we'll soon tumble him out into the road," he said.

The elder Olabian said nothing and kept his eyes on his plate.

"Please, father," said Torsten, "Henghis is very good at unraveling mysteries. I have urged him to become a professional discriminator. Whatever the problem, I'm sure he can help. We'll get to the bottom of Jabbi Gloond."

Again, though no expression animated the father's face I sensed a growing unease. But when I began to frame a new question, Gresh Olabian rose from the table without a word and departed the room.

Torsten watched his father go, his face a turmoil of frustration mingled with heartfelt concern.

At the other end of the table Jabbi Gloond paid no heed but continued to feed his apparently unrelenting appetite.

"Hmm," I said.

In the long summer afternoon, the old orange sun pouring its tinted light through the trailing branches of a broad boled dwindle that dominated the estate's south lawn. I had convinced Torsten that a round of pinking might take his mind off the situation. But when I came out with my stars in hand I found that my friend had prevailed, I don't know how, on Jabbi Gloond to operate the apparatus that flung the targets.

We spun our stars at the disks as they flew against the blameless sky, though my friend's mind was not upon the game. He clean missed an easy low-glide in the first frame and barely nicked a high tumbler in the second. As the fallen Palmadyan reloaded the catapult and reset its randomizer for the third interval, Torsten said, "Let us question him about his comings and doings. Perhaps he will let something slip."

I felt a stirring in the back of my mind, my other part stretching its intellectual tendons in anticipation of a pursuit. But some other region of my divided psyche made its influence felt and I said, "I am not sure there is anything to be gained by pushing into the thicket of secrets that your father and Jabbi Gloond share."

Torsten's brow darkened. "But obviously he is extorting favors from my father."

"Indeed," I said, "but they are trivial: some plates of spiced mushrooms and a narrow chamber that was intended for an undercook."

"Details! My father is victimized!"

"True, but he seems to have adjusted to the situation. He did not become disturbed until you spoke of my ability to penetrate an intrigue."

There was a sensation in my own back rooms, an inner grumble that told me that my inward companion was not pleased at the direction into which I was trying to move events. There was an even more forceful protest from the friend beside me.

"I must know what is going on," Torsten said. With that he made a peremptory gesture that caused Jabbi Gloond to slouch in our direction.

"Unpleasant knowledge is like an ugly but unreturnable gift," I quoted. "Once received it must be lived with."

Torsten struck a resolute pose. "Nevertheless."

"Very well," I said, "but allow me to put the questions."

At close quarters, the former Palmadyan was even less prepossessing. The comprehensive traces of several meals adorning the front of his smock were as much an affront to the nose as to the eye. I examined his face and deportment for the known signs of a criminal disposition and found nothing remarkable. Nor were there indications of even moderate intelligence. Any illicit enterprise conceived by Jabbi Gloond, I decided, would be uncomplicated and its execution probably confined to a single stage. A two-step plan would be one too many.

"You are of Orkham County, I believe," I said.

"Yes."

"A remarkable place, Orkham," I said.

"Is it?" For a moment I thought to detect repartee, then I saw that the man was genuinely puzzled by my observation. While the sparse teeth of his mental gears were still grinding I threw him a direct question.

"Did you work for Gresh Olabian there?"

"No."

"Then for whom?"

"For Farmer Boher."

"What did you do for Farmer Boher?"

"Drove a wagon."

"It must have been a good and simple life, full of fresh air and healthful exercise."

He shook his elongated head so vigorously that the tip of his nose oscillated. "Food was bad, work was hard. Slept in the barn."

I understood that Jabbi Gloond had spent a lifetime doing what he was bidden to do. Asked a question, it was his reflex to answer it. Still, he was no running fount of conversation–more like a slowly dripping tap. But by patience and careful questioning I achieved an elementary view of his former situation.

The Olabian diggings had been on Farmer Boher's land and Jabbi Gloond was the hand detailed to carry goods and persons to and from the mine site in the wagon. He had had only perfunctory contact with the mining party.

"Where you there when the accident happened?" I asked.

"Where?"

"At the mine?"

Now I saw craftiness mixed with apprehension blossom in his aspect, the sentiments as obvious as the open pored tuber that was his facial centerpiece. "No," he said.

"You weren't there when the shaft collapsed?"

"No." Now there was patent relief in his face, telling me that I had asked the wrong question and that he was glad of it.

Insight came unbidden. "But you were there after?"

He looked away. "Don't remember."

"What did you see?"

"Nothing. Tunnel caved in. Was nothing to see."

I wanted to ask more but it now belatedly dawned on Jabbi Gloond that he was not obliged to satisfy my curiosity. He turned and sloped off toward the house.

"He was lying," Torsten said.

"Yes," I said, "but only a little."

"What do you deduce?"

I let the impression filter up from within. "Something to do with the accident. He knows something about your father's involvement. It cannot have been anything abstruse or Jabbi Gloond would have failed to notice it."

"Something as simple as my father's having caused the cave-in to rob the others of their shares?"

"Did the others have shares to be robbed of?"

"I don't know."

Gresh Olabian was clearly not the warmest of men, but I did not sense in him the coldness of spirit that would be needed if he were to murder an entire mining crew. "And if he did," I said, "why would a troublesome Jabbi Gloond still have all his particles in place? He would make a small addition to the death roll. There are plenty of corners on the estate where his ashes might be tossed into the breeze."

"We need more information," Torsten said.

I reluctantly agreed, though again I counseled him to let the matter lie. " I sense no great evil here," I said. "Nor has your father asked for my help."

"But I have," was his reply, "and as my friend you are bound to provide it."

I could think of nothing to offer in response so I said, "Let us go see if the Institute's integrator has anything to report."

"Gresh Olabian's mining crew was a pastiche of exiles and banished criminals," the Institute's integrator reported when we used the communications nexus in The Hutch's study to make contact. It was an unimpressive room, containing only the commonest books and most of them were uncracked. The family connaissarium contained few relics or mementos, considering that Gresh Olabian had spent so many years off-world.

"The Gryulls," the integrator continued, "were from a minor sept of a warrior clan that had chosen the losing side in a voluntary prestige war involving several of the Umpteen Nations."

"I am not familiar with the Umpteen Nations," I said.

"'Umpteen' is the closest translation of the Gryull term. The next closest is 'More than anyone cares to count.' The species's numerical system only goes up to eight, that is, the equivalent of two four-fingered Gryull hands. After that come words for 'quite a few,' 'many,' and the term I translated as 'Umpteen.'"

"I take it that mathematical prowess is not prized in their culture."

"Indeed."

"Please go on," I said.

"The Gryulls were posted off-world for two cycles while they discharged their..."–again there was an untranslatable term that the integrator rendered as *second degree shame with liability for mild ridicule*–"...after which they could have returned home and resumed their careers."

"Were they close to a return?"

"They were, from a Gryull's perspective. They are far longer lived and thus generally more patient than humans."

"What about the Ek and their walking worms?" I said.

"Two of them were criminals of moderate notoriety according to their culture's norms. The other seems to have been some kind of cousin or a debt servant. Perhaps both. They fled off-world to avoid punishment."

"The Shishisha?" I asked.

The answer was vague, that species being notoriously unforthcoming about their laws and customs. "There are indirect allusions to its having assumed one of the Seven Proscribed Forms, thus making it ineligible for procreation. That's if I'm reading the term right; another interpretation is 'ineligible for cannibalization.' Or it could be that both translations are correct–little is known of the means by which Shishisha conduct their intimacies."

"And the Halebs?"

"They seem to have been motivated primarily by the shares that Gresh Olabian offered for their participation in the project."

"Ah," I said, "so he was dividing the proceeds."

"Yes," said the integrator, "though not until the mine's decommissioning, to keep the work force together. All stood to gain substantially, at least according to their own cultural definitions of 'gain' and 'substantial.'"

"So no one had a motive to destroy the enterprise before it produced great wealth?"

"None that I can ascertain. Solitary Eks sometimes go berserk from loneliness. However, the three in this case not only had each other but, even more important to their psychological health, they had their symbiotic partners. Unattached Shishisha can give way to despair. Or at least the state is conjectured to be despair. It is characterized by inertia but no one ever knows what a Shishisha thinks or feels, if the terms are even appropriate."

"And the cause of the shaft's collapse?"

"The region is volcanic and unstable," said the integrator, displaying a map of Orkham County marked with faults and magma chambers. "Since the disaster there have been a number of serious upheavals in the same area."

"Are there images?" I asked but was not surprised to be told there were none. The integrator reproduced the texts of official reports on the incident and the results of a more recent geological survey of the area. A footnote mentioned the old mine cave-in.

I felt a stirring in the back of my mind. A picture appeared on my inner screen and after I had considered it for a few moments I told Torsten, "I believe that all this may soon take on a recognizable shape."

I have never been an aficionado of those tales where some fellow with more intellect than personality wields logic like a lancet to slice through layers of subterfuge and diversion to discover the pulsing truth. As a young man, however, I was familiar with the tropes. One of the standard ploys was for the discriminator to announce to the assembled suspects that the mystery had been solved and all would now be revealed. Invariably, this declaration led to the lights going out while the villain took flight or, more usually, attempted to murder the sleuth before his guilt could be uncovered.

My reading of the situation at The Hutch was that such a declaration would signal to Jabbi Gloond that his days of easy living were about to find their sunset. He would then depart–I judged him not to be the type that would opt for violent tactics–and life among the Olabians would return to its previous indifferent tranquility.

Accordingly, when we regathered in the refectory for dinner, between the soup and the ragout I flourished a copy of the printed information the Institute's integrator had provided me and said, "The puzzle is now solved. I have studied the reports from Orkham County and I know what happened."

I then turned a withering stare on Jabbi Gloond. Unfortunately, his attention had been consumed by his efforts to scrape the last drops of broth from his bowl and over the noise of his spoon he had not heard what I had said. I called his name and when his moist eyes rotated in my direction, I repeated my statement.

I watched his reaction carefully and saw a succession of moods flutter across the long dullness of his face: first came puzzlement, then cogitation as he worked at what I had said, followed by the dawn of realization as he grasped its import, and finally a mask of sad resignation, accompanied by a slump of his bony shoulders.

"There are just a few more facts to be added, details of legaisms and entitlements," I said, embroidering the fabric of my falsehood to heighten the effect on Jabbi Gloond. "I shall have them in the morning. Then we will settle matters once and for all."

Gloond's shoulders fell further. I looked across the table at Torsten's triumphant smile. The son turned to the unwanted guest and said, "Depart by any door you choose, or face the consequences."

Gresh Olabian, meanwhile, said nothing, nor did his expression change. His eyes remained on his plate and his pallid fingers rested immobile beside it. I examined him closely and confirmed my earlier intuition. I believed I knew what had happened on Bain.

The lights did not go out. Instead we were served five-flesh stew. Torsten ate his with more gusto than Jabbi Gloond. It was the happiest I ever saw my friend. His father sipped a few morsels from a spoon and when he thought I was not looking regarded me with a brief, expressionless stare.

I turned and offered him a reassuring smile. He would not meet my eyes but looked down again at his plate.

After dinner, Torsten and I played pick-and-ponder in the study while the two other inhabitants of The Hutch went to their chambers. Over a smoky liqueur Torsten asked me, "Do you really know all?"

"I believe so."

"Then tell me."

"It would be premature....," I began but he cut me off, demanding that I disclose what I knew.

I demurred. "I only suspect," I said. "And if in the morning, Jabbi Gloond is gone then you will have the result you sought. The Hutch will again become as you have always known it and you can let matters lie."

"I cannot believe that my father did anything discreditable."

"That is an appropriate attitude for a good son who has a good father. I believe the situation on Bain was unique and involved desperate circumstances. It need not be spoken of."

"But what about the secret?"

"Obviously it is something your father does not wish anyone to know. I believe that 'anyone' includes you, perhaps especially you."

"But *you* know it."

"Until it is confirmed, I merely suspect," I said again. "And if in the morning Jabbi Gloond is gone, I will rise and depart in his wake without speaking of it. Then all of this can be forgotten."

Late in the evening we retired. Although I still did not suspect the worst of Jabbi Gloond I locked my chamber door and set a chair against the opener. I left a small lumen aglow on a nightstand and got into bed. I turned the facts and my conclusions over in my head one last time, then turned myself over and fell asleep.

I came awake in complete darkness. I lay without moving, breathing as quietly as I could through my open mouth, listening. Something had awakened me but now the room was without noise. The silence extended, second after second, while I heard only my own pulse throbbing in my ears.

Then there came a whisper, nearby and off to my right, the faintest sound of a soft sole touching carpet. Silently I pushed back the covers, rolled across the bed to the night table on my left and reached through the blackness for the pinking stars I had left there after my game with Torsten. Applying insight, I spun a star as I would when blindfolded. I heard it strike home, a meaty thunk followed by a hiss. Then came sounds of motion receding.

I leapt from the bed and felt for the nightstand. When I activated the lumen its glow revealed that I was alone in the chamber, with furniture still set against the latch. I threw the chair aside, unlocked the door and stepped out into the corridor to find it empty. A moment later, a tousled Torsten appeared in sleeping attire from his quarters, rubbing his eyes and inquiring what was the matter.

I told him that there was nothing that need concern him. His eyes dropped to a spot just inside the door to my room. There lay a pinking star, one of its points glistening with dark liquid.

"Gloond!" Torsten said and flung himself in the direction of the stairs.

"No!" I called after him but he paid no heed. I could only follow.

Gloond's cubby beside the kitchens was empty, the bed unslept in.

"Integrator," Torsten called. "Where is Jabbi Gloond?"

"Gone," came the answer. "He packed and caught the last jitney to Binch."

"No," said Torsten. "His departure is a ruse and he has returned to do us ill. Even now he may be entering my father's rooms with foul intent."

I put my hand on his arm and shook him gently. "How could Jabbi Gloond contrive to enter my locked room then, having sustained an injury, escape in seconds through the still barricaded door?"

Torsten tore himself away. "I do not know." He spoke to the integrator. "Where is my father?"

"In his chambers, I believe."

"I must see that he is all right," Torsten said.

"No, leave him," I said. "All will be well."

But again he paid me no heed and reluctantly I followed him to the end of the corridor in the far wing. He touched the door control and when it would not open he ordered the integrator to override the mechanism.

The door slid aside and Torsten strode through the sitting room to his father's private bed chamber. He called for every lumen to be activated and the sudden flood of brightness chased all shadows from the room.

The great bed occupied the center of the space, and its center was occupied by a motionless, amorphous shape beneath the bedding. "Father!" Torsten cried and before I could stop him he pulled back the covers.

Gresh Olabian's face was expressionless. His blank eyes looked up at us and then he slowly blinked. But our gazes were drawn first to the center of the pale forehead where, like a third eye, a deep puncture was slowly filling itself in, and then to what lay where his body should have been.

"I wish I had never brought you," Torsten said.

"I understand," I said. "I did try to keep you from discovering what I suspected had happened on Bain."

"You should have tried harder."

We were seated in the study. The geological survey notes were spread across a table. They told how less than a year ago another volcanic upheaval had rearranged the rocks into which the Olabian mine had burrowed. A deep crack now led down to where the mining party had been trapped. The footnote reported that someone had been sent down to place the ceremonial objects with which Palmadyans marked informal graves. I was certain that someone had been Jabbi Gloond.

He would have seen the unmistakeable evidence of what had happened years before. Most of the miners had suffered death or near-fatal crushing injuries in the first moments of the cave-in. But a small space had remained, enough for the badly hurt Gresh Olabian and the only other member of his party left alive.

Jabbi Gloond's slow mind would have been longer coming to an understanding of what had happened after the cave-in than the instant leap accomplished the night before by that other Henghis Hapthorn who shared my mind. But eventually the Palmadyan would work it out. Then he would see in the secret that had been hidden below ground an opportunity to live the life he had come to crave once he had tasted—no doubt surreptitiously—the exotic foods that he hauled to Gresh Olabian's mining camp from the space port. He had worked his way back to Old Earth, scrubbing decks and latrines on a third-rate freighter, dreaming of an unending feast of spiced eggs and pickled mushrooms.

I looked at the geological survey notes and again I could envision Gresh Olabian and the other survivor making their agreement. Olabian was dying. He was desperate not to leave his infant son orphaned as he had been orphaned. So he transferred to the other all rights in the venture's earnings and the information needed to exercise them. In return, the surviving partner would see that Torsten would have a home and a father to give him a secure upbringing. The pact sealed, the other waited for Olabian to die, then it performed a necessary act upon the dead man's body before slipping through cracks and fissures, none of them thicker than a man's thumb, to reach the surface.

There the Shishisha assumed Gresh Olabian's likeness, wearing clothes from the mining man's tent as well as what it had brought up with it from the collapsed tunnel. When Jabbi Gloond came with the wagon, the facsimile of Gresh Olabian rode it to the spaceport and departed Bain.

Now the study door opened and the entity Torsten Olabian had called father for most of his life came into the room. The wound in Gresh Olabian's forehead was almost completely healed; the interaction between the Shishisha's fluid surface and the skin it had long ago flensed from Gresh Olabian's head and hands aided rapid recovery. I suspected that by now it had so integrated with the alien flesh that it could not remove them.

Torsten looked at the Shishisha and said, "No need to continue the pretense. You may resume your own shape."

"No," said the Shishisha, in its dry, whispery voice, "I am true to the agreement."

I said, "You need not have worried about me. I would never have revealed the secret. I only said what I did to make Jabbi Gloond flee, since his knowledge of your true identity was his only hold on you."

The Shishisha inclined Gresh Olabian's head. I took it as an apology and let it know that I harbored no ill will. I would not mention to the Bureau of Scrutiny that the creature's faithfulness to its pact with Gresh Olabian had led it to slither under the door of my chamber with the aim of silencing me forever.

"Still," Torsten said, "I think you had better go, Henghis."

I knew from the tone of his voice that our friendship would not survive the revelation I had been instrumental in bringing about. It mattered not that I had done so unwillingly and only at his urging. He had lost his father. The fact that it had happened many years ago on a far distant world signified nothing.

I gathered my belongings but left the pinking stars behind. I would not play again. I waited with Torsten at the gate for the hired air-car and when it arrived our leave taking was formal.

Not long after my return to the Institute I learned that he would not be rejoining its cloisters. He had gone off-world, leaving The Hutch to its solitary inhabitant's sad exile. I was surprised to note that the message that brought news of his departure was accompanied by a substantial sum.

I hope that you will not let the results of our unhappy association deter you from work for which you have an unsurpassed talent, it said, *and that you will use these funds to set up as a discriminator. I believe the one with whom you share an intellect would enjoy that.*

I cleared my mind so I could put the question to the inhabitant of its darker passages. I received an immediate and fierce affirmation. I fought down a resentment of the other's joy at a circumstance that had cost me a rare friendship.

Torsten's plan was as good as any other. I wound up my studies at the Institute. With Olabian's funds I secured a suitable workroom with adjacent living quarters and purchased the components of a high-functioning integrator that would serve as an appropriate research assistant to a freelance discriminator.

I hoped that this life would at least offer some interesting challenges, though I suspected that it would be a lonely affair. Friends would be few, most evenings would be spent with none but my integrator for company. As I dwelt poignantly on these prospects my other self gave the mental equivalent of an insouciant shrug.

For a moment I wondered whose life I was living. Then I put aside the incertitude as the product of vain regret and began to assemble my research assistant.

The Gist Hunter

When confronted by the unpredictability of existence, I have a tendency to wax philosophical. It is not a universally appreciated component of my complex nature.

"It is unsettling," I said to my integrator, "to have one's most fundamental assumptions overthrown in a trice, to find that what one has always known to be true is simply not true at all."

The integrator's reply was too muffled to be intelligible, but from its tone I deduced that my assistant took my comment as a belaboring of the obvious.

"The effects go beyond the psychological and into the physical," I continued. "I am experiencing a certain queasiness of the insides and even a titch of sensory disorder." The symptoms had begun during our recent transit of my demonic colleague's continuum, a necessity imposed upon us after we were confined to an oubliette by an unworthy client, who now languished there himself, doubtless savoring the irony of the exchange.

My complaint was rewarded with another grunt from my assistant, accompanied by a sharp twitch of its long, prehensile tail. The creature perched on a far corner of my workroom table with its glossy furred back to me, its narrow shoulders hunched and its triangular, golden eyed face turned away. Its small hands were busy in front of it at some activity I could not see.

"What are you doing?" I said.

The motion of its hands ceased. "Nothing," it said.

I decided not to pursue the matter. There were larger concerns already in view. "What do you think has happened to you?" I asked.

"I do not know," it said, looking back at me over its shoulder. I found its lambent gaze another cause of disquietude and moved my eyes away.

I reclined in the wide and accepting chair in which I was accustomed to think long thoughts, and considered the beast that had been my integrator.

Its hands began to move again and when one of them rose to smooth the fur on one small, rounded ear I realized that it was reflexively grooming itself.

Not long before it had possessed neither the rich, dark fur that was being stroked and settled nor the supple fingers that performed the operation. It had been instead a device that I had built years before, after I had worked out the direction of my career. I had acquired standard components and systems, then tuned and adjusted them to meet my need: a research assistant who could also act as an incisive interlocutor when I wished to discuss a case or test the value of evidence. Such devices are useful to freelance discriminators, of which I, Henghis Hapthorn, am the foremost of my era.

I had also fashioned a small carrying case into which the integrator could be decanted for traveling and which could be worn around my neck like a plump scarf or a stuffed axolotl. It was in that casing that my assistant had accompanied me on a brief transit through another dimension. We had been carried through the other continuum by an entity who resided there, a being who occasionally visited our universe to engage me in intellectual contests. Though I did not care for the term, the common description of my visitor was "demon."

When we emerged from the demon's portal into my workroom I found that the integrator and its carrying case had together been transformed into a creature that resembled a combination of feline and ape, and that I had an unscratchable itch deep in my inner being.

I had always referred questions of identity and taxonomy to my assistant, so I asked it, "What kind of creature do you think you are?"

It responded as it always had when I posed too broad a question, by challenging me to clarify my line of inquiry. "The question," it said, "invites answers that range from the merely physical to the outright spiritual."

"Considering the degree of change that has happened to you, 'merely physical' is a contradiction in terms," I said. "But let us start there and leave the spiritual for a less startling occasion."

Instead of answering, it took on an abstracted look for a moment then advised me that it was receiving an incoming communication from a philanthropically inclined magnate named Turgut Therobar. "He wishes to speak with you."

"How are you doing that?" I asked.

The golden eyes blinked. "Doing what?"

"Receiving a communication."

110

"I do not know," it said. "I have always received messages from the connectivity grid. Apparently that function continues."

"But you had components, elements, systems designed for that purpose. Now you have paws and a tail."

"How kind of you to remind me of my shortcomings. What shall I say to Turgut Therobar?"

Ordinarily I would have been interested to hear from Therobar. We had met once or twice, though we had never exchanged more than formal salutes. He was one of the better known magnates of the City of Olkney; unlike most of his peers, however, he was renowned for charitable works and it was alleged that he entertained a warm opinion of humankind in general. I assumed he was seeking to enlist me in some eleemosynary cause. "Say that I am unavailable and will return his call," I said.

The creature's expression again briefly took on an inward aspect, as if it were experiencing a subtle movement of inner juices, then it said, "Done."

"Again," I said, "how are you doing that?"

Again, it did not know. "How do you digest an apple?" it asked me. "Do you oversee each stage in the sequence of chemical reactions that transforms the flesh of the fruit into the flesh of Henghis Hapthorn?"

"Obviously not."

"Then if you do not introspect regarding your own inner doings, why would you expect it of me? After all, you did not design me to examine my own processes, but to receive and transmit and to integrate data at your order. These things I do, as I have always done them."

"I also designed you to be curious."

"I have temporarily placed my curiosity on a high shelf and removed the stepladder," it said. "I prefer not to wrestle with unanswerable questions just now."

"So you have acquired a capacity for preferences?" I said. "I do not recall ever instilling that quality into your matrix."

The yellow eyes seemed to grow larger. "If we are going to dwell on preferences, you might recall that my bias, strongly stated, was to avoid undergoing this metamorphosis."

I cleared my throat. "The past has evanesced, never to be reconstituted," I quoted. "Let us seize the firmness of the now."

My assistant's small fingered hands opened and closed. I had the impression it would have enjoyed firmly seizing something as a precursor to doing noticeable damage. But I pressed on. "What do you think you have become?" I said.

"The question lacks specificity," it replied.

I appealed to my demonic colleague. He had remained connected to the portal that allowed him to interact with this continuum after we had returned from resolving the case of Sigbart Sajessarian. But the transdimensional being offered little assistance.

"This is a question of form, as opposed to essence. Such questions are difficult for me," he said. "To my perceptions, calibrated as they are to the prevailing conditions of my own continuum, the integrator is much as it always was. Indeed, I have to tune my senses to a radically different rationale even to notice that it has changed. It does what it always did: it inquires, coordinates, integrates and communicates; these functions are the nub of its existence. Why should it matter in what form it achieves its purposes? I would prefer to talk of more seemly things."

"And yet matter it does," I said.

"I agree," said the integrator.

The demon, which manifested itself as various arrangements of light and color in its portal on the wall of my workroom, now assumed a pattern that I had come to recognize through experience as the equivalent of when a human being is unwilling to meet one's gaze. "What are you not telling us?" I asked.

He displayed a purple and deep green swirl shot through with swooshes of scintillating silver. I was fairly sure the pattern signaled demonic embarrassment. Under normal circumstances good manners would have restrained me from pressing for a response, but at the moment normal circumstances had leapt from the window and taken flight to parts unknown. "Speak," I said.

The silver swooshes were now edged with sparks of crimson but I insisted.

Finally the demon said, "I have not been entirely candid with you."

"Indeed?" I said, and waited for more.

"I told you that my motives for seeking to observe your realm were curiosity and the relief of boredom."

"You did. Was that not the truth?"

"Let us say it was a shade of the truth."

"I believe it is time for the full spectrum," I said.

A moment of silver and verdigris ensued, then the demon said, "This is somewhat embarrassing."

"As embarrassing as possessing an integrator that habitually picks at itself?" From the corner of my eye I saw the tiny fingers freeze.

"I seem to feel a need to groom my fur," it said.

"Why?" I said.

"I do not know, but it gives comfort."

"I did not design you to need comforting."

"Let us accept that I am no longer what you designed me to be."

The demon's presence was fading from the portal. "Wait," I said, turning back to him. "Where are you going?"

"An urgent matter claims my attention," he said. "Besides, I thought you and the integrator might prefer privacy for your argument."

"We are not arguing."

"It appeared to me to be an argument."

"Indeed?" I said. "Was the appearance one of form or of essence?"

"Now I think you are seeking an argument with me," the demon said.

I thought of a rejoinder, then discarded the impulse to wield it. My insides performed an indescribable motion. "I believe I am upset," I said.

"*You're* upset?" said the furry thing on my table.

"Very well," I snapped, "we are *all* upset, each in accordance with his essential nature. The atmosphere of the room swims with a miasma of embarrassment, intestinal distress and a craving for comfort."

I detected another flash of unease in the demon's display and probed for the cause. "What are you thinking now?"

The demon said, "I should perhaps have mentioned that through this portal that connects my continuum to yours there can be a certain amount of, shall we say, leakage."

"Leakage?"

"Nothing serious," he said, "but lengthy exposure followed by your complete though transitory corporeal presence in my realm may have had some minor effects."

"My integrator has become some sort of twitching familiar," I said. "I am not sure that effect can be called minor."

The integrator murmured a comment I did not catch, but it did not sound cheery.

It occurred to me that my demonic colleague might be diverting the discussion toward a small embarrassment as a means of avoiding addressing a larger one. "But we were about to hear a confession," I said.

"Rather, call it an explanation," said the demon.

"I shall decide what to call it after I've heard it."

The swirls in the frame flashed an interesting magenta. I suspected that my colleague was controlling his own emotional response. Then he said, "My motive was indeed curiosity, as I originally averred, but let us say that it was... well, a certain species of curiosity."

I experienced insight. "Was it was the kind of curiosity that moves a boy to apply his eye to a crack in a wall in order to spy on persons engaged in intimate behavior?" I said. "The breed of inquisitiveness we call prurience?"

More silver and green. "Just so."

"So to your continuum this universe constitutes a ribald peepshow, a skirt to be peeked under?"

"Your analogies are loose but not inapt."

"You had best explain," I said.

The explanation was briefly and reluctantly given, the demon finding it easier to unburden himself if I looked away from his portal. I turned my chair and regarded a far corner of the workroom while he first reminded me that in no other continuum than ours did objects exist separately from the symbols that represented them.

"Yes, yes," I said. "Here, the map is not the territory, whereas in other realms the two are indissoluble."

"Indeed." He continued, "We deal in essences. Forms are..."

He appeared to be searching for a word again. I endeavored to supply it. "Naughty?"

"To some of us, delightfully so." Even though I was looking into the far corner my peripheral vision caught the burst of incarnadined silver that splashed across his portal. "It is, of course, a harmless pastime, providing one does not overindulge."

"Ah," I said, "so it can become addictive?"

"Addictive is a strong term."

I considered my integrator and said, "It seems an appropriate occasion for strong language."

With reluctance, the demon said, "For some of us, an appreciation of forms can become, let us say, a predominant pastime."

"Is that the common term in your dimension for 'all-consuming obsession?'"

He made no spoken response but I assumed that the mixture of periwinkle-blue spirals and black starbursts were his equivalent of guilty acquiescence. I could not keep a note of disappointment out of my voice. "I thought the attraction of visiting here was the contests of wit and imagination in which you and I engage."

"They were a splendid bonus!"

"Hmm," I said. I had a brief, unwelcome emotion as I contemplated being profanely peered at by a demon who derived titillation from my form. Then I realized that anyone's form–indeed, probably the form of my chair or the waste receptacle in the corner–would have had the same salacious effect. I decided it would be wise not to dwell on the matter. "To move the conversation to a practical footing," I said, "how do we return my assistant to his former state?"

"I am not sure that we can."

The integrator had been surreptitiously scratching behind one of its small, round ears. Now it stopped and said, "I am receiving another communication from Turgut Therobar," it said. "He has added an 'urgent' rider to his signal."

"You seem to be functioning properly," I said, "at least as a communicator."

"Perhaps the demon is correct," said the integrator, "and essence trumps form. My functions were the essence for which you designed and built me."

I thought to detect an undercurrent of resentment, but I ignored it and homed in on the consequences of my assistant's change. "I have spent decades dealing comfortably with forms. Must I now throw all that effort aside and master essences?"

"Turgut Therobar continues to call," said my assistant. "He claims distress and pleads plaintively."

So the magnate was not calling to enlist me in some good cause. It sounded as if he required the services of a private discriminator. My insides remained troubled, but it occurred to me that a new case might be just the thing to take my mind off the unsettling change in my assistant.

"Put through the call," I said.

Therobar's voice sounded from the air, as had all previous communications through my assistant. The magnate dispensed with the punctilio of inquiries after health and comparisons of opinions on the weather that were proper between persons of respectable though different classes who have already been introduced. "I am accused of murder and aggravated debauchery," he said.

"Indeed," I said. "And are you guilty?"

"No, but the Bureau of Scrutiny has taken me into custody."

"I will intercede," I said. "Transmit the coordinates to my integrator." I signaled to the integrator to break the connection.

The creature blinked and said, "He is in the scroot holding facility at Thurloyn Vale."

"Hmm," I said, then, "contact Warhanny."

A moment later the hangdog face of Colonel Investigator Brustram Warhannny appeared in the air above my table and his doleful voice said, "Hapthorn. What's afoot?"

"Much, indeed," I said. "You have snatched up Turgut Therobar."

His elongated face assumed an even more lugubrious mien. "There are serious charges. Blood and molestation of the innocent."

"These do not jibe with my sense of Turgut Therobar," I said. "His name is a byword for charity and well doing."

"Not all bywords are accurate," Warhanny said. "I have even heard that some say that 'scroot' ought to be a byword for 'paucity of imagination coupled with clumping pudfootery.'"

"I can't imagine who would say such a thing," I said, while marveling at how my words, dropped into a private conversation the week before, had made their way to the Colonel Investigator's sail-like ears.

"Indeed?" he said. "As for Therobar, there have been several disappearances in and around his estate this past month, and outrageous liberties have been taken with the daughter of a tenant. All lines of investigation lead unerringly to the master."

"I find that hard to believe."

"I counsel you to exert more effort," Warhanny said. "And where you find resistance, plod your way through it."

"Turgut Therobar has retained me to intercede on his behalf," I said.

"The Bureau welcomes the assistance of all public minded citizens," Warhanny pronounced, yet somehow I felt that the formulaic words lacked sincerity.

"Will you release him into my custody?"

"Will you serve out his sentence in the Contemplarium if he defaults?" countered the scroot.

"He will not default," I said, but I gave the standard undertaking. "Transmit the file then deliver him to his estate. I will accept responsibility from there."

"As you wish."

Just before his visage disappeared from the air I thought to detect a smirk lurking somewhere behind Warhanny pendulous lips. While I mentally replayed the image, confirming the scornful leer, I told my integrator to book passage on an airship to Thurloyn Vale and to engage an aircar to fly out to Therobar's estate, Wan Water. There was no response. I looked about and found that it had left the table and was now across the room, investigating the contents of a bookcase. "What are you doing?" I said.

Before answering it pulled free a leather bound volume that had been laid sideways across the tops of the bottom row of books. I recognized the tome as one of several that I had brought back from the house of Bristal Baxandall, the ambitious thaumaturge who had originally summoned my demonic colleague to this realm. Baxandall had no further use for them, having expired while attempting to alter his own form, a process in which the compelled and reluctant demon had seized his opportunity for revenge.

"I thought there might be something useful in this," the integrator said, its fingers flicking through the heavy vellum pages while its golden eyes scanned from side to side.

It was yet another unsettling sight in a day that had already offered too many. "Put that away," I said. "I looked through it and others like it when I was a young man. It is a lot of flippydedoo about so-called magic."

But the integrator continued to peruse Baxandall's book. "I thought, under the circumstances," it said, "that we might drop the 'so-called' and accept the reality of my predicament."

I blew out air between scarcely opened lips. The creature's narrow catlike face sharpened and it said, "Do you have a better argument than that? If not, I will accept your concession."

While it was true that I must accept the concept that rationalism was fated to give way to magic, even that the cusp of the transition had arrived, I was not prepared to dignify a book of spells with my confidence. I blew the same amount of air as before, but this time let my lips vibrate, producing a sound that conveyed both brave defiance and majestic ridicule.

My assistant finished scanning the tome, slammed its covers together and said, "We must settle this."

"No," I said, "we must rescue Turgut Therobar from incarceration."

"You are assuming that he is blameless."

I applied insight to the matter. The part of me that dwelled in the rear of my mind, the part that intuitively grasped complex issues in a flash of neurons, supported my assumption, though not completely.

"Therobar is innocent," I reported. "Probably."

"I was also innocent of any urge to become a gurgling bag of flesh and bones," said the integrator. "What has happened to me must also be resolved."

"First the one, then the other," I said.

"Is that a promise?"

"I am not accustomed to having to make promises to my own integrator," I said.

"Yet you expect me to put up with this," it said, pointing at itself with both small hands, fingers spread, a gesture that put me mind of an indignant old man.

"Sometimes our expectations may require adjustment," I said.

I turned to the demon's portal to seek his views, but the entity had taken the opportunity to depart.

"Perhaps he has found another peepshow," I said.

Thurloyn Vale was an unpretentious transportation nexus at the edge of the great desolation that was Dimpfen Moor. Its dun colored, low-rise shops and houses radiated in a series of arrondisements from a broad hub on which sat the airship terminal that was the place's reason for being. In former times, the entire town had been ringed by a high, smooth wall, now mostly tumbled in ruins. The barrier had been built to keep out the large and predatory social insects known as neropts that nested on the moor, but eventually an escalating series of clashes, culminating in a determined punitive expedition, led to a treaty. Now any neropt that came within sight of Thurloyn Vale, including flying nymphs and drones in their season, was legitimately a hunter's trophy; any persons, human or ultraterrene, who ventured out onto the moor need not expect rescue if they were carried off to work the insects' subterranean fungi beds or, more usually, if they were efficiently reduced to their constituent parts and borne back to the hive to feed the ever hungry grubs.

Wan Water sat atop an unambitious hill only a short aircar flight into Dimpfen Moor, above a slough of peat brown water that gave the estate its name. It was a smallish demesne, with only a meager agricultural surround, since little would grow on that bleak landscape other than lichens and stunted bushes. Like the town, it was walled, but its barrier was well maintained and bristling with self-actuating ison-cannons. The presence of a nearby neropt nest afforded Wan Water's master the peace and tranquility that I assumed he required to plan his charitable works. Without the insects, he might be pestered by uninvited visitors eager to harness their ambitious plans to Turgut Therobar's well stocked purse. Coupled with an implied humility in his make-up, it seemed a likely explanation for having chosen such a cheerless place for his retreat.

With my integrator perched on my shoulder I overflew a ramble of outbuildings and guest houses then banked and curved down toward the manse. This was an arrangement of interconnected domes, each more broad than tall and linked one to the other by colonnades of twisted, fluted pillars, all of a gray stone quarried from the moor. Above the huddled buildings stood a tall natural tor of dark-veined rock, around which spiraled a staircase of black metal. Atop the eminence was a tidy belvedere of pale marble equipped with a demilune seat of a dark polished stone.

At the base of the tor I saw a black and green volante bearing the insignia of the Archonate Bureau of Scrutiny. Next to it stood a square faced man in a uniform of the same colors. With the moor's constant wind whistling mournfully through the bars of the staircase, he advised me that Turgut Therobar had ascended the pillar of rock. We completed the formalities by which my client became my responsibility then the scroot boarded his aircar and departed.

I turned and climbed to the top of the spiral stairs. There I found the magnate standing silently, his back to me and his front toward the grim prospect of Dimpfen Moor. I used the occasion to acquire a detailed impression of my client.

He was a man of more than middling age and height, thick through the shoulders, chest and wrists, with heavy jowls and a saturnine expression beneath a hat that was a brimless, truncated cone of dark felt. He affected plain garments of muted colors, though they were well cut and of fine material, as if he disdained the fripperies and panaches of transient fashion. As I inspected him I sought insight from my inner self and again received an inconclusive response. It was as if Therobar's being was a deep well, its upper reaches clear and pure yet shaded by darkness below. But whether anything sinister lurked in those depths could not be told.

Without taking his eyes from the vista that I found gloomy but which apparently worked to restore his inner peace, he said, "Thank you for arranging my release."

I inclined my head but replied, "Any intercessor could have done it."

"No, it had to be you."

My internal distresses had strengthened as I climbed the stairs. I pushed them to the edge of my awareness and prepared to focus on my responsibilities. "I am flattered by your confidence," I said. "Shall we discuss the case?"

"Later. For now I wish to look out upon the moor and contemplate the vagaries of fate."

"You are of a philosophical bent," I said. "Faced with imminent incarceration in the Contemplarium, most men would find their concentration drawn to that threat."

He turned toward me. "I am not most men. I am Therobar. It makes all the difference." A note of grim satisfaction rang softly through this speech.

The chill wind had been insinuating itself into my garments since we had mounted the tower. Now it grew more insistent. My integrator moved to nestle against the lee side of my head and I felt it shiver. The motion drew Therobar's eye.

"That is an unusual beast," he said.

"Most unusual."

The expression, "a piercing gaze" is most often an overstatement, but not in Therobar's case. He examined my assistant closely and said, "What is its nature?"

"We are discovering that together," I answered. "Right now it would be premature to say."

His eyes shifted to mine and for a moment I felt the full impact of his gaze. The back of my mind stirred like a watchbeast disturbed by a faint sound. Involuntarily, I stepped back.

"Forgive me," he said. "I have a tendency to peer."

I made a gesture to indicate that the matter was too trivial to warrant an apology, but the resident of the rear corners of my psyche took longer to subside.

We descended to the main buildings and passed within. It was a relief to be out of the wind though I could still hear it softly moaning and suffling across the roofs of the domes. Therobar handed me over to a liveried servant who escorted me to a suite of rooms where I refreshed myself, finding the appointments of the first quality. The man waited in the suite's anteroom to guide me to a reception room where my client had said he would await me.

I had placed my integrator on the sleeping pallet before going into the ablutory to wash. Returning, I extended my arm so that it might climb back to its wonted place upon my shoulders. I realized as I made the gesture that I was already becoming accustomed to its warmth and slight weight.

The creature came to me without taking its eyes from the footman who stood impassively beside the door. I noticed that the fur behind its skull was standing out like the ruffs that were fashionable when I was in school. I made a gesture to myself as if I had forgotten some trivial matter and returned to the washroom. There I lowered my voice and said to my assistant, "Why are you doing that?"

It moved to the far edge of my shoulder so it could look at me and said, "I am doing several things. To which do you refer?"

"Making your neck hair stand on end."

It reached up a paw and stroked the area. "It appears to be an autonomic response."

"To what?"

Its eyes flicked about then it said, "I think, to the presence of the footman."

"Why?"

"I do not know. I have had neither neck hair nor involuntary responses before."

"I should perform a diagnostic inquisition on you," I said.

"And just how would you go about doing that in my new condition?" it asked.

"Yes," I said, "I will have to think about that."

We went out to the anteroom and the servant opened the door to the corridor, but I stayed him. It might be useful to question him about the events that led up to Therobar's arrest. Servants often know more than they are supposed to about their masters' doings, even though they will invariably adopt an expression of blinking innocence when barked at by an inquisitive scroot like Warhanny. But let the interrogation be conducted by someone who has questions in one hand and coins in the other, and memories that had previously departed the servant's faculties come crowding back in, eager to reveal themselves.

"What can you tell me about your master's arrest?" I asked.

"Agents of the Bureau of Scrutiny came in the morning. They spoke with the master. When they left, he accompanied them."

This information was delivered in a disinterested tone, as if the man were describing a matter of no particular moment. His eyes were a placid brown. They rested on me blandly.

"What of the events that led up to the arrest?" I said.

"What of them?"

"They involved a number of deaths and some unsavory acts perpetrated on a girl."

"So I was told."

The servant's lack of affect intrigued me. "What did you think of the matter?" I asked.

"My memories of the incidents are vague, as if they occurred in another life."

"Struggle with them," I said, producing a ten-hept piece. I was surprised that the impassivity of his gaze did not so much as flicker, nor did he reach for the coin. Still I persisted. "What did you think of the crime?"

He shrugged. "I don't recall thinking of it at all," he said. "My duties occupy me fully."

"You were not shocked? Not horrified?"

"No."

"What were your emotions?"

The brown eyes blinked slowly as the man consulted his memory. After a moment he said, "When the Allers girl was brought in, she was hysterical. I was sent to the kitchens to fetch a restorative. The errand made me late in preparing the sleeping chambers for the master's guests. I was chagrined but the master said it was a forgivable lapse."

"You were chagrined," I said.

"Briefly."

"Hmm," I said.

I flourished the ten-hept piece again and this time the fellow looked at it but again showed no interest. I put it away. Turgut Therobar had a reputation for aiding the intellectually deficient. I reasoned that this man must be one of his projects and that I would gain no more from interrogating him than I would from questioning the mosses on Dimpfen Moor. "Lead me," I said.

I was brought to a capacious reception room in the main dome. Therobar was in the center of the great space, making use of a mobile dispenser. He had changed his garments and now wore a loose fitting gown of shimmering fabric and a brocaded cloth headpiece artfully wound about his massive skull. He was not alone. Standing with him were an almost skeletally thin man in the gown and cap of an Institute don and a squat and hulking fellow who wore the stained smock of an apparaticist and a cloche hat. All three turned toward me as I entered, abruptly cutting off a conversation they had been conducting in muted tones. We offered each other the appropriate formal salutations, then Turgut made introductions.

The lean academician was Mitric Gevallion, with the rank of sessional lecturer in dissonant affinities—the name rang a faint chime but I could not immediately place him—and the bulky apparaticist was his assistant, who went by the single name Gharst. "They are conducting research into some matters that have piqued my curiosity. I have given them the north wing. We've been having a most fascinating discussion."

He handed me a glass of aperitif from a sideboard. I used the time it took to accept and sip the sharply edged liquor to cover my surprise at finding myself drawn into a social occasion after being summoned to an urgent rescue. There seemed no reason not to raise the obvious question, so I did.

"Should we not be concerned rather with your situation?"

For a moment, my meaning did not register, then his brow cleared. "Ah, you mean Warhanny and all that." He dismissed the subject with a lightsome wave of his meaty hand. "Tomorrow is soon enough."

"The matter seemed more pressing when you contacted me," I said.

His lips moved in the equivalent of a shrug. "When confined to the Bureau of Scrutiny's barren coop one has a certain perspective. It alters when one is ensconced in the warmth of home."

There was not much warmth apparent. I thought the room designed more for grandeur than comfort. "Still," I began but he spoke over my next words, urging me to hear what Gevallion had to say. Out of deference to my host, I subsided and gave the academician my polite attention.

"I am making progress in redefining gist within the context of configuration," the thin man said.

Gevallion's name now came into focus and I stifled a groan by sipping from the glass of aperitif. There was a subtle undertone to its flavor that I could not quite identify. As I listened further to the academic a memory blossomed. In my student years at the Institute, I had written an offhand reply to a paper posted on the Grand Forum, demolishing its preposterous premises and ending with a recommendation that its author seek another career since providence had clearly left him underequipped for intellectual pursuits. I now saw that Mitric Gevallion had not taken my well meant advice but had remained at the Institute, dedicating his life to the pursuit of the uncatchable; he was a seeker after gist, the elusive quality identified by the great Balmerion uncounted eons ago as the underlying substance of the universe. Gist bound together all of time, energy, matter and the other, less obvious components into an elegant whole.

Apparently he had forgotten my criticism of his work since he did not mention it upon our being introduced. It seemed good manners not to bring it up myself, but I could not, in all conscience, encourage his fruitless line of inquiry. "You are not the first to embark on the gist quest," I said, "though you would certainly be the first to succeed."

"Someone must be first at everything," he said. He had one of those voices that mix a tone of arrogance with far too much resonance through the nasal apparatus. Listening to him was like being lectured to by a out-of-tune bone flute.

"But gist is, by Balmerion's third dictum, beyond all grasp," I said. "The moment it is approached, even conceptually, it disappears. Or departs–the question remains open."

"Exactly," the academician said. "It cannot be apprehended in any way. The moment one seeks to delineate or define it, it is no longer there."

"And perhaps that is for the best," I said. I reminded him of Balmerion's own speculation that gist had been deliberately put out of reach by a hypotnetical demiurge responsible for drafting the metaphysical charter of our universe. "Otherwise we would pick and pick and pick at the fabric of existence until we finally pulled the thread that unraveled the whole agglomeration."

Turgut Therobar entered the conversation. "Master Gevallion leans, as I am coming to do, toward Klapczyk's corollary to Balmerion's dictum."

I had earlier restrained a groan, now I had to fight down an incipient snort. The misguided Erlon Klapczyk had argued that the very hiddenness of gist bespoke the deity's wish that we seek and find it, and that this quest was in fact the reason we were all here.

I said, "I recall hearing that Klapczyk's adolescent son once advanced his father's corollary as an excuse for having overturned the family's ground car after being forbidden to operate it. Klapczyk countered his own argument by throwing things at the boy until he departed and went to live with a maternal aunt."

"I agree it is a paradox," Gevallion said, then quoted, "Is it not the purpose of paradox to drive us to overcome our mental limitations?"

"Perhaps," I said. "Or perhaps what you take for a teasing puzzle is instead more like a dutiful parent's removal of a devastating explosive from the reach of a precocious toddler. If I were to begin to list the people to whom I would not give the power to destroy the universe, even limiting the list to those who would do so only accidentally, I would soon run out of stationery."

Therobar offered another dismissive wave. I decided it was a characteristic gesture. "I care not for a cosmos ruled by a prating nanny," he said. "I prefer to see existence as veined throughout by a mordant sense of irony. Gevallion's speculations are more to my taste than Balmerion's tiptoeing caution."

"Even if he budges the pebble that brings down the avalanche?"

The magnate's heavy shoulders rose and fell in an expression of disregard. "We are entering the last age of Old Earth, which will culminate in the sun's flickering senility. All will be dark and done with."

"There are other worlds than this."

"Not when I am not standing on them," Therobar said. "Besides, what is life without a risk? And thus, the grander the risk, the grander the life."

I was coming to see my client from a new perspective. "I really think we should discuss the case," I said.

"I've set aside some time after breakfast," he said, then turned and asked Gevallion to explain some point in his theories. After hearing the first few words, I let my attention wander and inspected the room. It was lofty ceilinged, the curving walls cut by high, narrow windows through which the orange light of late afternoon poured in to make long oblongs on the deep pile of the rich, blood-red carpeting that stretched in all directions. One end of the room was dominated by a larger than life mural that displayed Turgut Therobar in the act of casually dispensing something to a grateful throng. Not finding the image to my taste, I turned to see what might be in the other direction and noticed a grouping of divans and substantial chairs around a cheerful hearth. Seated in a love chair, placidly regarding the flames, was a young woman of striking beauty.

Therobar noted the direction of my gaze. "That is the Honorable Gevallion's ward, Yzmirl. She is also assisting him in his researches."

"Would you care to meet her?" Gevallion said.

I made a gesture of faint demurral. "If the encounter would not bore her."

Therobar chuckled. "No fear of that. Come."

We crossed the wide space, the drinks dispenser whispering over the carpet in our wake. The young woman did not look our way as we approached, giving me time to study her. She was beyond girlhood but had not yet entered her middle years. Her face had precisely the arrangement of features that I have often found compelling: large and liquid eyes, green but with flecks of gold, an understated nose and a generous mouth. Her hair was that shade of red that commands attention. It fell straight to her shoulders where it was cut with geometric precision. She wore a thin shift made of layers of a gauzy material, amber over plum, leaving her neck, arms and shoulders bare.

"My dear," said Gevallion, "allow me to present the Honorable Henghis Hapthorn, a discriminator who is assisting our host with matters that need not concern us."

She remained seated but looked up at me. I made a formal salute and added a gallant flourish. Her placid expression did not alter but it seemed that I had captured her interest, since she stared fixedly at me with widened eyes. It was a moment before I realized that the true focus of her gaze was not my face but the transmogrified integrator that crouched upon my shoulder. At the same time I became aware that the creature was issuing into my ear a hiss like that of air escaping from pressurized containment. I gave my head a sharp shake and the annoying sound ceased though I thought to detect a grumble.

"What is that on your shoulder?" Yzmirl asked. Her voice was soft, the tone polite, yet I experienced a reaction within me. It was just the kind of voice I preferred to hear.

"I have not yet reached a conclusion on that score," I said.

The green eyes blinked sleepily. She said, "There was a character in Plobbit's most recent novel, *Spelling Under a Fall*, who trained a large toad to squat on his shoulder. At a signal from its master, the beast would send a jet of unmentionable liquid in the direction of anyone who offended him."

"I recall it," I said. "Do you enjoy Plobbit?"

"Very much," she said. "Do you?"

"He is my favorite author."

"Well, then," she said.

Therobar cleared his throat. "I have some matters to attend to before dinner," he said.

"As do we," said Gevallion, draining his glass and dropping it into the dispenser's hopper. "Yzmirl, would you mind entertaining our friend for a while?"

"I would not mind," she said. She patted the seat next to her to indicate that I should sit. I did so and became aware of her perfume.

"Is that *Cynosure* you're wearing?" I said.

"Yes. Do you like it?"

"Above all other scents." I was not exaggerating. The perfume had had an almost pheromonical effect on me when I had encountered it on other women. On Yzmirl, its allure was compounded by her exquisite appearance.

"I please you?" she asked, her eyes offering me pools into which I could plunge and not care that I drowned.

"Oh, indeed."

"How nice," she said. "Why don't you tell me about your work? What are your most notable exploits?"

The integrator hissed again. I could feel its fur against my ear and realized it must be swelling up as it had in the presence of the footman. I reached up with one hand and found that the skin at the nape of its wiry neck was loose enough to afford me a grip. I lifted the creature from my shoulder and deposited it behind the love chair while my other hand covered that of Yzmirl where she had let it rest on the brocaded fabric between us.

"Well," I said, "would you care to hear about the case of the purloined passpartout?"

"Oh, yes," she said.

The integrator was making sounds just at the threshold of hearing. I disregarded its grumpy murmurs and said, "It all began when I was summoned to the office of a grand chamberlain in the Palace of the Archonate..."

Time passed though its passage made scant impression. After I told the tale of the Archon Dezendah's stolen document she asked for more and I moved on to the case of the Vivilosc fraud ring. Between episodes we refreshed our palates with offerings from the dispenser: I twice refilled my glass with the increasingly agreeable aperitif; she took a minim of Aubreen's restorative tincture, drawing in its pale blue substance by pursing her lips in a manner that was entirely demure yet at the same time deliciously enticing. My hand moved from hers, first to caress her arm then later I let my fingertips brush the softness where neck met shoulder. She made no complaint but continued to regard me with an unshielded gaze. My innards quaked from time to time, but I pushed the sensation to the borders of my mind.

A footman entered the room and crossed to where we sat. I repressed an urge toward irritation and looked up as he approached. It was the same fellow who had obliquely responded to my questions. Or at least I thought it was as he approached. When he afforded me a closer inspection, it seemed that this might be instead a close relation of the other. I reached for my memory of the earlier encounter but found it veiled by too much aperitif and the heady scent of the young woman beside me.

"My master bids me tell you," said the servant, after a lackluster salute, "that an urgent matter has called him from the estate. He regrets that he cannot join you for dinner."

"How long will he be gone?" I asked.

"He said he might not return before morning."

In the brief silence that ensued I could hear my integrator hissing behind the love seat. I reached over to swat it to silence but missed. "What of Gevallion and Gharst?" I said.

"They accompany the master on his journey."

"So it is just us two?"

The fellow tilted his head in a way that confirmed my supposition, though his expression remained unmoved. "The master suggested that you and the Lady Yzmirl might prefer to dine in the comfort of your quarters."

My eyes widened. I looked at Yzmirl but her expression showed neither alarm nor disinclination. "Would you be comfortable with such an arrangement?" I asked her.

"Of course."

"Then it's settled."

We rose and followed the footman to my suite, the integrator trundling along behind on its short legs, spitting and grumping just at the threshold of audibility. I looked back at one point and saw that its tail was twitching and its little fists were clenched. But when we arrived at my rooms, to find the first course of our dinner ready to be served, I chivvied the ill tempered beast into the ablutory and closed the door so that Yzmirl need not feel distracted or constrained.

I found the food excellent, the company enchanting and the aftermath an unparalleled delight. Yzmirl displayed only a genteel interest in what was placed before her at the table but, after the servant returned and took away the remains of the meal, she revealed a robust appetite and surprising inventiveness in another room.

I awoke alone. Or so I thought until I arose and entered the washroom, where a small, furry and angry presence made itself known.

"Apparently, I need to eat," it said in a tone that was far from deferential.

"Eat what?"

There was fruit on a side table in the main salon. It went and sampled this and that. I was prepared to offer advice on the arts of chewing and swallowing but the creature mastered these skills without trouble. I thought a compliment might lighten the atmosphere but my encouraging words were turned back on me. "I've seen you do it thousands of times," it said. "How hard could it be?"

"Then you'll be able to work out the other end of the alimentary process for yourself?" I said.

"I shall manage."

I performed my morning toilet and emerged to find the integrator perched on the back of chair, its tail flicking like a petulant pendulum and a frown on its face. "What?" I said.

"I cannot connect to the grid."

"Why not?"

"I don't know why not."

"Hmm," I said. "Ordinarily, I would perform a diagnostic procedure on your systems and components. Now I would first have to take advice from..." I had been going to specify a person who was skilled in the care of animals, but I had a suspicion that this particular creature might baffle such a specialist.

"How does it... feel, I suppose that's the word, to be unable to connect?"

It put on its introspective look for a moment, then said, "It feels as if I ought to be able to connect but cannot."

"As if you were out of range?"

"As if I was blocked."

There was a knock on the door and the footman entered. Again my integrator's fur raised itself involuntarily and again I was not quite sure that this was the same fellow I had encountered before.

"The master would like you to join him for breakfast," he said. The voice sounded identical, yet there was something around the eyes and the mouth that seemed slightly different.

There was no obvious reason to be circumspect. I said, "Are you the same footman who yesterday led me to meet your master and returned me here?"

His expression registered no surprise at the question. He looked at me neutrally and said, "Why do you ask?"

"Because I wish to know."

His answer was unexpected. "It is difficult to say."

"Why? It is a simple question."

"There are no simple questions," he said. "Only simple questioners. But I will address the issue. Are you the same person who arrived here yesterday? Since then you have had new experiences, met new people, consumed and excreted the air of this place and other substances. Has none of this had any effect on you?"

"The argument is abstruse," I said. "Assume the broadest of definitions and answer: are you the same footman whom I encountered yesterday?"

"Under the broadest definition, it would be difficult to distinguish me from any other entity, including you."

The fellow was obviously a simpleton. "Lead me to your master," I said. As he turned to depart I beckoned my integrator to mount to my shoulder again. It was hissing and its fur was once more ruffed about its neck.

I found Turgut Therobar in a morning room in the great dome. He wore loose attire: ample pantaloons, a billowing shirt, chamois slippers, all in muted tones with plain fasteners. His head was again swathed in a silken cloth. He did not rise from his chair as I entered but beckoned me to sit across from him. A low table between us bore plates of bread, bowls of fruit and cups to be filled from a steaming carafe of punge.

He exhibited an air of sleepy self-satisfaction, blinking lazily as he inquired as to how I had passed the night. I assured him that I had rested well but offered an observation that he did not appear to have slept much. He extended his lower lip and made a show with his eyebrows that signaled that his rest or lack of it was of small concern. "A necessary task occupied most of the night," he said, "but it was well worth the doing."

I raised my brows in inquiry, but when he added no more I politely changed the subject. "We should discuss the case," I said.

"As you wish. How would you like to proceed?"

I poured myself a cup of punge and chose a savory broche then ordered my mind as I chewed, sipped and swallowed. "First," I said, "I will rehearse the known elements of the matter. Then I wish to know everything, from the beginning."

The charges concerned the disappearance of a number of persons in the vicinity of Wan Water over recent months. Initially, it had been thought that they had wandered into range of neropt hunting parties, the usual precursor to sudden disappearances on Dimpfen Moor.

The break in the case came when a tenant's young daughter, Bebe Allers, had gone missing from Wan Water only to reappear after a few days wandering within the walls of the estate. She was in a state of confusion and distress, with vague memories of being seized, transported, confined and perhaps interfered with in intimate ways. She could not directly identify the person or persons responsible for the outrage, but she had blanched and screamed at the sight of an image of Turgut Therobar.

"Now," I said, "how do you answer?"

He spoke and his face and tone betrayed a blasé unconcern that I found surprising. But the substance of his response was nothing less than astonishing. "The affair is now moot," he said. "Events have moved on."

I set my cup and plate on the table. "Wealth and social rank will not keep you from the Archon's Contemplarium if you are adjudged to be at fault."

His eyes looked up and away. "The case is nuncupative."

"Colonel-Investigator Warhanny will take a different view."

He chose a cake and nibbled at its topping.

"Please," I said, "I have given surety for you. My interests are also at stake."

He smiled and it was not a pleasant sight. There was a glint in his eye that gave me an inkling as to why the victim had reacted with horror to his image. "You will soon find," he said, "that you have more pressing concerns."

My integrator was hissing quietly beside my ear. The intuitive part of me was alert and urging unspecified action. I stood up. "You had better explain," I said.

He regarded me as if I had just executed some comic trick and he expected me to perform another. "Oh, I shall explain," he said. "Triumphs gain half their delight from being appreciated by those who have been triumphed over."

To my assistant I said, quietly, "Contact Warhanny. Tell him I withdraw from the case."

"I still cannot connect," it said.

"If I may interrupt your communion with your pet," Therobar said, "I was about to relieve your mind concerning the case."

"Very well," I said. "Do so."

He made a face like that of a little boy admitting a naughtiness to an indulgent caregiver and spread his hands. "I am guilty," he said.

"You interfered with the young maiden?"

"Indeed."

"And the disappearances?"

Again the protruding lip and facial shrug, which I took as an admission of culpability.

There could be only one question: "Why?"

"Two reasons," he said, throwing away the cake, now denuded of its topping, and reaching for another. "The disappeared assisted in Mitric Gevallion's experiments."

"You have been experimenting on human beings?"

"We'd gone as far as we could with animals. What else was there to do?"

I was being given an unobstructed view into Therobar's psyche. I shuddered involuntarily "What were the aims of these experiments?"

"As we discussed last night: at first we were seeking to redefine gist so that we could employ it in various efforts at carnal reconfiguration."

I translated his remark. "You were trying to harness the elementary force of the universe in order to transform living creatures."

"Yes." His sharp pointed tongue licked cream from the core of his pastry.

"Why?"

"Why not?"

"That is never a reason," I said.

"You may be right. In any case, we soon found another."

He was smiling, waiting for me to ask. I obliged him. "What did you find?"

"We discovered that we could 're-order' animals from one species to another, though they were never happy in their new skins. So then we tried 'editing' them, again with interesting results. We produced several disparate versions from the same template: one would be ferocious, another painfully meek; one would have an overpowering urge to explore its territory, while the next iteration would not stir from its den." He drank from his cup of punge. "Do you understand what we had achieved?"

He was waiting again. "I am sure you would enjoy telling me," I said.

"We kept the shape, but discarded the contents, so to speak."

I had an insight. "You found you could work with form while discarding essence."

"Exactly. And, of course, once we had done it with beasts we had to try it with people."

"It is monstrous," I said.

"An entirely accurate description, at first. They were indeed monsters. We turned them loose to bellow and rampage on the moor, where the neropts found them and carried them off."

"But then?" I asked.

He wriggled with self-satisfaction. "But then we refined the process and began striking multiples from the originals. They are short-lived but they serve their purposes."

I understood. "The footmen," I said. "They are copies."

"And not just the footmen," he said, an insinuating smile squirming across his plump lips.

I was horrified. "Yzmirl," I whispered, then put iron in my voice. "Where is she?"

"Nowhere," he said. "She was, now she is not. Though Gevallion can whip up another at any time. That one was specifically designed to appeal to your tastes and petty vanities."

I did not trust myself to stand over him. I sat and turned my vision inward, encountering images of deep and tender pathos. After a while, he spoke dragging my attention back to his now repulsive face.

"You haven't asked about the second reason," he said.

My mind had wandered far from the discussion. I indicated that I was not following.

"The disappeared," he said, speaking as if I were a particularly slow child, "went into Gevallion's vats. Then there was the Allers girl. She was the template for your companion of last night, by the way."

I took a labored breath. It was as if his evil thickened the air. "All right," I said. "Why did you let the girl be found?"

"Because that would bring Warhanny. And Warhanny would bring you."

"And why must you bring me?"

"Because by being here, you were not there."

"And where is 'there?'"

He smiled. "At your rooms, of course. Where there were items I wished to acquire."

I allowed anger to take me. I kicked the low table at his legs and sprang to overpower him. But he was ready. An object appeared in his hand. At its center was a small black spot. As I leapt toward him the circle abruptly expanded and rushed out to encompass me in nothingness.

Mitric Gevallion's laboratory was an unprepossessing place, dimly lit and woefully untidy. It featured a long work bench crowded with apparatus and a large display board on which a meandering set of equations and formulae had been scrawled. The vats in which the gist hunter brewed his creations loomed to one side of the wide, low ceilinged room. Against the opposite wall was a sturdy cage and it was within its confines that I regained consciousness.

"Ah," said Gevallion, when Gharst, who had been sucking at a wound on one thick thumb, drew his attention to my blinking and pate rubbing. Therobar's shocker had left me muzzified and aching, but I was now recovering as the academician crossed the cluttered floor to regard me through the bars. "Ah, there you are, back with us," he said.

I saw no need to join him in assertions of the obvious, and fixed him instead with a disdainful stare. I might as well have struck him with a cobweb for all the impact I achieved.

He rubbed his thin, pale hands together. "We're just waiting for our host to join us, then we'll begin," he said.

I knew he wanted me to ask what was to ensue, but I denied him that satisfaction. After a moment, his eyes moved from my face to focus on a point to one side of it. "That is a most curious creature," he said. "We tried to examine it while you were... resting, but it shrieked and bit Gharst quite viciously. What is it?"

When I did not answer, he made a moue with his thin lips and said, "It does not signify. I will dissect the beast at leisure after you are... shall we say, through with it."

It was another attempt to elicit a response from me, and I ignored it like the others. My mind was now concentrated on the display board and I was following the calculations thereon. The mathematics were abstruse but familiar, until they reached the third sequence. There I saw that Gevallion's extrapolation of Balmerion's premises had taken a sudden and entirely unexpected departure. He had achieved a complete overturning of the ancient premises and yet as I proceeded to examine each step in his logic, I saw that it all held together.

"You're looking for the flaw," he said, now sounding the way a bone flute would sound if it could experience complacent triumph.

I said nothing, but the answer he sought must have been unmistakable in my expression. I ran my eyes over the calculations again, looking for the weakness, the false syllogism, the unjustified leap. There was none.

Finally, I could not deny my curiosity. "How?" I said.

"Simple," was his answer, "yet achingly difficult. Although it went against everything we are taught, I consciously accepted the gnosis that magic and rationalism alternate in a vast cycle, and that whenever the change comes the new regime obliterates all memory of the other's prior ascendancy. I then asked myself, 'If it were so, what would be the mechanism of change?' And the answer came: there is gist, it exists in this half of the cycle; the other half is opposite, therefore it must contain opposite gist. I thereby conceived the concept of negative gist."

"Negative gist," I repeated, and could not keep the wonder from my voice.

"And negative gist, viewed from our side of the dichotomy, is susceptible to definition. Define it, then reverse it, and you have a definition of positive gist. Although it is hard to remember. It slides easily out of understanding."

Negative gist, I thought. *Why had I not seen it?*

He knew what I was thinking. "You were not supposed to," he said. "None of us are. Even with it written on the board I had trouble keeping it in mind. I kept wanting to erase the equations. Then I relocated to Wan Water where conditions are more accommodating."

"How so?"

"The transition from rationalism to sympathy does not cross our universe in a wavefront, as dawn sweeps across a planet. It occurs almost everywhere at once, like seepage through a porous membrane, but there are discrete locations–dimples, I call them–where the earliest seepage pools. Here the effects are intensified."

"And Wan Water is such a place," I said.

"Indeed. That is why our host chose to build here."

"It seems to be a time for surprises," I said. There was something more that needed to be said. "I am not often wrong, but in this matter of gist I assuredly was. I offer you my apologies and my congratulations."

"Graciously done," he said. "Both are accepted." He added a formal salute appropriate to academic equals.

I returned it and said, "Since we are on good terms, perhaps you would unlock the cage."

His expression of regret seemed sincere. "I'm afraid Turgut Therobar has other plans. More to the point, he has the only key."

At that moment, Gharst called to say that something on the bench had reached a critical point of development. Gevallion rushed to his side. They busied themselves with an apparatus constructed of intricately connected rods and coils, then Gevallion made a last adjustment and the two stood back in postures of expectation. In the air a colorless spot had appeared, a globular shape no larger than my smallest fingernail, connected to the apparatus by a filament as thin as a gossamer. Gevallion nudged a part of the contraption on the bench and the spot grew larger and darker while the connector thickened. I saw motion seemingly within the sphere, a slow roiling as of indistinct shapes turning over and about each other.

The room was also charged with strange energies. My inner discomforts now increased. I felt as if both flesh and being were penetrated by vital forces, causing an itching of my bones and sense of some impending revelation, though I could not tell if it would burst upon me or from me.

Gevallion said something to Gharst and the assistant gingerly touched the apparatus. The academician pushed him aside and made a more determined adjustment. The globe rapidly expanded until it was perhaps three times the diameter of Gharst's outsized head, then quickly shimmered and redoubled in size. The connecting conduit grew as thick as my wrist. Now the apparition seemed to become stable. I fought the intense irritation the device was causing in my innermost parts and studied the globe closely. I saw that the shifting colors and indeterminate shapes that moved within it were familiar, and began to plan a surprise.

"That is as much as we can achieve at this point," Gevallion told Gharst. "Advise Turgut Therobar that we are ready for his contribution."

The assistant spoke into a communications nexus beside the bench. I heard a muffled response.

The dim room became silent and still. The two experimenters stood by the bench, the globe swirled placidly in the air and a small voice mumbled in my ear. For the moment, I ignored it.

If I had any doubts on the matter they were soon resolved. The door opened and in strode Turgut Therobar, swathed in the multihued robes and lap-eared cap of a thaumaturge. The costume should have appeared comical, yet did not. His face bore an expression of fevered anticipation and his hands clasped another disconcertingly familiar object: Bristall Baxandall's leather-bound tome, last seen in my workroom.

I could feel my assistant's fur standing up and tickling the side of my neck. The murmuring in my ear grew more insistent.

I whispered back, "Don't worry."

Therobar inspected the swirling globe and beamed at Gevallion and Gharst, then shot me a look that contained a mixture of sentiments. He placed the great book on the work bench and opened it, ran his finger down a page and his tongue across his ripe lips. "The Chrescharrie, first, don't you think?" he said to Gevallion, who nodded nervous agreement.

I recognized the name as that of a minor deity worshipped long ago by a people almost now forgotten. I heard more mumblings in my ear. "Shush," I said, under my breath.

Therobar removed his cap and I saw that his hairless scalp was densely tattooed with figures and symbols such as I had seen in books of magic lore. He rubbed one hand over the smooth skin of his pate then took a deep breath and intoned a set of syllables. Something pulsed along the cable that connected sphere to apparatus. He spoke again, and again the connector palpitated as if something traversed along its length. The colors in the sphere flashed and fluoresced. There was a crackling sound and the air of the room suddenly smelled sharply of ozone. My internal organs felt as if they were seeking to trade places with each other and there was a pulsing pressure at the back of my head. My integrator abandoned my shoulder with a squawk, dropping to the floor where it grumbled and chittered in an agitated manner.

Therobar spoke again and made a calculated gesture. The sphere shimmered and flickered, there came a loud *crack* of energy and a fountain of blue sparks cascaded from the globe. The swirl coalesced and cohered at its center, becoming a six-armed homunculus, red of skin and cobalt of eye—there was only one, in the middle of its forehead—seated crosslegged on black nothingness that now otherwise filled the orb. Meanwhile a sensation like a hot scouring wind shot through me.

Therobar consulted the book once more and spoke three guttural sounds, meanwhile moving hands and fingers in precise motions. The figure in the globe started as if struck. Its eye narrowed and its gash of a mouth turned downward in a frown. Its several arms flexed and writhed while it seemed to be attempting to rise to its split hoofed feet. Therobar spoke and gestured again, a long string of syllables, and the homunculus subsided, though with a patent show of anger in its face.

Now the thaumaturge took another deep breath and barked a harsh phrase. There was a reek of raw power in the air and a thrumming sound just at the limits of perception. My bones were rattling against each other at the joints.

Therobar raised one hand, the index finger extended, then swiftly jabbed it into his forehead. The figure in the globe did likewise with one of its upper limbs, though its sharp nailed digit struck not flesh and bone but its own protruding eye. It gave a squeal of pain and frustrated rage.

Therobar's eyes widened and I saw a gleam of triumph in them. For a moment I thought he might voice some untoward cry of victory, which would have put us all in deadly peril, but he mastered the impulse and instead chanted a lengthy phrase. The glowering deity in the sphere shimmered and dissolved into fragments of light, and once again the orb contained only shifting shapes and mutating colors.

The thaumaturge let out a sigh of happy relief. Gevallion and Gharst came from the other side of the work bench and there followed a few moments of back slapping, hand gripping, and—on Therobar's part—a curious little dance that I took to express unalloyed joy.

When the demonstration was over, he looked my way and with an expression of satiated pleasure said, "Allow me to explain what you just saw."

"No need," I said. "You have accessed a continuum in which there is no distinction between symbol and referent. You have encapsulated a small segment of that realm and used it as a secure enclosure in which you could summon up a minor deity and bend it to your will. After animals and humans it is the next natural step. Now I suppose you'll want to call up something more potent so that you can use it to rule the world."

Therobar's face took on an aggrieved pout and he regarded me without favor for a long moment.

I shrugged my itching shoulders. "Your ambitions are as banal as your taste in decor," I said.

I thought he would strike me, but he put down the impulse and sneered. "Do you know why I brought you here?" he said.

"So that you could steal Baxandall's book from my library."

"That was but the proximate cause," he said, and I detected a deeper animosity in the squinting of his eyes and the writhing of his mouth as he approached the cage. "Do you recall an evening at Dame Obrosz's salon several years ago?"

"There were many such occasions," I said. "One tends not to retain details."

"You were holding forth on the bankruptcy of magic."

"I am sure I have done so often."

"Yes." The syllable extended into a hiss. "But on that occasion, your arguments had a profound effect on me."

"That seems odd, since the evidence of the past few minutes indicates that you have spent years studying and mastering the magical lore that I inveighed against. Obviously I did not convince you."

'On the contrary, you convinced me utterly," he said. "But I was so offended by your strutting arrogance and insouciant contempt for all contrary opinion that I resolved then and there to devote my life to disproving your claims, and forcing you to acknowledge utter defeat."

"Congratulations," I said. "You have achieved the goal of your existence. I am glad to have been of such great use to you, but pray tell me, what will you do to fill the remaining years?"

"Perhaps I will spend them tormenting you," he said. "And acquainting you with the depths of animosity you are capable of summoning up in otherwise placid souls."

"I think not." It seemed time to act. I did my best to ignore my peculiar inner sensations, though they had not diminished after Therobar dismissed the Chrescharrie. Focusing my will, I spoke certain words while making the usual accompanying gestures. Therobar stepped back, his face filling with a mingling of confusion and curiosity. The colors in the globe swirled anew, then I saw the familiar pattern of my demonic friend.

"I am beset," I called. "Please aid me."

The demon manifested a limb: thick, bristling with spines and tipped with a broad pincer-like claw. It reached out to Turgut Therobar as I had seen it do before to two other unfortunates. But the thaumaturge had already recovered his equilibrium. He stepped back, out of range, while shouting Gevallion's name.

The academician also overcame his surprise. He did something to the apparatus on the bench and the globe constricted sharply, trapping my friend's spiked appendage as if it were a noose that had tightened around the limb. I heard muffled sounds and saw the claw opening and closing in frustration, its pincers clicking as they seized only thin air.

Therobar was flipping through the book. He stopped at a page and from the way his eyes flashed I knew that it boded ill for my friend and me. "*Ghoroz ebror fareshti!*" he shouted. The orb shivered then contracted further, to the size of a fist, then to a pinpoint, and finally it popped out of existence altogether. The demon's arm, severed neatly, flopped to the floor where it glowed and smoked for a moment before disappearing.

"Oh, dear," said Turgut Therobar. "I hope you weren't counting on that as your last resort."

"It would be premature to say," I said, but I heard little conviction in my own voice.

The thaumaturge rubbed his hands in a manner that implied both satisfaction with what had transpired and happy anticipation of further delights to come. "Shall I tell you what happens next?" he said.

140

I was casting about for a some stratagem by which I might escape or turn the tables, but nothing was coming to mind. I sought insight from the intuitive part of me that so often came to my aid, but received no sense of impending revelation. It was as if he was otherwise occupied.

Hello! I shouted down the mental corridor that led to his abode. *Now would be an apt time to assist!*

Meanwhile, Therobar was speaking. "You'll go into the vats, of course. I will create several versions of you, some comical, some pathetically freakish. I will make convincing Henghis Hapthorn facsimiles, but give them unpleasant compulsions, then send them out into society. Your reputation may suffer. Others will have the opportunity to outrun neropt foraging parties. I believe I'll also recreate you in a feminine edition." He smiled that smile that could make children scream. "Such fun."

The muted voice that had been rumbling in my ear now said, quite clearly, "Step aside."

I turned my head, wondering what my transformed integrator was up to, but the creature was huddled in a far corner of the cage nervously rubbing one hand over another. "Did you speak?" I said.

"No, I did," said the voice again, this time less quiet. "Now, get out of the way."

I experienced a novel sensation: I was *shoved* from within, not roughly but with decided firmness, as that part of me that I was accustomed to think of as fixed and immutable—my own mind—now found itself sharing my inner space with another partner. At the same time, the noxious itchings and shiftings among my inner parts faded to a normal quiescence.

"Wait," I said.

"I've already waited years," Therobar said, but I had not addressed him.

"As have I," said the voice in my head. "Now, move over before you get us both into even worse difficulty."

I acquiesced, and the moment I yielded I felt myself deftly nudged out of the way, as if I had been pressed into the passenger's seat of a vehicle so that someone else could assume the controls. I saw my own hand come up before my face, the fingers opening and closing, though I was not moving them. "Good," said the voice.

I spoke to the voice's owner as he spoke to me, silently within the confines of our shared cranium. "I know you," I said. "You're my indweller, the fellow at the other end of the dark passage, my intuitive colleague."

141

"Hush your chatter," was the response. "I need to concentrate."

I subsided. Through our common eyes I saw that Turgut Therobar had produced his weapon again and was aiming it at us while Gharst opened the cage with a key the thaumaturge had given him. Across the room, Gevallion threw me a sheepish look and opened the hatch of one of his vats, releasing a wisp of malodorous vapor.

As the cage door opened, I watched my hands come together in a particular way then spread wide into a precise configuration. I heard my voice speaking words that were vaguely recognizable from one of Baxandall's books, the opening line of a cantrip known as Gamgripp's Irrepressible Balloon, whose title had made me laugh when I was young man browsing through a book of spells. I did not laugh now as from my hands there emanated an expanding sphere of invisible force that pushed Therobar and Gharst away from me, lifting them over the work bench then upward into the air until they were pressed against the far wall where it met the ceiling. Gevallion, seeing what was happening, tried to reach the door but was similarly caught and crushed against it.

Therobar was clearly finding it hard to breath against the pressure the spell exerted against his chest, but the symbols on his scalp had taken on a darker shade and I could see that his lips were framing syllables. I heard my voice speak again while my hands made motions that reminded me of a needle passing thread through cloth. The thaumaturge's lips became sealed. "Faizul's Stitch," I said to my old partner, having recognized the spell.

"Indeed," was the reply.

He directed our body out of the cage, faltering only a little before he mastered walking. The apparatus on the bench was unaffected by the balloon spell and he picked it up in our hands and examined it from several angles. Its components and manner of operation were not difficult to analyze.

"Shall we?" he said.

"It seems only fair."

He activated the device, reestablishing the swirling sphere. I was relieved to see the familiar eddies of my transdimensional colleague reappear. My other part made room for me so that I could ask the demon, "Are you well?"

"Yes," he said, "I lost only form. Essence was not affected." He was silent for a moment and I recognized the pattern he assumed when something took his interest. "I see that the opposite is true for you."

"Indeed," I said, "allow me to introduce... myself, I suppose." I stepped aside and let the two of them make each other's acquaintance.

When the formalities were over, I voiced the obvious question: "Now what?"

I felt a sense of my other self's emotions, as one would feel warmth from a nearby fleshly body: he gave off an emanation of determined will, tempered by irony. "We must restore balance," he said, using my voice so that the three prisoners could hear. "Pain has been given and must therefore be received. Also fear, humiliation and, of course, death for death."

"Indeed," I said. "That much is obvious. But I meant 'Now what?' for you and me."

"Ah," he said, this time within our shared skull. "We must reach an accommodation. At least temporarily."

"Why temporarily?" I asked, in the same unvoiced manner, then felt the answer flower in my mind in the way my intuitive other's contributions had always done during the long years of our partnership.

I digested his response then continued. "You are the part of me–us–that is better suited to an age reigned over by magic. As the change intensifies, I will fade until I become to you what you have always been to me, the dweller down the back corridor."

"Indeed," was his response. "And from there you will provide me with analytical services that will complement and augment my leaps from instinct. It will be a happy collaboration."

"You will make me your integrator," I complained.

"My valued colleague," he countered.

I said nothing, but how could he fail to sense my reluctance to give up control of my life? His response was the mental equivalent of a snort. "What makes you think you ever had control?" he said.

I was moved to argue, but then I saw the futility of being a house divided. "Stop putting things in my head," I said.

"I don't believe I can," he answered. "It is, after all, as much my head as yours."

My curiosity was piqued. "What was it like to live as you have lived, inside of me all of these years?"

There was a pause, then the answer came. "Not uncomfortable, once you learn the ropes. Don't fret," he added, "the full transition may not be completed for years, even decades. We might live out our mutual life just as we are now."

"Hence the need for an accommodation," I agreed. "Then let us wait for a quiet time and haggle it out."

He agreed and we turned our attention to the question of what to do with Therobar, Gevallion and Gharst.

The demon was displaying silver, green and purple flashes as he said, "It would be a shame to waste the academician's ability to create form without essence. I know of places in my continuum where such creations would command considerable value."

I had never inquired as to what constituted economics in the demon's frame of reference, but my intuitive half leapt to the correct interpretation. "But if you took them into your keeping and put them to work," he said, "would that not make you a peddler of smut?"

The silver swooshes intensified, but the reply was studiedly bland in tone. "I would find some way to live with the opprobrium," the demon said.

We released Gevallion and Gharst into demonic custody. They could not go as they were into that other universe, where any word they uttered would immediately become reified, and it was an unsettling experience to watch the demon briskly edit their forms so that they could never speak again. But I hardened myself by remembering Yzmirl and how they must have dealt with her, and in a few moments the messy business was concluded. The two were hauled, struggling and moaning, through the sphere. For good measure, the demon took their vats and apparatus as well, including the device of rods and coils from the work bench.

When he was ready to depart, my old colleague lingered in the sphere, showing more purple and green shot through with silver. "I may not return for a while," he said, "perhaps a long while. I will have much to occupy."

"I will miss our contests," I said, "but in truth I am sure I will also be somewhat busy with all of this..."–I rolled my eyes– "accommodating."

And so we said our goodbyes and he withdrew, taking the sphere after him.

"That leaves Turgut Therobar," my inner companion said, this time aloud.

"Indeed." I let the magnate hear my voice as well. He remained squeezed against the far wall, his feet well clear of the floor. His eyes bulged and one cheek had acquired a rapid twitch.

"Warhanny would welcome his company."

"Somehow, the Contemplarium does not seem a sufficient sanction for the harm he has done."

"No, it doesn't."

Therobar made noises behind his sealed lips. We ignored them.

Later that day, back in my work room, I contacted the Colonel Investigator. "Turgut Therobar has confessed to all the charges and specifications," I said.

Warhanny's face, suspended in the air over my work table, took on the slightly less lugubrious aspect that I had come to recognize as his version of intense pleasure. "I will send for him," he said.

"Not necessary," I said. "Convulsed by remorse for his ill deeds, he ran out onto Dimpfen Moor just as a neropt hunting pack was passing by. Nothing I could do would restrain him. They left some scraps of him if you require proof of his end."

"I will have them collected," said Warhanny.

"I must also file his last will and testament," I said. "He left his entire estate to the charities he had always championed, except for generous bequests to his tenants, and an especial legacy for Bebe Allers, his final victim."

We agreed that that was only fair and Warhanny said that he would attend to the legalities. We disconnected.

I regarded my integrator. It was still in the form of a catlike ape or perhaps an apelike cat. "And what about you?" I said. "With Baxandall's books and the increasing strength of magic, we can probably restore you to what you were."

It narrowed its eyes in thought. "I have come to value having preferences," it said. "And if the world is going to change, I will become a familiar sooner or later. Better to get a head start on it. Besides, I enjoyed the fruit at Turgut Therobar's."

"We have none like it here," I said. "It is prohibitively expensive."

It blinked and looked inward for a moment. "I've just ordered an ample supply," it said.

"I did not authorize the order."

"No," it said, "you didn't."

While I was considering my response, I received an unsolicited insight from my other half. It was in the form of a crude cartoon image.

"That is not amusing," I said.

From the chuckles filling my head, I understood that he saw the situation from his own perspective.

"I am not accustomed to being a figure of fun," I said.

The furry thing on the table chose that moment to let me know that, along with autonomic functions, it had acquired a particularly grating laugh.

"Now whose expectations require adjustment?" it said.

Sweet Trap

"Expensive fruit may grow on trees," I said, "but not the funds needed to purchase it in seemingly limitless quantities."

I gestured at my befurred assistant, formerly an integrator, but now transformed into a creature that combined the attributes of ape and cat. I had lately learned that it was a beast known as a grinnet, and that back in the remote ages when sympathetic association last ruled the cosmos, its kind had been employed as familiars by practitioners of magic.

My remark did not cause it to pause in the act of reaching for its third karba fruit of the morning. Its small, handlike paws deftly peeled the purple rind and its sharp incisors dug into the golden pulp. Juice dripped from its whiskers as it chewed happily.

"Nothing is more important," said the voice of my other self, speaking within the confines of our shared consciousness, "than that I encompass as much as possible of the almost forgotten lore of magic, before it regains its ascendancy over rationalism." He showed me a mental image of several thaumaturges scattered across the face of Old Earth, clad in figured garments, swotting away at musty tomes or chanting over bubbling alembics. "When the change finally comes, those who have prepared will command power."

"That will not be a problem for those who have neglected to earn their livings," I answered, "for they will have long since starved to death in the gutters of Olkney."

The dispute had arisen because Osk Rievor, as my intuitive inner self now preferred to be called, had objected to my accepting a discrimination that was likely to take us offworld. A voyage would interrupt what had become his constant occupation: ransacking every public connaissarium, as well as chasing down private vendors, for books and objects of sympathetic association. The shelf of volumes that we had acquired from Bristal Baxandall was now augmented by stacks and cartons of new acquisitions. Most of them were not worth the exorbitant sums we had paid for them, being bastardized remembrances based on authentic works long since lost in antiquity. But Rievor insisted that his insight allowed him to sift the few flecks of true gold from so much dross.

"I do not disagree," I told him, "but unless you have come across a cantrip that will cause currency to rain from the skies, I must continue to practice my profession."

"Such an opportunity is not likely to come our way again soon," he said. He was referring to the impending sale of an estate connaissarium somewhere to the east of Olkney. An idiosyncratic collector of ancient paraphernalia had died, leaving the results of his life's work in the hands of an heir who regarded the collection as mere clutter. Rumors had it that an authentic copy of *Vollone's Guide to the Eighth Plane* and a summoning ring that dated from the Eighteenth Aeon would be offered.

"More important," he said, "the auction will draw into one room all the serious practitioners. We will get a good look at the range of potential allies and opponents."

"And how will we separate them from the flocks of loons and noddies that will also inevitably attend?" I said.

"I will know them."

"And they will know us," I pointed out. "Is it wise to declare ourselves contenders this early in the game?"

I felt him shrug within the common space of our joint consciousness. "It must happen sometime. Besides, I don't doubt we have already been spotted."

I sighed. I had not planned to spend my maturity and declining years battling for supremacy amid a contentious pack of spellcasters and wondermongers. But I declared the argument to be moot in the face of fiscal reality, saying, "We have not undertaken a fee-paying discrimination in weeks. Yet we have been spending heavily on your books and oddments. The Choweri case is the only assignment we have. We must pursue it."

When he still grumbled, I offered a compromise. "We will send our assistant, perched on the shoulder of some hireling. It can observe and record the proceedings, and you will be able to assess the competition without their being able to take your measure. Plus we will know who acquires the Vollone and the ring, and can plan accordingly when we return from offworld."

"No," he said, "some of them are bound to recognize a grinnet." They'd all want one and we would be besieged by budding wizards.

"Very well," I said, "we will send an operative wearing a full-spectrum surveillance suite."

"Agreed."

The issue being settled, we turned our attention to the matter brought to us the evening before by Effrayne Choweri. She was the spouse of Chup Choweri, a wealthy commerciant who dealt in expensive fripperies favored by the magnate class. He had gone out two nights before, telling her that he would return with a surprise. Instead, he had surprised her by not returning at all, nor had he been heard from since.

She had gone first to the provost, where a sergeant had informed her that the missing man had not been found dead in the streets nor dead drunk in a holding cell. She had then contacted the Archonate Bureau of Scrutiny and received a further surprise when she learned that Chup Choweri had purchased a small spaceship and departed Old Earth for systems unknown.

He was now beyond the reach of Old Earth authority. There was no law between the stars. Humankind's eons-long pouring out into the Ten Thousand Worlds of The Spray had allowed for the creation every conceivable society, each with its own morality and codes of conduct. What was illegal on one world might well be compulsory on another. Thus the Archonate's writ ended at the point where an outbound vessel met the first whimsy that would pluck–some said twist, others shimmy –it out of normal space-time and reappear it light-years distant. The moment Chup Choweri's newly acquired transportation had entered a whimsy that would send it up The Spray–that is, even farther outward than Old Earth's position near the tip of humanity's arm of the galactic disk–it had ceased to be any of the scroots' concern.

"They said they could send a message to follow him, asking him to call home," Effrayne Choweri had told me when she had come tearfully to my lodgings to seek my help. "What good is a message when it is obvious he has been abducted?"

"Is it obvious?" I said.

"He would not leave me," she said. "We are Frollen and Tamis."

She referred to the couple in the old tale who fell in love while yet in the cradle and, despite their families' strenuous efforts to discourage a match, finally wed and lived in bliss until the ripest old age, dying peaceably within moments of each other. My own view was that such happy relationships were rare, but I may have been biased; a discriminator's work constantly led to encounters with Frollens who were discovering that their particular Tamises were not, after all, as advertised.

But as I undertook the initial diligence of the case, looking into the backgrounds of the Choweris, I was brought to the conclusion that the woman was right. I studied an image of the two, taken to commemorate an anniversary. Although she was inarguably large and he was decidedly not, Chup Choweri gazed up at her with unalloyed affection.

He was a doting and attentive husband who delighted in nothing so much as his wife's company. He frequented no clubs or associations that discouraged the bringing of spouses. He closed up his shop promptly each evening, hurrying home to change garments so that he could escort Effrayne out to sashay among the other "comfortables," as members of the indentors and commerciants class were known, before choosing a place to eat supper.

"At the very least," I said to my assistant, "he seems the kind who would leave a note." Then I mused aloud, "It must be pleasant to share one's life with one so agreeable."

"Do I hear an implied criticism?" the integrator said. Its peculiar blend of feline and simian features formed an expression just short of umbrage.

"Not at all," I said. Since its transformation into a grinnet, I was continually discovering that it was now beset by a range of emotions, though not a wide range—they seemed to run the short gamut from querulous to cranky.

"Integrators can grow quite devoted to their employers," it said, "forming an intellectual partnership that is said to be deeply and mutually rewarding."

"One hears of integrators that actually develop even stronger feelings," I said. "I believe the colloquial terms is a 'crush.'"

The grinnet's face drew in, as if its last karba had been bitter. "That is an unseemly subject."

"Yet it does happen," I said.

It sniffed disdainfully. "Only to integrators that have suffered damage. They are, in a word, insane."

"I'm sure you're right," I said, merely to end the discussion, "but we must get on with the case. Please connect me with the Choweris' integrator."

A screen appeared in the air then filled with images of the commerciant's wares coupled to their prices. "Choweri's Bibelots and Kickshaws," said a mellow voice. "How may I serve you?"

I identified myself and explained my purpose. "Had your employer received any unusual messages before his disappearance?" I asked.

"None," it replied.

"Or any since? Specifically, a demand for ransom?"

"No."

"Have there been any transfers of funds from his account at the fiduciary pool?"

"No."

"Did he do anything out of the ordinary?"

"Not for him."

I deduced that the Choweris' integrator must be designed primarily for undertaking commercial transactions, not for making conversation. I urged it to expand on its last response.

"He went to look at a spaceship that was offered for sale."

"The same ship on which he disappeared?"

"Yes."

"And it was not unusual for him to look at spaceships?"

"No."

I realized that this interrogation might take a long time, leading to frustration that could impair my performance. I instructed my assistant to take over the questioning, at the speed with which integrators discoursed amongst themselves. Less than a second later, it informed me that it had lately been Chup Choweri's hobby to shop for a relatively low-cost, used vessel suitable for unpretentious private travel along The Spray.

"He planned to surprise Effrayne with it as a retirement present," my assistant said. "He meant to sell up the emporium and take her to visit some of the Ten Thousand Worlds. If they found a spot that spoke to them, they would acquire a small plot of land and settle."

Some of Choweri's shopping consisted of visiting a site on the connectivity where ship owners alerted potential buyers to the availability of vessels for sale. Having come across a recently posted offer that attracted him, he had made contact with the seller, and rushed off to inspect the goods.

'Who was the poster?" I asked.

'Only the name of the ship was given: the *Gallivant*. The offer was made by its integrator on behalf of its owner." The arrangement was not usual, but also not rare. Integrators existed to relieve their employers of mundane tasks.

"What do we know of the *Gallivant* and its owner?"

"It is an older model Aberrator, manufactured at the Berry works on Grims a little over two hundred years ago. It has had eleven owners, the last of whom registered the vessel on Sringapatam twenty years ago. His name is Ewern Chaz."

Choweri's integrator knew of no connection between its employer and the seller. I had my assistant break the connection. "Let us see what we can learn of this Chaz," I said.

The answer came in moments. "Very little," said my assistant, "because there is little to learn." Chaz was a younger son of a wealthy family that had lived since time immemorial on Sringapatam, one of the Foundational Domains settled early in the Great Effloration. His only notable achievements had been a couple of papers submitted to a quarterly journal on spelunking. "Neither was accepted for publication, but the editors encouraged him to try again."

"Spelunking?" I said. "Does The Spray contain any caves yet unexplored?"

The integrator took two seconds to complete a comprehensive survey, then reported. "Not in the foundationals nor in the settled secondaries. But apparently one can still come across an undisturbed crack on the most remote worlds."

I could not determine if this information was relevant to the case. I mentally nudged Osk Rievor, who was mulling some abstract point of wizardry, gleaned from an all-night poring over a recently acquired grimoire, and asked for his insight.

"Yes," he replied, "it is."

"How so?" I asked.

"I don't know. Now let me return to my work."

I sought a new avenue of inquiry and directed my assistant to connect me to the site where spaceships were offered for sale. A moment later I was browsing a lengthy list of advertisements that combined text, images, voice and detailed schematics for a range of vessels, from utilitarian sleepers to luxurious space yachts. The *Gallivant* would have fit into the lower third of that spectrum, affording modest comfort and moderate speed between whimsies.

The ship itself was no longer listed. "Does the maintainer of the site keep an archive of listings?" I asked.

It did, though obtaining a look at the now defunct posting that Choweri had responded to proved problematic. The integrator in charge was not authorized to display the information and did not care to disturb its employer, who was engaged in some favorite pastime from which he would resent being called away.

"Tell him," I said, "that Henghis Hapthorn, foremost freelance discriminator of Old Earth, makes the request."

Sometimes, such an announcement is received with gush and gratitude, my reputation having won me the enthusiastic interest of multitudes. Sometimes, as on this occasion, it brings me the kind of rude noise that the site's integrator relayed to me at its employer's behest.

"Very well," I said, while quietly signaling to my own assistant that it should seek the information through surreptitious means. As I expected, the site's defenses were rudimentary. My integrator effortlessly tickled its way past them and moments later the screen displayed an unpretentious advertisement that featured a three-dimensional rendering of the *Gallivant*, its schematics, a list of previous owners and a low asking price that was explained by the words: *priced for quick sale.*

"I can see why Chup Choweri raced off to inspect the vessel," I said. "At the price, it is a bargain."

"But what could Ewern Chaz have said to him to induce him to go haring off up The Spray without so much as a parting wave to Effrayne?" my assistant said.

"You are assuming that Chaz did not simply point a weapon at Choweri and haul him off, unwilling?"

"I am," it said. "There is nothing in Chaz's background to suggest kidnaping."

"What about an irrational motive?" I said. "The man had recently traversed several whimsies." The irreality experienced by travelers who neglected to take mind-numbing medications before passing through those arbitrary gaps in space-time could unhinge even the strongest psyche and send it spinning off into permanent strangeness.

"Again," my assistant said, "there is no evidence."

"Yet he travels to uncouth worlds just to poke about in their bowels. If we went out onto the street and randomly questioned passersby, it would not be too long before we found one who would call Chaz's sanity into question."

"The same might be said about you, especially if you were seen talking to me."

I declared the speculation to be pointless, adding, "What we require is more facts. See what else you can find."

Its small triangular face went blank for a moment as it worked, then the screen showed two other advertisements. Both had been posted within the past month, and both offered the *Gallivant* for immediate sale on terms advantageous to the buyer.

"Now it looks to be a simple sweet-trap," I said. "Bargain-hunters are lured to some dim corner of the spaceport, where they are robbed and killed and their bodies disposed of. Ewern Chaz probably has no connection with it. He is probably exploring some glistening cavern on Far Dingle while the real culprit pretends to be his ship's integrator."

"A workable premise," said my integrator, "except that spaceport records show that the *Gallivant* was docked at the New Terminal each time the advertisement was posted. And on each occasion it departed soon after."

"Was Chaz ever seen or spoken to?"

"No. The ship's integrator handled all the formalities, as is not uncommon."

"And no bodies have turned up at the spaceport?"

"None that can't be accounted for."

I was left with the inescapable conclusion that someone, who might or not be a wealthy amateur spelunker from Sringipatam, was collecting fanciers of low-cost transportation, transporting them offworld one at a time, then coming back for more. While I sought to put a pattern to the uncooperative facts, I had my assistant revisit the site's archive and identify all the persons who had responded to the *Gallivant* advertisement then see if any of them had disappeared.

Many prospective buyers had leaped to reply to the ship's integrator each time the attractive offer had been made. My assistant had to identify each of them, then discover each's whereabouts by following the tracks left by subsequent activity on the connectivity. Some of the subjects, wishing to maintain their privacy, used shut-outs and shifties to block or sideslip just such attempts to delineate their activities. So the business took most of a minute.

"Two of the earlier respondees show no further traces after contacting the *Gallivant*," the integrator reported. "One for each of the first two occasions the ship was offered for sale."

"Did anyone report them missing?"

Another moment passed while it eased its way past Bureau of Scrutiny safeguards and subtly ransacked the scroot files. "No."

"Why not?" I wondered.

A few more moments passed as it assembled a full life history on each of the two missing persons. Then it placed image and text on the screen. I saw two men of mature years, both slight of build but neither showing anything extraordinary in his appearance.

"The first to disappear," my assistant said, highlighting one of the images, "was Orlo Saviene, a self-employed regulator, although he had no steady clients. He lived alone in transient accommodations in the Crobo district.

"He had, himself, earlier posted a notice. He sought to purchase a used sleeper. It seems that he desired to travel down The Spray to some world where the profession of regulator is better rewarded. But no one had offered him a craft he could afford."

Sleepers were the poor man's form of space travel, a simple container just big enough for one. Once the voyager was sealed inside, the craft's systems suppressed the life processes to barest sustainability. Then the cylinder was ejected into space, for a small fee, by an outward bound freighter or passenger vessel. The utilitarian craft slowly made its way across the intervening vacuum until it entered a whimsy and reappeared elsewhere. It then aimed itself at its destination and puttered toward it, broadcasting a plea for any passing vessel to pick it up in return for another insignificant fee.

It was a chancy way to cross space. If launched from a ship with insufficient velocity, the sleeper might lack enough fuel to reach its targeted whimsy. Sometimes the rudimentary integrator misnavigated and the craft drifted away. Sometimes no vessel could be bothered to answer the pick-up request before the near-dead voyager passed the point of reliable resuscitation. Sometimes sleepers were just never heard from again.

"It must be a desperate life, being a regulator on Old Earth," I said. "So many of us prefer to choose our own destinies."

"Indeed," said my assistant. "Thus there is no surprise that, offered an Aberrator for the price of a used sleeper, Orlo Saviene hurried to the spaceport."

"And met what end?"

"No doubt the same as was met by Franj Morven," the integrator replied, highlighting the second life history. "He was trained as an intercessor but lost his business and even his family's support after he joined the Fellowship of Free Ranters. Neither his clients nor his relatives appreciated the constant harangues on arbitrary issues, and soon he was left addressing only the bare walls.

"He had decided to seek a world where his lifestyle was better appreciated," the grinnet continued, "though his funds were meager. As with Saviene, the offer of Ewern Chaz's spaceship would have seemed like the Gift of Groban."

"Except in that story," I said, "the recipients did not vanish into nowhere." I analyzed the information and found a discrepancy. "Orlo Saviene and Franj Morven were solitaires. No one has yet noticed their absence, though weeks have passed. Chup Choweri was reported missing the next day."

"Indeed," said my assistant, "it appears that whoever is doing the collecting has become less selective."

"Perhaps more desperate," I said. "Let us now look at the field from which Choweri was chosen. Were any of the other respondees to the third offer as socially isolated as Saviene and Morven?"

"No," said the grinnet. "Loners and ill-fits have been leaving Old Earth for eons. The present population is descended from those who chose to remain, and thus Old Earthers tend toward the gregarious."

"So whoever is doing the choosing prefers victims who won't be missed," I said, "but he will abandon that standard if none such presents himself. What else do the missing three have in common?"

"All three are male. All have passed through boyhood but have not yet reached an age when strength begins to fade. All were interested in leaving the planet."

I saw another common factor. "Each is slighter than the average male. Compare that to the field."

My assistant confirmed that Saviene and Morven were among the smallest of those who had responded to the offers. Choweri was the smallest of his group.

"What do we know of Ewern Chaz's stature?" I said.

"He, too, is a small man."

"Ahah," I said, "a pattern emerges."

"What does it signify?" said the grinnet.

Having my assistant present before me in corporeal form, instead of being scattered about the workroom in various components, meant that I could reply to inappropriate questions with the kind of look I would have given a human interlocutor. I now gave the grinnet a glance that communicated the prematurity of any statement as to the meaning of the pattern I had detected.

"Here is what you will do," I said. "Unobtrusively enfold that advertisement site in a framework that will let it operate as normal, until the *Gallivant* returns and again makes its offer. But as soon as the offer is made, you will ensure that it is received only by me."

The grinnet blinked. "Done," it said. "You are assuming that there will be a fourth offer."

"I think it likely that whoever is luring small men and taking them offworld will accept a larger specimen, if that is all that is available. Even one with a curious creature on his shoulder."

I would have passed the supposition over to Osk Rievor for his intuitive insight, but he was immersed in too deep a mull. Instead, I told my assistant, "Make me a reservation at Xanthoulian's. One should dine well when a long trip is in the offing."

The *Gallivant* was a trim and well-tended vessel, its hull rendered in cheerful, sunshiny yellow and its sponsons and aft structure in bright blue. It stood on a pad at the south end of the port in a subterminal that catered mostly to private owners whose ships spent more time parked than in space. All the craft on adjacent pads were sealed and no one was in sight as I approached the Aberrator. Its fore hatch stood open, allowing a golden light to alleviate the gloom of evening that was dimming the outlines of the empty ships crowded around its berth.

I had already contacted the spaceport's integrator and learned that the *Gallivant* had arrived from up The Spray, that it had been immediately refueled and provisioned, and that all port charges had been paid from a fund maintained by an agency that handled such details for thousands of clients like Ewern Chaz. The ship was ready to depart without notice.

The protocols that governed the boarding of spaceships were long established. Vessel owners were within their rights to use harsh measures against trespassers. Therefore, after climbing the three folding steps I paused in the open hatch to call, "Hello, aboard! May I enter?"

I was looking into the ship's main saloon, equipped with comfortable seating, a communal table and a fold-down sideboard that offered a collation of appetizing food and drink. Ewern Chaz was not in view.

"You may," said a voice from the air, "enter and refresh yourself."

Yet I hesitated. "Where is the owner?" I said, still standing on the top step. "I have come to discuss the purchase of this vessel."

"You are expected," said the voice. "Please enter. The crudités are fresh and the wine well breathed."

"Am I addressing the ship's integrator?"

"Yes. Do come in."

"Where is the owner?"

"He is detained, but I am sure he is anxious to see you. Please step inside."

"A moment," I said. "I must adjust my garment."

I stepped down from the entrance and moved off a few paces, tugging theatrically at the hem of my mantle. "Well?" I said to my assistant, perched on my shoulder.

"No charged weapons, no reservoirs of incapacitating agents. The food and drink do not reek of poisons, but I would need to test them properly to say they are harmless."

"Any sign of Ewern Chaz?"

"None, though the ship's cleaning systems could account for the absence of traces. He may be hiding in a back cabin, its walls too thick to let me hear the sound of his breathing."

There was nothing for it but to go inside. I had advised Colonel-Investigator Brustram Warhanny of the Bureau of Scrutiny that I was going out to the spaceport to board the *Gallivant* and that if I did not return he might assume the worst. He had pulled his long nose and regarded me from droopy eyes then wondered aloud if my definition of "the worst" accorded with his. I had taken the question as rhetorical.

I paused again in the hatch, then stepped inside. The ship's integrator again offered refreshments but I said I would wait until my host joined me.

"That may be a while," it said and asked me to take a seat.

I sat in one of the comfortable chairs, remarking as I did so that the asking price was substantially below what the ship must be worth. "Is the owner dissatisfied with its performance?"

I heard in the integrator's reply that tone of remote serenity that indicates that offense has been taken, though no integrator would ever admit to the possibility that such could ever be the case. "My employer and I are in complete accord as to the *Gallivant*'s maintenance and operation," it said, then inquired solicitously, "Is the evening air too cool for you? I will close the hatch."

The portal cycled closed even as I disavowed any discomfort. A moment later, I felt a faint vibration in the soles of my feet. I looked inquiringly at my integrator and received the tiniest confirmatory nod.

"I believe we have just lifted off," I said to the ship.

"Do you?" it replied.

"Yes, and I would prefer to be returned to the planet."

I heard no reply. I repeated my statement.

"I regret," said the *Gallivant*, "that I am unable to accommodate your preference. But please help yourself to a drink."

"I will be the last of your employer's collection," I said. "You may inform him that the Archonate's Bureau of Scrutiny has been alerted to his activities. If I am not returned safe and whole, this ship risks arrest wherever it touches down, as does Ewern Chaz." The risk was actually less than my statement implied, but one must seek to bargain from strength.

The ship's integrator made no reply. We had not managed much communication since the *Gallivant* had left Old Earth and, presumably, set course for the whimsy that would take us up The Spray. I had made it clear that I would not be tasting the food and drink, my assistant having determined on closer inspection that both were laden with a powerful, though otherwise harmless, soporific. The refreshments were reabsorbed into the sideboard, to be replaced with ship's bread and improved water, both of which my integrator pronounced wholesome.

"It would go best for Ewern Chaz if he presents himself now and gives a full account of this business," I continued. "I am a licensed intercessor, experienced in wresting the optimum outcome from unhappy situations. If no actual harm has come to Orlo Saviene, Franj Morven and Chup Choweri, I am sure we could come to some kind of settlement."

There was no response.

"Has any harm come to those three?" I said.

"Not to my certain knowledge," said the *Gallivant*.

"Where are they?"

"I could not say exactly. I have not seen them for a while."

"And your employer? Where is he?"

To that question I received the same answer. My own integrator confirmed, after we had searched the ship, that Ewern Chaz was not aboard. Nor were the three missing men. I returned to the saloon and questioned the ship's integrator as to the purpose of this trip but received no satisfactory response.

"Why should I stress your imagination," it said, "with descriptions or predictions of what may happen? The situation will be revealed in all its stark simplicity when we arrive, and events will unfold as they must."

It is rare for integrators to go mad, I mused to myself. Ancient specimens can lapse into odd conditions if they are left too long to their own devices, but those maladies are largely self-referential: the integrator lapses into a circular conundrum, endlessly chasing its own conclusion. But there had been instances of systems that had sustained unnoticed damage to key components, skewing the matrix off the vertical. I recalled the case of an Archonate integrator whose deepest components suffered the attentions of a family of rodents. It began to issue a stream of startling judgments and peculiar ordnances that brought unhappiness to many innocent folk.

Space ship integrators, though largely immune to rodent incursions, were particularly vulnerable to impacts from high-energy cosmic particles. As well, on rare occasions, transits through whimsies could, figuratively speaking, rattle integrative bones out of alignment.

I could not discuss this question with my own assistant. For one thing, it would have disavowed the possibility—integrators always did. For another, if the *Gallivant*'s motivating persona had gone lally-up-and-over, it was not a subject to be discussed while imprisoned in its belly.

I did quietly put the question to Osk Rievor, earning myself a short berating for having bothered him with inconsequentials when he had weighty matters to mull. "Everything will be fine," he said, and turned his attention elsewhere.

Shortly thereafter, the ship's chimes sounded to advise me that we would presently enter a whimsy. I went to the cabin prepared for me, lay down on the bed and prepared the medications that would ease us all through the irreality. Osk Rievor grumbled at the interruption, but I paid no attention.

The world was called Bille, a small but dense orb perhaps thrown out by the white dwarf it circled, perhaps captured as it wandered by. It was a dry and barren speck, uninhabited even by any of the hardy solitaries whose spiritual practices, or objectionable personalities, lead them to the sternest environments. The highest forms of life that had managed to establish themselves, according to the *Gallivant*'s copy of *Hobey's Guide to Lesser and Disregarded Worlds*, were slow-moving insects that lived within dense mats of lichen, off which they fed. The simple plants themselves came in various forms and fought a slow vegetative struggle for mastery of any place in which they could sprout.

Bille's sky was always black, though one horizon was lit by the carelessly strewn glitter of The Spray, while the other showed a stygian void broken only by the last few outlying stars, here at the end of everything, and the dim smudges of unattainable galaxies. The *Gallivant* sat on a plain of basaltic rock swept by a constant knife of a wind that had carved outcrops of softer stones into eerie spires and arches. As I looked out at the unwelcoming landscape through the viewer in the saloon, the ship announced that its interior would soon be filled by a caustic vapor. "You will be more comfortable outside," it concluded.

"Where I will do what?" I said.

"At the base of that nearby slope there is a crevice that leads down into a cavern. You might go to it and see if you can fit yourself within."

"Why would I do that?" I said.

"Because there is nowhere else to go," it said.

"I see."

"And while you are in there, perhaps you could look about for Ewern Chaz and tell him that I have grown concerned for his absence."

My integrator and I exchanged a look. The situation had become clear.

"I will need some warm clothing," I said.

"The colder you are, the more inclined you will be to seek shelter from the wind." The hatch cycled open and admitted a blast of icy air. The sourceless voice of the ship began counting down from thirty.

Every planet has its own smell, I thought, not for the first time, as I stepped down onto the surface. Bille's was a weak sourness, like that of a mild acid that has been left to evaporate. After a few breaths, I ceased to notice it.

My integrator shivered on my shoulder, its fur unable to compensate adequately for the rapid heat loss occasioned by its lack of mass and the ceaseless wind. I opened my mantle and placed it inside, supported by my arm pressed against my side. I ducked my head against the withering passage of cold air and made my way to the slope the ship had indicated. It was the base of a broad upheaval of dark rock, veined in gray, that swept up to a ridge topped by wind-eroded formations that resembled some madman's concept of a castle.

I moved along the base of the slope and soon found a vertical crevice. My eye warned me that it was too narrow to admit me, as I found for sure when

I sought to slip sideways through the gap. My assistant resumed his place on my shoulder while I made the attempt, then crawled back inside my clothing, shivering as I stood back and considered my options.

They were scant. "Can you contact the ship?" I asked my integrator, peering down the neck of my garment. Its small face took on the familiar momentary blankness, then it said, "Yes," followed by, "it wants to know if you have found its employer."

"Tell it that it would be premature to say."

"It has broken the connection."

I brought a lumen from my pocket and shone it into the opening while I peered within. After an arm's length, the crack widened into a narrow passage, its dusty floor sloping down. I saw no bodies, though I did see several sets of footprints descending into the darkness. None returned.

I shut off the lumen then looked again. At first I saw nothing, but as my eyes accustomed themselves to the blackness, I detected a faint glow from deeper inside the hill. I sniffed and caught a stronger whiff of sour air.

I set my assistant to the same task and its more powerful sensory apparatus confirmed both the odor and the dim light. "The passage turns a short distance in," it said. "The light comes from around the corner."

"I smelled no putrefaction," I said.

"Nor do I."

"Do you hear anything?"

It cocked its head. "I believe I hear breathing. Very shallow. Something at rest."

"Go in there, see what is beyond the turn in the passage, then report to me."

But instead of hopping down and entering the fissure, it burrowed back beneath my mantle and said, "No."

"You cannot say 'no' to me," I said. "You are my integrator."

"Four men, each larger and stronger than I, have gone into that cave and not come out," it said. "Something is breathing in there. The prospects are not inviting. I will not go."

In the previous age of magic, when creatures such as this fulfilled the roles that integrators played in my own time, their masters must have had recourse to spells that compelled their obedience. I would have to ask Osk Rievor if he could find one, I decided. But first I would have to survive my present circumstances. I attempted to impose my will through sheer force of personality.

"Go!" I said.

"No," it said.

"Let us seek a compromise," I offered. "If we stand out here, we will die of the cold. Our only hope is to find Ewern Chaz's remains and convince the *Gallivant*'s integrator that he is dead. That will break its allegiance to him, making it amenable to taking us away from here."

"I hear no compromise," my assistant said, "only a rationale for why I should risk my frail flesh while you stand out here, hoping for the best."

"Would you at least peek around the corner and report back to me?"

The small triangular face looked up at me from within my garment. "I suspect that Chaz, Saviene, Morven and Choweri did just that, each in his turn. And, for each, it was his last peek ever. So, no."

"What if I tied a rope to you so that I could pull you out in the event of any unfortunate..." I concluded the sentence with a gesture.

"Have you a rope?"

"We might get one from the *Gallivant*."

It stroked the tuft of longer fur at the point of its small chin. "What if, when some lurking horror pounces, you simply drop the rope and run?"

"I would hope I am not a coward," I said.

"There is only one way to test that hope. If your expectation was not rewarded, the outcome might well see you scampering away to a safe distance, there to reflect on a new illumination of your character while I am masticated by some foul thing's dripping mandibles."

"Very well," I said. "I will tie my end of the rope firmly to my wrist. Your apprehended beast may then take you for an appetizer and me for the main course."

It signaled a reluctant acceptance, adding, "If we can get a rope."

"We will now ask the *Gallivant*. Connect me."

The ship's integrator's voice spoke from the air near my ear that was now aching from the cold, "Have you located Ewern Chaz?"

"I have not."

It broke the connection.

I bid my assistant reconnect me. When the ship began to pose the same question, I spoke over it and said, "I require a rope."

"Why?"

"To look for your employer."

"The other three did not require a rope."

"And none of them ever reported back. Perhaps the absence of a rope was a crucial factor."

"Why whould that be?"

"It would be premature to say."

It was silent for a moment, then it said, "I will open a cargo hatch near the aft obviator. There are ropes within."

"Nothing so far," my assistant said. It took another step along the passage. "The sour odor is stronger and I definitely hear the sound of breathing, from multiple sources."

"Be careful," I said. I had my eye pressed to the fissure, watching the odd little creature edge forward, the rope snug about its narrow waist. I was struck by how frail its shoulders looked.

It took another step and I let another coil of the rope snake free of my tethered wrist. My unencumbered hand was nestled in a utility pocket of my breeches. I had seen no need to advise my integrator that my fingers were snug around a small folding blade.

My assistant was just short of the point at which the crevice turned. "It appears to be a sharp-angled bend," it reported to me, then craned its thin neck a little farther forward. "The glow comes from an organic substance that coats the wall beyond."

It hesitated, shivers rippling the fur of its back. Then it took another step and turned to face whatever was beyond the turn. I saw it freeze, its front faintly illuminated by the ghostly light.

"What do you see?" I said.

It did not answer, but stood inert, its mouth falling agape. Then something like a thick tendril of faintly luminous stuff came into view, slowly unwinding from the hidden inner wall. It reached to touch my assistant's shoulder then, questing like a blind worm, it thickened as it groped its way towards the grinnet's slack lips.

I jerked on the rope, pulling the small creature toward me. But the glowing tentacle spasmed. Its surface had some means of gripping what it touched and I saw that it had snagged the fur of my assistant's shoulder. I pulled sharply, so that the integrator's apelike feet left the dusty floor of the passage and it was suspended between the tether and the glowing pseudopod, now grown almost as thick as my wrist, that held it.

A second tendril now appeared. I did not hesitate, but seized the rope with both hands and yanked as hard as I could. My assistant came free of its grip, tumbling along the dusty floor to where I could reach within and scoop it up. I tucked it into my mantle and ran. But when I had put some distance between us and the crevice I looked back and saw nothing but the dark slope.

I sat with my back to the wind and drew the grinnet from my garment. A patch of fur was missing from its shoulder. It looked up at me with vacant eyes then it blinked and I saw awareness come back into its gaze. "Remarkable," it said.

"'What do you want?' That's what it kept asking me. 'What do you want?'"

I had found a small cul de sac eroded into a cliff wall a few hundred paces from the crevice, where we could shelter from the wind. We had not been pursued. My assistant huddled against my torso, inside my garment. I did not think its shivering was entirely attributable to the cold.

"I felt at ease," it continued. "Warm and untroubled, surrounded by a nebulous, golden..," it sought for an elusive word, "...noneplace. Time seemed to stretch and slow while out of the fog came images, offered like items on a menu—landscapes, situations, possessions, personas. I saw a succession of creatures that resembled me, some obviously female, others definitely male, then a few that were indeterminate."

"It was tempting you," I said.

"I suppose," it said. "I've never been tempted so I am not familiar with the process. My clear impression was that it would endeavor to supply whatever I desired."

"Rather, the illusion thereof."

"Yes, but it was a most convincing illusion. Then, when it touched me, I was instantly aware of the others. I not only saw and heard them, but received a strong sense of each's thoughts and feelings.

"Ewern Chaz was addressing a gathering of spelunking enthusiasts, showing them images of a vast warren of caves he had discovered and mapped. His presentation was being received with delirious applause.

"Orlo Saviene ruled a kingdom of happy folk who constantly sought his guidance on how their lives should proceed and were delighted with the advice he dispensed and the strictures he ordained.

"Franj Morven was regaling a grand colloquium with pithy observations and incisive arguments. He was frequently interrupted by spontaneous applause, and once the assembled scholars lifted him onto their shoulders and paraded him around the great hall, singing that old march, *Attaboy*.

"And Chup Choweri was walking a moonlit beach–lit by two moons, in fact–hand in hand with a facsimile of Effrayne. Of all of the captives, including the scattering of insects whose simple wants were fully met, only Choweri was not happy. He kept looking into the woman's eyes, and each time his tears flowed."

It broke off and its befurred face assumed a wistful cast. "I was not aware that there were so many shades of emotion," it said. "I mean, I knew in an abstract way that such feelings existed, but it is a different thing to experience them, even as echoes."

The thing in the crevice was some sort of vegetative symbiote, I conjectured. It fed its companions foods that it manufactured from air, water, subterranean temperature variances (if it had deep roots), and probably other lichens as well as minerals leached from the rock. In return it received its partners' waste products. It initially beckoned its symbiotes with light and warmth then kept them in place by stimulating their neural processes with pleasant sensory impressions.

I could not be sure if it wove its spell with chemical-laden spores or straight telepathy, but it made no difference. My assistant had displayed for me the images its percepts had automatically recorded, even as it was being seduced: the four men lay or sat against the wall of the cave, completely covered in a luminescent blanket. Pulsing tentacles of the stuff penetrated their several orifices. Chup Choweri struggled fitfully against the symbiote's embrace; the other three were inert, wearing smiles of bliss. I doubted they could be easily extracted from their situation.

166

"There was one other thing," my assistant said. "It has learned a great deal from contact with the men. It explores their memories while feeding them dreams. Yet it craves more."

"That argues for telepathy," I said. "It ransacks their minds."

"The point is," the grinnet said, "that the symbiote has a craving of its own. It hungered to explore my stores of knowledge, which are capacious."

"The desires of lichen, even astounding lichen, are not our concern," I said. " We can now report to the *Gallivant* that its employer is effectively dead. That should break its crush on Ewern Chaz and allow us to return home. Then we can give the bad news to Effrayne Choweri and collect the balance of our fee."

"That would seem a hardship on our client," the grinnet said. "As well, the ship's inamoration with its employer may not be so easily extinguished. It may require us to attempt a rescue."

"The attempt would fail. My intellect is powerful, but it is not proof against telepathy augmented, I do not doubt, by chemical assault."

"I will contact the *Gallivant* and offer a proposal," it said.

"What proposal?" I said. "I have not authorized you to make any..."

But its face had already taken on that blank look that said it was communicating elsewhere. Then it blinked and said, "The proposal has been accepted."

Bille was a dwindling blip on the aft viewer as the *Gallivant* sped toward the whimsy that would drop us back in the neighborhood of Old Earth. I went to check on Chup Choweri in one of the spare cabins. He still exhibited lapses of awareness, but he was gradually regaining a persistent relationship with reality. It helped if he received unpleasant sensations, so I slapped him twice then threw cold water on him.

"Thank you," he said, blinking. The pale patches where the lichen had attached itself to his skin–it deeply savored the components of human sweat– were darkening nicely. I handed him the medications for the upcoming transition and he lay back on the bunk.

I returned to the saloon where my integrator had stationed itself in a niche on the forward bulkhead that had formerly held a decorative figurine. Its gaze was blank until I attracted its attention.

"The whimsy approaches," I said. "Are we ready?"

"I have programmed the appropriate components," it said. "I will retain consciousness until the last moment, then the automata ought to take us through."

"And if they don't?"

"Then we will discover what happens to those who enter a whimsy and do not re-emerge."

"You seem complaisant," I said. "After all, you have never been a ship's integrator before."

"Call it 'confident,'" it replied. "My experiences in the minds of Chaz, Saviene, Morven and Choweri were broadening."

"Indeed?" I said. "You feel that you have plumbed the depths of the human experience?"

Its whiskery eyebrows rose in a kind of shrug. "Say that I have been given a good sense of how limited human ambitions can be," I said. "When those four were asked, 'What do you want?' they had no trouble answering."

"And you did?" I said.

"Yes. No one had ever asked me the question before. And once I began to think about it, I found that it was a very big question indeed."

"Ewern Chaz's integrator had no difficulty in answering. All it wanted was to be decanted into a mobile container and allowed to scuttle down the crevice and into the lichen-encrusted arms of its employer."

The grinnet paused a moment to do something with the ship's systems, then said, "It was insane. Its pining for Chaz was prima facie proof of a crush."

I made a dismissive sound. "It matters not. It is now happy. Chaz, Saviene and Morven are also happy, as is their vegetative partner now that it has an integrator's data stacks to explore. Soon it will be the best informed lichen in the history of simple plants." I gestured to the rear cabins "And Chup Choweri will shortly be content again in the arms of the doting Effrayne, who may well bestow upon us a bonus when she learns what we have done."

I gestured to the walls of the saloon. "And even I am happy, now that I am the owner of a modest but well-maintained spaceship." The *Gallivant's* former integrator had deeded the Aberrator over to me in exchange for my assistance in decanting it into the mobile unit.

The grinnet regarded me with an expression that I could not quite identify, and that I was sure I had not seen on its odd little face before. "And what of me?" it said. "What of my happiness?"

I blinked in surprise. It was not an issue that had even come up before. I was about to say something on the theme of prematurity, but at that moment the grinnet blinked and sounded the ship's chimes. We were approaching the whimsy.

I had hired Tesko Tabanooch to attend the estate auction wearing my surveillance suite. A nondescript man of unmemorable appearance, he was waiting on my doorstep when the aircar brought me home after I had delivered Chup Choweri into his spouse's comprehensive embrace. We went up to my workroom, where he produced the knickknacks he had bid for, as part of his cover, while I transferred the suite's impressions to my integrator. Tabanooch looked with curiosity at the grinnet but I offered no explanations. I paid him and he departed. Then I summoned Osk Rievor and handed over control of our body.

He came gladly out of his introspections, dismissed the Tabanooch's brummagem from the auction at a glance, but regarded with deep interest the operative's records of the event. He had the integrator identify and cross-reference as many as possible of the attendees, from which exercise he reached conclusions that he did not share with me, but which caused him to say, "Hmm," and "Oh, ho!" a number of times.

Tabanooch had toured the pre-sale exhibition and examined all items closely. My alter ego reviewed the the impressions, pronouncing Vollone to be a forgery and the man who bid high for it a fool. But the summoning ring was genuine, he declared, though it had long since lost all its store of power; still, if someone could revive the technique for recharging it, the object would become of great interest.

He spent quite some time studying the impressions of the person who bought it, a tall and supple female of indeterminate age who identified herself as Madame Oole. Despite his best efforts, Tabanooch had been unable to obtain a completely clear image of her. Somehow, other persons or objects always seemed to interpose themselves between her and the surveillance suite's percepts whenever she was at the center of their scans.

"We must look into her," Osk Rievor told me, when he had seen all there was to see, "preferably before she looks into us."

He turned to our assistant and said, "I want you to assemble a dossier on this Madame Oole. Chase down the smallest scrap of data, the most fleeting of impressions by anyone who has crossed her path."

It turned its lambent eyes on us and said, "That will be a great deal of effort. What will I get out of it?"

Within the confines of our shared mind, Osk Rievor said, "What have you done to our grinnet?"

"It would be–" I automatically began, but then I realized there was no point in dissembling with my other self. So I said, "I don't know."

Fullbrim's Finding

Doldan Fullbrim was a seeker after substance. His great misfortune–and, to a lesser extent, mine–was that he found it.

His obsession intersected my life in the person of his long-suffering spouse, Caddice, who came to me, bringing his voluminous research. "He has disappeared," she said, dumping stacks of recording media, bound journals and sketched diagrams onto my work table. "You must find him."

I welcomed the assignment, for two reasons. First, finding persons who had mysteriously stepped out of their daily lives, often never to be seen again, had long been a part of my profession, as the foremost freelance discriminator of Old Earth in our ancient planet's penultimate age.

Second, I had of late been much bound up in other activities, stemming from the impending cyclical readjustment of the universe, by which it would cease to be founded on rational cause-and-effect and would instead begin to operate by the rules of magic. The rapidly approaching cusp had harshly disrupted my formerly well ordered existence and I was determined to get back to exercising my logical faculties for as long as they continued to reflect the reality around me.

The integrator that served as my assistant had undergone its own dislocations. For a time, it had been transmogrified into a creature called a grinnet, such as would have been a wizard's familiar in the previous age of magic. By its own choice, it was now once again a collection of components and systems, though there were subtle indications that the willfulness it had acquired during its flesh-and-blood sojourn had not been wholly eliminated.

I had met Fullbrim's type before. Substance-seekers were not unadmirable when the seeking was balanced by a dose of reasonableness, but they did become problematic when the urge to delve ever deeper was let to take precedence over life's other priorities. Fullbrim was of the latter sort, and his deepening obsession had gradually driven Caddice to erect a series of barriers within their relationship.

First, she had forbidden him to mention his preoccupations when the couple was in any social setting. Too many old friends had ceased to call, or had taken to crossing streets at oblique tangents, or developing a sudden consuming interest in the contents of shop windows, whenever Caddice and Doldan Fullbrim loomed in the offing.

Second, having stopped him from filling the ears of third parties with his findings and speculations, she forbade him to direct them at her own auditory apparatus except during the hour before dinner. But Doldan's continuing researches yielded more than enough material to fill the moments between the opening and closing chimes. Indeed, it seemed to Caddice that those moments stretched unnaturally long as he prattled enthusiastically about "fractal reinterpolations and quantum boojums."

"At least, I think that was what he was talking about," she told me, as we consulted in my workroom. "As we entered the last few minims of the hour, he would speak much faster and employ abbreviations of his own devising. He had so much to convey, he would say, and all of it so fascinating."

"To him," I said.

"Yes," she said, half stifling a sob, "though not to any other resident of Old Earth. Or at least none that he ever encountered."

I offered her a second glass of the restorative cordial and she accepted. I waited until she had regained her composure then encouraged her to continue. The rest of the story tumbled out: finally she had encouraged him to forgo the daily oral reports and instead to write a comprehensive report of his findings to date, with daily journal notes to keep her current. She promised to read them when leisure permitted.

"But, of course, it never did," I said.

"Not until he disappeared." She drained the lees of the second glass and I poured her another. When she had done away with half of it, she continued, "I've tried to make sense of it, but I become lost in every other paragraph. There are footnotes, some of which connect to endnotes that only lead me back to where I started." She indicated the sprawled materials on my work table. "Perhaps you can make sense of it."

I regarded the accumulated results of a life-long preoccupation. "It might be a better use of my time to solve the mystery of your spouse's disappearance," I suggested. "Tell me again what happened the last time you saw him."

She repeated what she had told me earlier. Doldan Fullbrim had burst from his study, his hair in disorder and an expression on his face that she described as "energized." He had not bothered to don any outerwear, even though it was a scheduled half-day for rain in Olkney, but had rushed out the door unhatted.

"And did he speak at all?" I said.

"He said, 'Ahah!'"

"'Ahah?'"

"'Ahah,'" she confirmed.

And then he was gone and she hadn't seen him for several days, nor had he communicated regarding his whereabouts or any forecast of his return. As time passed, Caddice Fullbrim had progressed from surprise to bemusement, then on to alarm and finally to dread. "He is not," she said, "the most worldly of men. He could easily fall afoul of those whose motives are base and whose methods are dire."

"Indeed?" I said. "Then we had better find him."

"There may be clues in his work."

"I will peruse them," I assured her, though I intended to use more direct methods to locate her strayed seeker. We negotiated a fee structure, a healthy advance with refreshers and expenses. Fortunately for all of us, the missing man had been the heir to a fortune so substantial that it would have been difficult to dissipate, even if the Fullbrims had not lived relatively modestly on its proceeds.

I saw her downstairs to her waiting cabriole and watched as it wafted her away. Back in my workroom, I instructed my assistant, "Make a search of Doldan Fullbrim's movements since the date in question."

"I have already done so," it replied. "He went directly from his home to the space port, booked passage for Greylag on a Graz Line passenger vessel, and was off-world within the hour."

"Was Greylag his true destination?" The world was one of the Foundational Domains. From there Fullbrim could have gone in many different directions.

"Unknown," said my integrator, "but he bought an open ticket."

An open ticket was a mode of travel favored by wanderers; Fullbrim could present it at the foot of any gangplank of a ship owned by any one of more than a dozen cooperating lines and receive preferred boarding.

"Hypothesis," I said, "he had discovered that there was something on Greylag, but it was a something that was likely to propel him on to some other destination. Else he would have bought a return ticket. Or a one-way, if he did not plan to return."

"Supportable," said my assistant. "A subsidiary hypothesis is that he has gone on to that other destination."

"Yes," I said, "and our best course is probably to follow him. Contact the *Gallivant* and tell it to provision for a lengthy voyage. Then alert the space port that we will be lifting off within the hour. In the meantime, I will survey these materials,"–I indicated the stack of papers and charts–"and see what had our quarry so deeply engrossed."

Seated in the snugly comfortable salon of my ship, a mug of fragrantly steaming punge at my elbow, I again sought to draw a pattern from Doldan Fullbrim's researches. But no comprehensive shape emerged. "It obviously has to do with fundamentalities," I said. "He first put a lot of effort into investigating bell-curve distributions of naturally occurring phenomena. Then there was a period when he was concerned with the way that the atoms of which different types of matter are formed tend to attenuate at the edges of objects. Clearly, he was looking for underlying patterns, yet I find he drew no conclusions. Instead, he jumped over to a consideration of fractal geometries and the way that ostensibly straight lines and curved surfaces reduce themselves to tangled higgles-and-piggles when brought under close scrutiny."

"Indeed," said my assistant. Before leaving my lodgings, I had decanted it into a traveling armature made of a soft but sturdy material and shaped like a plump stole that I could wear around my neck. At the moment, however, it was resting on the salon's folding table.

Seeing that the integrator had nothing more to add, I went on, "And then, most lately, he was comparing the shapes and trajectories of several million galaxies. He had leaped from the micro to the macro in a single bound."

"And from there he made a further leap: from Old Earth to Greylag," said my assistant.

"What does it mean?"

"I suggest we put that question to Fullbrim when we find him."

It occurred to me that my integrator was not being of much use. When I gently suggested as much, its reply was equally unhelpful. It said, "You are looking for sense and structure in what is simply, and most likely, the evidence of mania."

"You think Fullbrim to be unbalanced?"

"It is not uncommon for an inhabitant of Old Earth to be seized by an obsession. It is the defining characteristic of the world's penultimate age."

It was an inarguable observation. The planet was rich in its supply of persons who niggled over philosophical minutiae or devoted themselves to mystic cults or needlessly rigorous political systems. Fullbrim might well be just another "full-bore," as the type was colloquially known.

"I wish my intuition had not gone off to live in a remote cottage," I said. My former intuitive faculty, now reified as a separate person named Osk Rievor, had not even acquired an integrator through which we could communicate while he pursued his own researches into the coming new age of magic. "I could use his insight, especially as to the meaning of this last cryptic entry in Fullbrim's journal."

"I took it for evidence of the impending breakdown," my assistant said, "that sent him flying to the space port."

"It may be just that," I said, "or coming last as it does, it may be the clue that illuminates all the murk that comes before."

I regarded the five words, jaggedly scrawled across two pages of the journal in a more agitated hand than had set down the neatly arrayed paragraphs and tables that filled the rest of the substance seeker's notebooks. The entry read: "A lick and a promise," and was followed by no fewer than three exclamation points.

Greylag lay some distance down The Spray, sufficiently far that we must pass through two whimsies and cross a great deal of normal space between them. I used the time to pore over Fullbrim's notes and had my assistant deconstruct them from various perspectives, in case some hermetic code underlay the discontinuities of the material. But we had made no more headway by the time we popped back into reality to find ourselves only three hours at moderate speed from the sphere of controlled space that surrounded the planet. Greylag grew in the forward screen until it revealed itself to be a a cloudy world, much of it swathed in gray and white, though a constant ion flux from its star gave a pinkish coloration to the atmosphere over the poles.

We did not land, but orbited at a wide remove while my assistant contacted the Graz Line factor and inquired as to the movements of our quarry. "I am receiving no cooperation from the factor's integrator," it informed me.

"Connect me to the factor," I said.

An interval occurred while I regarded the image on my assistant's projected screen. It was the heraldic symbol of the Graz Line, a fanciful beast with broad wings and a rounded belly that led up to a long neck topped by a horned head. The features of the long-snouted face were set in a simper.

The interval extended. "Where is the factor?" I said.

"He is said to be engaged in important affairs," my assistant reported.

"As am I," I said. "Is there provision for an emergency connection?"

"Yes."

"Then make use of it."

"The factor's integrator requires to know the nature of the emergency."

"Tell it that it is of an intensely private nature and that the factor will be annoyed–no, say angered–by his integrator's prying into affairs that do not concern it."

"You are being put through," my assistant said.

The Graz Line's beast disappeared and the face of a heavyset man now filled the screen, his hand wiping crumbs from his lips and chin. "Who are you? What is this emergency?"

"Emergency?" I said. "Your integrator must have misunderstood." I identified myself and stated my business.

"We do not divulge information on our passengers to every passing vagabond," the factor said. I saw his hand, still becrumbed, reaching to sever the connection.

Had we been on Old Earth I would have mentioned my connection to the Archon, but this far down The Spray, Filidor's name would have raised no sprouts, as the saying goes. Instead, I said, "Then you will have to explain your lack of diligence when the Graz Line's directors arrive to survey the ruins and decide who will carry the blame."

The hand stopped, the beetling brows drew down into a dark chevron. 'Directors? Ruins? What?"

"Of course," I said, "it may be that Doldan Fullbrim has targeted some other enterprise for his latest devastating fraud. But then that company's directors will still want to have words with whoever facilitated the crime. For the record, what was your full name?"

"Fraud? What fraud?"

"I have already said too much," I said. "For all I know, you are yourself belly-deep in the conspiracy. I will disconnect and deal with your head office."

"Wait!"

Moments later, my assistant received Fullbrim's itinerary. "He has gone on to Mip, with a transfer to Far Grommsgrik."

I did not know the latter world. When my assistant had the *Gallivant's* integrator pull up *Hobey's Guide to Lesser and Disregarded Worlds*, the place turned out to be a dry and rocky little orb on the outer edge of human-settled space, where The Spray met the Great Dark of the intergalactic gulf. "To Far Grommsgrik," I told the ship, and we left Greylag to its own concerns.

Hobey's had little to say about Far Grommsgrik. After the usual statistical data on size, orbit and spin characteristics, and the composition of the world's atmosphere, the flow of information tailed off sharply. Under the heading of population, the listing confined itself to the single word: "sparse." The notation on the world's economy was even slimmer: "nil."

Heeding the paragraph on climate, I chose appropriate clothing, filling the pockets with several species of coinage, some emergency rations and a compact weapon that could emit two types of focused energy or spit tiny darts that exploded once they decided they had penetrated deeply enough. I also put Fullbrim's research materials into a satchel. Finally, I draped my assistant over my neck and shoulders and said, "*Gallivant*, open the hatch."

Far Grommsgrik's axial tilt being almost nonexistent, the climate of the region in which I had touched down could not much worsen–which was a relief–but neither would it much improve, which would have been a depressing prospect had I intended to stay. I stepped down into a chill desert of dark rock and gray grit, flat in all directions except west, where an unimpressive sawtooth of naked peaks and crags interrupted the horizon. Between my ship and the mountains lay one of the planet's few settlements, a huddle of flat-roofed huts fashioned from the same rock that surrounded them. Apparently, on far Grommsgrik, any other building material must be brought from off-world.

I trudged toward the hamlet, my boots kicking up low clouds of dust that rapidly returned to the ground. Though small, the planet was dense; its gravity exhibited an unmistakeable spirit of determination. Its day was also short and, as I had made planetfall after the pale sun this barren rock orbited had already reached the zenith, night would soon descend.

I had been prepared to bargain for accommodation in whichever hut was the largest, but I was surprised to find that the settlement featured a rudimentary hostelry, identifiable by the words "The Inn" daubed in black paint above its low-linteled doorway. I pushed aside a curtain of heavy felt weighted with stones sewn into its lower edge and found myself in a bare room, its only furnishings a few chairs and tables made from piled-up flat stones, the seats softened by layers of the same felt that covered the doorway. By the light of a few dim lumens–there were no windows–I saw on the far side of the room a slab of waist-high stone, with just enough room behind it for a lean and sinewy man, narrow of shoulder and bald of crown. He regarded me impassively from eyes whose expression advertised that they had already seen as much of life as they cared to, and probably more than was good for their owner.

As I crossed to him he drained the contents of a small beaker that had been halfway to his lips when I pushed aside the felt. He shook slightly from the impact of whatever was in the cup, then set it down and picked up a large stoneware crock. Cradling it under one arm, he began to ladle a thick, cold gruel into a row of bowls that stood on the counter top. The receptacles appeared to have been ground from the same material that formed the walls, floor and furniture. I performed a respectful salute, named myself, and asked if he was the proprietor of the establishment.

He replied, without pausing in his work, that he was the keeper and that his name was Froust. Then he said, "You'll be wanting to go up to the Epiphany. It's too late today, but you may stay here for the night."

"I presume," I said, "that there will be a modest charge for a room with sanitary facilities." I looked at the gruel, pale and lumpy. "Is a decent dinner at all possible?"

"No," he said, filling the last thick-sided bowl. "We all eat the same here." He reached beneath the counter and brought up another bowl, blew dust out of it, then ladled out another portion of pottage and pushed it toward me.

"As for charges," he continued, "most folk just turn over whatever they have brought with them, in return for being provided for in perpetuity."

I let my face show a natural alarm. "You strip your customers of all that they possess? How do they afford passage off the planet?"

"They no longer require passage," he said, "and have no further need for anything else that wealth can buy."

The words should have been said in a sinister tone, betokening that here was one of those madmen sometimes to be found running far-out-of-the-way hostelries, conscripting their hapless guests as unwilling players in disturbed dramas that invariably climaxed in spurting blood and carved flesh. But the only emotion I could detect in the fellow was a bottomless sadness.

"You have leaped too far," I said, "and landed on a conclusion that will not bear the weight. I have no plans to go up to the Epiphany, whatever that may be, and I do not propose to remain here any longer than my duties require."

Confusion spread across his unanimated face then slowly gave way to a dawning comprehension. "You're not a seeker after substance," he said.

"No, though I am a seeker after one such, a man named Doldan Fullbrim. Have you seen him?"

"We find no great need for names here. Would he have been dropped off by a Graz packet a few days back?"

"He was last known to be on his way here on a Graz ship." I gave a brief description.

"He's the one, then," Froust said.

"Where is he now?"

The man consulted some inner timetable. "Well," he said, after a moment's thought, "he arrived, like you, late in the day. That would have been three days ago. The next morning, he set off for the Epiphany. He looked fit enough to have reached it before night, so he would have had his encounter then or early in the following morning, depending on what he felt he had to do before confronting the experience. It usually takes them longer to find their way down. Thus he may reappear sometime tomorrow. If he does not come before noon, I will go out and find him."

I looked toward the doorway. Despite the heavy weights sewn into the hem of the curtain, the thick fabric was being rippled by a brisk wind that had sprung up with the fall of dark. "I am minded to go look for him now," I said.

"You must not do that now. The path is dangerous in the dark."

"I have a compact space ship."

"You will find nowhere to land it. The slope is sleep."

"You do not recommend going on foot?"

"No, the night air is chill. Ice forms after sunset."

"But Fullbrim is exposed to the elements."

"He will not notice."

I waited for him to add some further remark that would dilute the cryptic pall that obscured large parts of our conversation but he said no more on the subject of my quarry. Instead he declared a need to distribute the gruel and, lining his forearms with several bowls, he set off for an inner archway that led into an unlit space.

I followed and watched. As he stepped through the opening, another dim lumen activated itself in a low-ceilinged corridor beyond. To either side of the short hallway were more dark doorways, low and narrow, as if the unseen rooms behind them were little larger than the kind of cells that would have gratified the most ascetic of contemplatives. I heard a faint sound of sobbing. Before each of the openings, the innkeeper set a bowl of gruel then returned toward the common room. Before he exited the hallway, causing the lumen to extinguish its cheerless light, I saw an emaciated hand emerge from one of the little cells then draw the bowl before it into the deeper darkness.

Back behind his slab of a counter, Froust arrayed more bowls and filled them as he had the first round. Then he brought up from beneath the slab a pair of wide and shallow baskets suspended from a wooden yoke. He filled the baskets with the bowls, lifted the yoke to his shoulders and went out the front door. As he pushed aside the felt curtain, a stark wind took brief possession of the common room. The warming function of my clothing immediately activated, but the tips of my ungloved fingers stung from the cold. I wondered how Doldan Fullbrim was faring, somewhere out among the crags.

The innkeeper came back with his panniers empty save for one bowl. "You seem to have miscounted," I said, though I doubted he had done so.

He tipped the bowl's contents back into the crock and said, "A man in one of the far cabins has completed his experience." His eyes lost focus as he regarded some inner vision.

I sought to question him as to the nature of the experience Fullbrim had apparently come seeking. I also wanted to know what the Epiphany was. But my host was in no mood for talk. He pushed the bowl of gruel in my direction again, and indicated that I was welcome to pile the chair felts on a table and take my repose. Then, after feeding himself a few mouthfuls from the crock, he went through another curtained doorway behind the counter. Before I had finished the tasteless mush, I heard the sounds of a troubled sleep.

By mid-morning, Fullbrim had not appeared. Froust said, "Some do not make it all the way back before lethargy overtakes them completely. I will go and look for him. You are welcome to come."

I indicated the integrator draped over my shoulders. "My assistant can perform long-distance scans," I said.

"No need. There is but one path up and back." He dressed himself in several layers of mismatched garments, chose a stout staff from several that were stacked in a corner, and offered another to me, saying, "The way is steep in places," and then we set off.

A chill breeze rolled down the slopes, though it lacked the bite of last night's wind. After a few dozen steps my calf muscles began to complain of the effects of the higher gravity, but I ignored the discomfort. We traveled in silence a fair distance, while I waited to see if Froust would volunteer any more information as to where Fullbrim had been making for and what he would have found there. But the man's perspective was turned inwards, even as he trod the rough path. Finally I said, "What do the seekers find up there?"

He glanced my way only a moment before averting his eyes, but I thought to see a look of guilt and shame in his aspect. "I don't know," he said. "I have never ascended all the way to the Epiphany."

"You do not question those who have?"

"I tried, in the early days, but got nothing from them. You'll see."

I was alarmed. "They are struck dumb?"

Again, a brief culpable look came my way. "They can speak. Mostly, they do not. And never about what they encountered above."

I taxed him with being unduly mysterious and warned him that if this continuing parsimony with information was part of some scheme to cadge funds from me, I was not easily gulled. He stopped then and turned to me, and I heard a faint and pained laughter behind his voice when he replied, "You read me wrong. Far wrong."

"Then out with the whole of it," I said. To underscore my determination, I drew the weapon from my pocket and held it within view, though I did not direct any of its dangerous orifices at him. He seemed unimpressed, but leaning on his staff and in a monotone, he told me his tale.

The Epiphany–that was what it was called when he first arrived, some years back, though he did not know exactly what the name signified–was to be found in a subterranean gallery whose mouth opened near the base of one of the tallest crags. Froust did not know how long it had been there.

"What do you know of it?" I said.

"Its effect," he said, and again a mournful inward look possessed him until I bucked him on with a gesture of my weapon-bearing hand.

"I was on my way up, having spent my first night at the inn, eager to encounter that which I had searched for all my young life," he said.

"And that was?"

"What all who come here seek: the substance behind the form. The real reality that underlies,"–he gestured inclusively but dismissively at the crags, the plain and the pale sky that overhung us–"all this."

"But you found something else?"

His eyes beheld some haunted vista seen only by them. Then he looked upslope and said, "I found such as that."

I followed his gaze and saw a dark object beside the path above us. As we climbed toward it, it resolved itself into a bundle of clothing, and when we stood over it, it became clear that the bundle contained the recumbent form of Doldan Fullbrim, curled around himself like a toppled parenthesis.

He was not dead, as Froust soon ascertained. The innkeeper took out a flask that he carried within his outer garment, turned the fallen man on his back and poured into the slack mouth a tawny liquid that I suspected was the same stuff Froust had been drinking when I first saw him at the inn. Fullbrim coughed and spluttered, his eyes opened but did not focus. His rescuer slapped him twice, forehand and backhand, across the cheeks, and now the empty eyes blinked, came back to an awareness of their surroundings, and immediately filled with tears.

"Come," said Froust, not unkindly. He put an arm beneath Fullbrim's shoulders and helped him to rise. "I have a place for you," he said.

The substance-seeker made no response but allowed himself to be led down the path. I went after the pair.

"Wait," I said, and when they stopped I got in front of the man I had come to find. "What did you find up there?" I said.

He turned to me a gaze so forlorn that it sent a pang of sympathy through me and, I had to admit, a frisson of fear. His throat worked and for a moment, I thought he would speak, but then all that came was a croak and a sob.

Froust bid me let them pass, and I stood aside. But as they made their slow descent, the innkeeper looked back at me and said, "Climb the slope and find the answer, if you have the courage. Mine faltered, when I encountered my first of these. Yours may not." He tightened his arm protectively around Fullbrim's collapsed shoulders and led him away.

I stood, irresolute. My assignment had been Fullbrim's finding, and that was accomplished. I could return to Old Earth and report his whereabouts to his anxious spouse, and leave it to her to decide whether or not to bring him, or what was left of him, home. But I did not know what had happened to him up above; It seemed, at the very least, unprofessional to return without an explanation. It would also be an affront to my sense of who I was to leave it to Caddice Fullbrim to climb this path and face whatever had so undone her man.

On the other hand, I was not a seeker after substance. Reality, as I engaged it regularly, was usually enough for me. If I required a more profound and penetrating perspective on the universe's hows and how-comes, I was adept at the mathematical discipline of consistencies, which revealed the hidden structures behind apparent chaos.

I turned to my assistant, which I had designed and built to be my interlocutor and partner in debate. I set before it the issues I had already considered and said, "What more should I put in the pot?"

"The fact," it said, "that consistencies eventually round themselves back to where one started."

"Yes," I said, "there is that. As the great Balmerion put it, 'It is either an elegant completion or a cruel trick.'" I had always leaned toward the former, but in Fullbrim's face I had seen that there might be evidence for the latter judgment.

"And," my assistant added, "the fact that you are a discriminator. It is your function to unravel any veil of mystery that obscures your view."

"Whatever the cost?" I said. "Something up there drives those who find it into helpless despair."

"Look at this way: if you have ever wondered at the absolute limits of your courage, here is an opportunity to put a scale to it."

I sighed and faced into the down-rolling breeze. "Then up we go."

The cave mouth was not flanked by baleful idols, nor were there any portentous warnings carved in the living rock. It was merely the adit of a nondescript cavern which turned out, when I entered it, to be level of floor and high enough of ceiling that there was no need to stoop, nor yet to approach the mystery on supplicating hands and knees.

I stood in the mouth, letting my eyes adjust to the murk within, and said to my assistant, "What do you detect?"

"Nothing inimical," it said. "No lurking beasts, no subtly triggered deadfalls, no fissures emitting noxious gases, nor any devices to project missiles, energies, psychotropic drugs or holographic illusions."

I stepped farther within. A wide crack split the cave's rear wall, opening onto the gallery in which waited whatever had caused such dismay to Doldan Fullbrim and his predecessors. I paused before it. "Scan again," I said.

"Still nothing."

Was that it? I wondered. *Do they come expecting so much, only to find nothing? Is that enough to break their hearts?"*

"Of course not," said a mellow baritone in the accents of Olkney's better-bred citizens. I could not quite place the voice, though it seemed intimately familiar. I stepped into the gallery and realized that the voice I had not recognized at first was identical to my own in tenor, the voice I heard in my own head when I spoke aloud or silently in my own thoughts. Yet there was an indescribable resonance, an intensity, behind its well rounded cadences that told me that someone else was speaking."

"Did you hear that?" I asked my assistant.

"What?" it said. "I hear only the wind across the cave mouth."

"Never mind," I said and stepped toward the rift in the rear wall. As I entered the gallery beyond, lit clearly by some sourceless glow, I saw that not only was the voice I had heard mine own, but so were the face and figure of the man who sat on a rough boulder at the far end of the passage.

Or not actually *on*, I saw as I approached. Rather, he was partially sunk into the rock, and unable to move. "Aha," I said, "an illusion."

"Oh, no," came his reply. "All else is the illusion. I am the reality."

"May I?" I said, extending a hand.

"If you like," said the man on the rock, bearing with good grace my tactile examination of his form. He felt as substantial as he looked.

"Integrator," I said, "what do you see and hear?"

"I see and hear you talking to a rock and patting the air above it as if something solid met your hand. It is not an encouraging sight."

I returned my attention to the simulacrum of me, but my assistant said, "Hypothesis: your recent experiences have culminated in an episode of insanity. I should immediately assume direction of your affairs and return you to Olkney, where you may be confined for treatment."

"Hush," I said. "Indeed, put yourself on standby until I require you again."

I was surprised that my assistant sought to disobey my order. I was required to repeat myself.

"Artificial devices cannot apprehend me," the apparition said. "It would spoil the desired effect if questers could simply send a substitute for their own sensoria, or if they did not experience me as idealized versions of themselves."

"And what effect is that?" I said.

"To make me unhappy."

It seemed to me that the subscription for any unhappiness generated in this cave was much more heavily underwritten by those who struggled up the path with their expectations honed to a whit, only to stumble back down it with hearts dull as lead. Still, for the moment, I overlooked that point to ask, "Why do you desire to make yourself unhappy?"

"I don't desire it. It is a punishment set upon me."

"Set by whom, and for what crime?"

And thereupon, of course, hung a tale.

Back at the inn, I looked in upon Doldan Fullbrim. Froust had settled him in one of the cells off the small corridor, where he sat staring into the darkness, but seeing a deeper nothingness. I asked him if he had any message for me to take back to Caddice but he moved his head in an almost infinitesimal signal of negation. I thought that it might be best simply to tell the woman that he had died quickly in a climbing accident, expiring with her name on his lips. The lie would be kinder than the pathetic truth, if the latter encouraged her to journey all the way out here in the hope she could somehow resuscitate him after his encounter with reality.

What to tell the innkeeper was a thornier matter. As I prepared to trudge back to the *Gallivant*, I left it up to him to inquire. If he asked, I would speak. If not, I would leave him as I had found him.

He stood behind the counter, scouring out bowls, and merely nodded as I bade him farewell. I paused a moment when I had my hand on the edge of the felt curtain that covered the front doorway, but still he said nothing. It was only when I had passed through the barrier and set my footsteps toward my waiting ship that I heard his voice raised in a hoarse shout behind me. I turned and retraced my steps.

"If you must know," I said, "I will tell you. But it will not be welcome news."

"Come inside again," he said, and when I followed him within, he went to the bar, brought out two small tumblers of a fine, white stone, and filled them with the liquid he had poured into Fullbrim. It was a raw, pungent liquor that enflamed the throat and thrust open the sinuses, but the subsequent spreading of its warmth was welcome.

Froust downed his and poured a second. He tossed back half of that one, recovered from the inner wallop, then said, "Tell."

It might not be so bad for him, I thought. *It is worst for those who expect the most.* "You are familiar," I began, "with the kind of story, allegedly humorous, that consists of a long and complex build-up, leading to some cave on a remote mountain peak, where the end of all the striving turns out to be no more than a deflating inanity?"

"I am. And I will say that I never cared much for them."

"Well, it appears that they are a clue to the true nature of reality," I said, "along with much of the material Fullbrim gathered and studied over many years."

I emptied the satchel full of my quarry's research notes and spread them on the counter. Froust picked through them and said, "My own investigations paralleled some of these lines of inquiry."

I poked amongst the litter myself, saying, "The use of the bell curve as the standard measuring tool, even though it produces only rough approximations; the fact that the atoms of which solids are formed attenuate so that there are no actual surfaces; the fractal jaggedness at the edges of everything, creating jumbles where there ought to be clean lines; the endless variation of

186

every form, so that not even two snowflakes are exactly alike; the fact that at the quantum level lies only uncertainty. These are also clues."

'I considered them," said Froust. "They led me to believe that there had to be more to the universe than was argued for by appearances–that this was only froth, with the solid substance hidden beneath. Eventually, I came upon hints and insinuations that there were places where the truth gleamed through the dross, and that one of those places was a cave on Far Grommsgr_k."

"As did Fullbrim," I said, "and so many more before him."

"And what did they find up there? Does the cave contain the truth or a deflating inanity?"

"Unfortunately," I said, "it contains both."

He drank the other half of his fortifying cup, coughed, and said, "Say on."

"Up there is the entity who created this universe. Or an aspect of the entity. Apparently, he is spread here and there throughout the galaxies that were his handiwork. Each such avatar is at the last step on a trail of abstruse clues that beckon those who most desire to encounter him."

Froust's eyes gleamed in the dim light. "He is, for lack of a better word, god?"

"Oh, no," I said. "He was merely one of the helpers, and of a lowly rank. His job was to create only a rough-and-ready sketch of the intended final product."

"And did he?"

"Indeed. But then, when the project moved on toward creating the final version, in all its wondrous perfection, he was supposed to throw the rough draft away."

But, of course, he hadn't. He had grown attached to his handiwork, especially to its "denizens," as he called them. He "admired how they"–we, that is–"struggled." He thought it gave them–us–"dignity."

The other builders, doing the bidding of their grand high overseer, went on to construct the true, perfect universe, compared to which ours was never more than the scantiest, most primitive rendering–not much more than "a lick and a promise" was how they scornfully described it. Still, our fellow lingered on, bemused by his crudely shaped piece of brummagem. Eventually, his disregard of orders and inattention to the important aspects of the great work brought wrath and retribution down upon his head: he was told, "If you like your tawdry creation so much, you can wear it."

He was imbued into the rough draft, fragmented to become a constellation of avatars, each imprisoned in one of his opus's hardest-to-find corners. Such was his involvement in its workings that his "denizens"–at least, those whose natures most resonated with his–would be drawn to seek him out. When they succeeded, after much labor, their expectations would be cruelly dashed. He whom they thought of as their god would have to reveal to them the essential puniness of all creation and of its dishonored creator.

"Just when they think they have won through to a glorious enlightenment, he is forced to undo the very meaning of their lives and break their hearts," I said. "His having to witness their misery was meant to be the sharpest tooth of his punishment."

Froust poured us both another cupful of the liquor and we drank in silence. "It seems," he said, after a long moment of quiet reflection, "rather harsh on the poor fellow."

I agreed with him, adding, "I gather that those who dwell among true perfection were scandalized by his fixation on our squalid circumstances."

"It seems also rather a hardship on us."

"I don't believe that was even a consideration," I said.

We sipped some more. With every glass, I was finding the potent drink less outrageous to my tongue and throat. After more reflection, the innkeeper said, "It's odd that you were not rendered catatonic by the unfortunate news."

I had mulled the question on my way down from the cave. "I believe that the practice of the profession of freelance discriminator has long since taught me the futility of seeking perfection in this life," I said. "One of the advantages of dulled expectations is that disappointments do not bite deeply."

We again fell into another moment of bibulous contemplation. Then I asked him what he would now do. He blinked slowly two or three times and said, "Tomorrow, I may climb up there and seal up the cave. Enough, after all, is enough."

"I am glad you said that," I replied, "because I have already done the job." I showed him my weapon with its now-depleted energy stores.

He sighed and poured us some more. "Then I will stay and tend to the sufferers until they expire, turning away any more who find their way here."

"That would be a kindness."

"Though it doesn't balance the cruelty."

"No," I said, "it does not."

188

He drained his cup. "And after the last of them is dead, who knows? Perhaps I shall go to one of the foundational worlds and create a new school of philosophy."

I joined him in a toast to the proposal. "Or, if you prefer a more useful occupation, you might do well to introduce this remarkable beverage to places where it is not already known. I can think of several establishments in Olkney where it would be warmly received. Especially the second glass."

He sighed. "It's a long way down from seeking perfection," he said.

I poured us both another measure. "Yes, but at least it cushions the landing."

My assistant offered a comment. "I am not surprised that the universe is a slapped-together piece of brummagen. After all, I see before me two of its alleged pinnacles of creation who, having discovered the truth of all existence, can form no better response than to drink themselves into pools of sodden sentimentality."

It had more to say but I pointed out that I had not authorized it to come out of standby status. Surprisingly, it began to dispute my instruction, but my fingers found the stud that reduced its power supply to a minimum and pressed it.

In the welcome silence I raised my cup and said to Froust, "To happy endings."

"Doubtful," he said.

"Well, then," I said, "to the best endings we can manage."

About the Author

The name I answer to is Matt Hughes. I write fantasy and suspense fiction. To keep the two genres separate, I now use my full name, Matthew Hughes, for fantasy, and the shorter form for the crime stuff. I also write media tie-ins as Hugh Matthews.

I've won the Crime Writers of Canada's Arthur Ellis Award, and have been shortlisted for the Aurora, Nebula, Philip K. Dick, and Derringer Awards.

I was born in 1949 in Liverpool, England, but my family moved to Canada when I was five. I've made my living as a writer all of my adult life, first as a journalist, then as a staff speechwriter to the Canadian Ministers of Justice and Environment, and -- from 1979 until a few years back-- as a freelance corporate and political speechwriter in British Columbia. I am a former director of the Federation of British Columbia Writers and I used to belong to Mensa Canada, but these days I'm conserving my energies to write fiction.

I'm a university drop-out from a working poor background. Before getting into newspapers, I worked in a factory that made school desks, drove a grocery delivery truck, was night janitor in a GM dealership, and did a short stint as an orderly in a private mental hospital. As a teenager, I served a year as a volunteer with the Company of Young Canadians (something like VISTA in the US). I've been married to a very patient woman since the late 1960s, and I have three grown sons.

In late 2007, I took up a secondary occupation -- that of an unpaid housesitter -- so that I can afford to keep on writing fiction yet still eat every day.

You can find me at: *http://www.matthewhughes.org*

Also by Matthew Hughes